HAUNTED

HAUNTED

WiLLIAM HUSSEY

OXFORD
UNIVERSITY PRESS

OXFORD
UNIVERSITY PRESS

Great Clarendon Street, Oxford OX2 6DP
Oxford University Press is a department of the University of Oxford.
It furthers the University's objective of excellence in research, scholarship,
and education by publishing worldwide in

Oxford New York

Auckland Cape Town Dar es Salaam Hong Kong Karachi
Kuala Lumpur Madrid Melbourne Mexico City Nairobi
New Delhi Shanghai Taipei Toronto

With offices in

Argentina Austria Brazil Chile Czech Republic France Greece
Guatemala Hungary Italy Japan Poland Portugal Singapore
South Korea Switzerland Thailand Turkey Ukraine Vietnam

Oxford is a registered trade mark of Oxford University Press
in the UK and in certain other countries

First published 2013

British Library Cataloguing in Publication Data

Data available

ISBN: 978-0-19-273250-7

3 5 7 9 10 8 6 4 2

Printed in Great Britain

Paper used in the production of this book is a natural,
recyclable product made from wood grown in sustainable forests.
The manufacturing process conforms to the environmental
regulations of the country of origin.

For my niece Lyla, brightest of bright souls.

And for the five good witches: Deborah Chaffey, Veronique Baxter, Jasmine Richards, Laura West and Clare Whitston, in gratitude for their encouragement, wisdom and uncanny alchemy.

While yet a boy I sought for ghosts, and sped
Through many a listening chamber, cave and ruin,
And starlight wood, with fearful steps pursuing
Hopes of high talk with the departed dead.

Percy Bysshe Shelley, *Hymn to Intellectual Beauty*

PROLOGUE

UNLAND

'You gotta bring them back the head, Henry, or it won't count. Good luck.'

Henry Torve sidestepped through a gap in the rusted bars, his teeth clenching at the clatter-clang of the gate. Ever since he'd heard the stories about this place, most of them told by his cousin Emma, he had dreamed of this moment: his leg reaching through the gate, his foot touching down upon the cursed earth, and then . . . he shivered. Henry wouldn't let go of the bars, not yet, the others might notice how his hands shook.

'C'mon, Sas,' he sighed. 'Stop looking at me like that.'

Tall as a sixth-former and built like a rugby fullback, Brandon Lorne towered over the rest of the Chainsaw Gang. Henry had been mates with Bigfoot Bran, or 'Sas' as he was more commonly known (short for Sasquatch, naturally), ever since that fateful day at preschool when they'd teamed up to push Suzie Stark into the duck pond. Now they were thirteen and still playing what Henry's father described as 'damn fool games'.

'Like what?'

'Like you want to come with me.'

'You kidding?' Sas laughed. 'Once was enough for me.'

'You want to come,' Henry insisted, 'because you think I'm scared.'

'It's not that, bro . . . But listen, maybe I could talk to Freakazoid, say you don't know the layout of the park. He might let me come with.'

'I'm *not* scared.' *Liar*, said a little voice at the back of Henry's head. 'And anyway, there's a map the size of your mum's arse right over there.'

He pointed to the billboard that stood beside the gate. A decade of wind and rain had stripped much of the paintwork but the map's main features stood out clear enough—the Corkscrew Rollercoaster, Dizzy Daisy's Teacup Ride, the Lazy Laguna Log Flume, and there, at the end of a snaking path, Hiram's Hellish Horror House.

'Only one way into the Chainsaw Gang,' Henry said. 'You run the Funland Gauntlet, and you run it alone.'

Sas gave a reluctant nod. His spade-like hand reached through the bars and slapped Henry on the back. 'Just don't forget the head.'

It was as Henry started down the wide promenade that served as the entry point to the park that he noticed the shadows: six black letters quivering at his feet. He turned and looked back at the gate. All those years he and Sas had dared each other to run the mile and a half through Black

Acre Forest to stand breathless in the weed-cracked car park of Funland, and he'd never noticed the missing letter before. Now he saw that the metallic name arcing over the gate was incomplete and that a haunting word had been left behind—*unland.*

Henry moved past the boarded windows of bars and restaurants, gift shops and ice cream parlours, ticket booths and coffee stalls, all mocked up to look like the main street of a Wild West town. Eleven years ago hordes of over-excited children had swarmed down this promenade, little hearts aflutter. Now the place was empty, desolate, *un*made.

Turning right, he stepped onto a narrower path that sloped gently downwards. On one side stood the rusted rollercoaster, its spindly legs trousered with vines; on the other, a swaybacked helter-skelter jacketed with moss. Only once had Henry heard a grown-up talk about what had happened here. Every fortnight his mother's friends would take over the sitting room for an hour of what his father called 'womanly twittering'. Usually Henry avoided these get-togethers like the plague, but passing the door he had heard Mrs Glock, the doctor's wife, mention the name 'Hiram Sparrow'. Everyone in Milton Lake knew the story, of course, but in the presence of children the town's shame was never mentioned. Not only had Mrs Glock gone to school with Hiram Sparrow, her husband had been the first to examine his body when they found it—Henry swallowed—in the ghost train.

'Hiram had *always* been peculiar,' said Mrs Glock. 'But when he inherited that big plot of land in the forest and decided to build an amusement park, well, you could've knocked me down with a feather.'

'Why did he build it, I wonder?' Henry's mother frowned.

'You ask me, he was planning it from the start.' Mrs Glock nibbled at her teacake. 'He'd had a miserable childhood, cooped up in that lonely old house on Connolly Avenue, only his sour-faced father for company. I think he wanted the world to sit up and take notice. Wanted everyone to know the name Hiram Sparrow.'

'But if he'd planned it all along why didn't he do it sooner? The park had been open for years before—'

'Ah, but it was only really successful that last season when he installed the rollercoaster. That was when the big crowds came. He wanted as large an audience as possible. And afterwards? Well, daydreams are a funny thing. You fantasize about something for years, lay your plans, then, when it's done, you realize it wasn't what you wanted after all. In the dark of the train, with all those screams ringing in his ears, maybe Hiram came to his senses. Maybe that's why he—'

'Henry!'

His mother had seen the shadow at the door and sent Henry to his room. It didn't matter, he knew what Mrs Glock was going to say next. The last act of the Funland tragedy had been in all the newspapers.

Henry came to the end of the path and stood before the ghost train. Stood, and stared, and shivered. It was Sas who'd got him into this. Sas who'd joined the Chainsaw Gang at the start of term and who wouldn't take no for an answer.

'We've always done everything together, bro, you just gotta join.'

They'd approached Sas a few months back, offering membership if he ran the Funland Gauntlet and returned with a poster from the ticket booth as proof of his guts. Despite its name, the gang was about as terrifying as one of Henry's mother's coffee mornings. Freddie Liszt, Freakazoid Fred as he liked to be known, was the leader and typical of the other nine members—skinny, pimple-plagued geeks who spent too much time in sunless rooms slaughtering zombies on their games consoles. Henry had had no interest in the gang, his levels of cool were pitiful enough without associating with the 'Chainers', but it clearly meant a lot to Sas, and so it was important to him too. In Freakazoid's musty-smelling bedroom, he had drawn from a collection of paper slips stuffed inside a Darth Vader-shaped biscuit barrel.

'The ghost train,' Sas sighed when Henry unfolded the slip. 'OK, Fred, what'll he have to bring back . . . ?'

Like the rest of the park, the ghost train was a ruin. The front of the ride had been designed to look like a medieval castle, all wooden turrets and cut-out arrow slits painted to resemble ancient stone. An arched doorway, complete with portcullis, made up the entrance, above which, in faded green paint, the words 'HIRAM'S HELLISH HORROR HOUSE' had been daubed.

The setting sun streamed over Funland and sparkled against the first snowfall. It was getting colder by the minute, dark was coming, and this head wasn't going to detach itself.

Henry pulled down a lungful of midwinter air and marched into the horror house.

A wide corridor divided by queuing rails opened out into the ride's boarding station. Cobwebbed carriages stood around a semicircle of track, safety bars pushed up as if, after eleven long years, the ghost train still expected passengers. On the opposite side of the station twenty or more cars lined up in front of a cloth-draped doorway. It wasn't completely dark; needles of sunlight broke through holes in the worm-eaten ceiling and showed Henry that he would have to venture further if he was to prove his guts.

He jumped down from the platform and picked his way around the track until he stood at the nose of the last carriage. The drape brushed against his face like a leathery wing as he pushed through. Here, inside the ghost train proper, the ceiling had held up better than in the boarding station. With no holes for daylight, Henry took out his phone and used its screen to illuminate a maze of dripping plywood walls. His heart skipped. If only Sas was with him. Sas or his cousin, Emma. Daredevil Emma Rhodes would take his hand and, with laughter in those bright green eyes, race him through his fear and out the other side. His cousin was just about the bravest person Henry knew. Or she had been, until the accident . . .

Stumbling to a halt, Henry cried out. It was the smell that had begun to unsettle him, a faint citric odour that stirred a recent memory. Then, turning with the track, he had stepped into a chamber filled with people. Hands trembling, he refreshed the phone light and swept it around the gallery of frozen faces. Stupid! He'd been expecting them at every turn, so why had they frightened him?

There were a dozen mannequins in all, each standing on its own plinth with the track weaving between them. Here was a bloody-lipped vampire in mildewed evening dress; a snout-nosed werewolf in slashed jeans and T-shirt; a mummy rising from its sarcophagus; an evil-eyed witch stirring her cauldron; a lake monster bedecked with seaweed, a graveyard ghoul, a white sheet ghost, a zombie, a Frankenstein monster, a hunchback, a mad scientist, a masked killer complete with butcher's knife—every horror cliché present and correct. Henry made his choice.

Stepping onto the platform behind the mummy, he dug his fingers under the creature's threadbare bandages. The phone made his movements clumsy so he decided to pocket it. The screen light continued to glow through the fabric of his trousers but the waxwork chamber was now plunged into near darkness. Henry's fingers scrabbled at the mummy's neck as the long seconds ticked by.

'Come on, come on.'

Finally he found the slit that ran round the mannequin's neck. With one hand worrying at the join, he locked an arm round the mummy's head. He could feel it start to give. One good tug and it would—

Brrrring Brrrring; Brrrring Brrrring.

This time Henry did not cry out. The shriek was there all right, speeding out of his lungs and whipping into his windpipe, but it got stuck somewhere in his throat. Arm still latched round the mummy's head, he teetered backwards.

The mannequin fell with him in a sprawl of bandages and broken plastic limbs—a foot went one way, a finger another, a hand skittered off into the gloom. Only the monster's head remained stubbornly attached to its torso. Flat on his back, Henry listened to the ringing.

'S just my phone, he thought. *Sas probably checking if I'm OK . . . But . . .*

Brrrring Brrrring; Brrrring Brrrring. That wasn't *his* ringtone.

Sweat formed on Henry's brow, snaked coldly down his temples and slipped under his collar. All the strength went out of his arm and he dropped the mummy's head. Over the ringing he could hear the creak of rotten floorboards. Someone was moving around in the next chamber. Maybe it was a tramp, some homeless man who wasn't frightened by the stories of Hiram Sparrow, and who'd made a home for himself in the abandoned horror house. A tramp whose ringtone sounded like an old-fashioned phone . . .

The ringing stopped. Small sounds began to fill up the stillness—the groan of damp wood, the wet pop as Henry moistened his lips, the drip of water through the worm-eaten ceiling. But wait a minute. There were no holes in the chamber ceiling, that was why it was so dark. *Tuck-tuck-tuck.* Liquid falling on the wooden floor not far from Henry's head. *Tuck . . . Tuck-tuck . . . Tuck . . .* Liquid thicker than water. His hand closed round the phone in his pocket. *Tuck-tuck-tuck.* And now Henry heard other sounds—the shamble of heavy boots and a low, guttural choke as if from the throat of a drowning man. Was it the tramp? No, listening carefully he could still make out movement coming from the other room. Whoever—whatever—was now inside the chamber with him it was something *other.*

Just as Henry found a button to illuminate the phone, a splodge of wetness dropped onto his hand and greased the screen. The liquid felt oily on his skin . . . and suddenly he knew what it was, this thing that moved in the dark. Filtered through the liquid, the phone projected a pinkish glare across the chamber. It picked out the faces of monsters: the heavy-browed hunchback, the scaly lake beast, the headless man . . .

Every muscle in Henry's body braced. When he had entered the chamber he had counted twelve mannequins, so why—*for God's sake why*—were there now thirteen? Vampire, werewolf, lake creature, masked killer, Frankenstein monster, mad scientist, ghost, witch, zombie, hunchback, mummy, ghoul, and now . . . headless man.

The headless man that *moved.*

Investigators had estimated it had taken Hiram Sparrow all night to cut and hammer, melt and buckle, place and prime. Then, sitting alone in the ghost train, he'd used a remote control to detonate small charges at all the points he had weakened. Eyewitnesses said everything happened at once: tracks snapped, wires sheared through, carriages plummeted and people died. His work done, Hiram had stood alone in this darkened chamber, placed a shotgun under his jaw, and pulled the trigger . . .

Now, eleven years later, the murderer was back. Bathed in the glow of the phone, the faceless owner of Funland reached out to Henry. Despite the fact that he had no eyes with which to see, Hiram seemed to know where Henry lay, still tangled in the mummy's bandages. In the few seconds it took for Henry to come to his senses, he made out every solid detail of the ghost: the neck with its collar of ragged flesh; the blood-soaked overalls and heavy work boots; the battered toolbox and discarded shotgun.

Move! Henry told himself. *Just get to your feet and run.* But he couldn't. The message to his arms and legs seemed to get stuck, blocked by the strength-sapping fear that pumped through every fibre of his body. His fingers went numb and he dropped the phone. The light from the cracked screen flickered and threw Hiram's foreshortened shadow across the walls. Two more steps and the reaching hand would find him . . .

Hiram's boot landed on the ghost train's weaving track. The murderer had no mouth, he could not scream, and yet he did. The most terrible scream Henry had ever heard. Worse than any fake shriek from a horror movie; worse than the time Sas had snapped his leg falling from a tree; worse even than the scream his mother had made when the call came through from Emma's dad telling them about Richie. Hiram's hands clutched at his throat and moved up to his missing head. There came a sound like bacon frying in a pan, then the light died.

Move, he told himself again, and this time Henry did.

He pulled the last of the bandages from around his ankles and took to his heels, running through the corridors, stumbling over the tracks, through the black drapes and the empty boarding station, under the wooden portcullis and into the snowy twilight beyond. Thick white flakes melted against his cheeks so that, when he cannoned into Sas and the other Chainers on the promenade, they did not see his tears.

Freakazoid frowned. 'Where's the head?'

That's when Henry started laughing. A scary-sounding laugh that made the Chainers step back and Sas run to his side. He was there to catch him when Henry fell.

'Where's the head?' The laughter went out of Henry's eyes and he looked up at Sas with such fear the bigger boy shrank back. 'Where's the head? Where's the *head*? *WHERE'S THE HEAD?!'*

1

Emma's eyes never strayed from the pavement. *Step on a crack, break your mother's back.* The old playground rhyme ran through her head, but it was not a childish chant that kept her gaze fixed on the concrete. A small part of her wouldn't care if the chant was true—if she did step on a crack and, by some supernatural law, snap her mother's spine, it was no more than Rowan Rhodes deserved. Emma hadn't seen her mother for over a year; not since the night they pulled the plug. In her dreams, she still heard the bleeps of the heart monitor and the final prolonged *reeeeeeeeep* signalling that her brother was dead.

The doctors had said it was simply a matter of mechanics, and her father agreed. In time he'd even talked Emma's mother round. *Talked her round*, Emma hitched a bitter smile. There hadn't been much talking in those last weeks. It was all just shouting and silence, her mother adamant that Richie wasn't dead, that they could still save him if they looked hard enough. Look where? Bob Rhodes demanded. The doctors had scanned and scanned again, there was no activity registering in Richie's brain. He was just a body kept alive by wires and fed with a tube.

Stop it, Emma told herself, and focused again on the pavement.

Connolly Avenue was a wide suburban street shaded with rows of silver birch. Only a few weeks ago those wispy branches had been crowned with the golden glow of autumn; now they stood pale and stark, their papery bodies like the ghosts of winter. Emma remembered her mother—Rowan, she corrected herself—telling her that the birch was the tree of Venus and was supposed to protect against dark spirits and the evil eye. Behind each tree stood an identical two-storey townhouse put up when the street was redeveloped ten years ago. Only one Connolly Avenue residence stood out. The Sparrow House rose from the earth like a diseased root and threw a tall and twisted shadow over its neighbours.

Emma heard Mrs Glock, the doctor's wife, calling to her. There was no music coming through her iPod but Margery Glock didn't know that. She pressed the buds into her ears and moved on. Whenever she walked along Connolly Avenue she never looked up. The memories were there, on every stretch of tarmac, swinging around every lamppost, sitting in every bough. Everywhere she looked, Richie was waiting.

Skeeeeekurgh. Pffffssst.

The asthmatic gasp of the lorry's airbrakes hooked her attention. Before she could stop herself, Emma's gaze had flitted from the pavement. Parked outside the Sparrow House, the removal truck idled while two deliverymen jumped down from the cab and threw open the back doors. One of the men operated a loading platform while the other leant against the back wheel and picked his teeth. When the platform was high enough, they leapt up and began to unload.

A dank pile of tottering bricks, the old mansion had stood empty ever since Hiram Sparrow had gone mad and killed all those people at the amusement park. Like Funland, most of the kids in the Lake, and quite a few of the adults too, thought the house was haunted. Even in broad daylight people tended to cross the road rather than pass its picket fence. Emma's gaze strayed to the house and, just as she'd feared, memories crowded in . . .

Days like that one were rare in the Lake. Shrouded by the three hills that overlooked the valley, even the brightest of summers tended to be full of shadows. On that glorious afternoon, however, the sun had lingered directly over the town, as if someone had reached out and pinned it to the blue. Emma, Richie, their cousin Henry, and his sidekick Sas had decided to spend the morning at the lake. They found most of the town kids already there, playing tag along the shore, disappearing in and out of Black Acre Forest, or simply sunbathing on the bank. That was what Chantelle, Madeleine, and Lola were doing when they arrived. Emma had known Chantelle McGarry since primary school, a friendship cemented when a lonely Emma had helped the kindly but somewhat empty-headed Chan with her maths homework. Madeleine Chow and Lola Flick were Chan's friends, and although Emma remained sociable with them for Chan's sake, she had never truly felt accepted by the other girls. Fascinated by fashion and spellbound by boys, Lola and Mads didn't really know what to make of the tomboyish Emma Rhodes. A fact borne out moments later when Emma decided to climb the rickety diving board that yawned over the lake. They all told her she was crazy. Lola repeated an urban myth in which a kid had jumped off the board only to end up buried headfirst in the sludge of the lakebed. Emma had just laughed, scaled the slimy ladder, saluted the spectators, and somersaulted off.

That was the day Miles Taggart noticed her. A few weeks later he asked her out.

The day ran forward in her mind: Emma and Richie sitting on the lawn outside their house. By the time they reached home, the lake water had dried from her hair and the sun had finally managed to unstick itself from the sky. The hills were tucking their shadows into Connolly Avenue when Richie made his announcement—

'Girls shouldn't be braver than boys.'

'Huh?' Emma waggled her head. There was still a bit of Milton Lake whooshing around in her ear.

'I'm the boy. People should be saying I'm the bravest, not you.'

'You're four years old, little man. No four year olds are brave.'

'But I *am.*'

'Then prove it.'

'How's I'm assupposed to do that?'

Emma grinned. 'Easy. Go ring the doorbell of the Sparrow House.'

Richie's mouth dropped open. He was too young to know what had happened at Funland, and her parents had forbidden Emma, on pain of eternal grounding, to tell the tale. Even so, Richie was wise enough to know that a bad, bad man had once lived in the big empty house across the street. He also knew that the Sparrow House was absolutely definitely haunted.

'I can't go over there. I'm not assupposed to cross the road by myself.'

'No problem.' Emma jumped to her feet. 'I'll go with you.'

The neighbourhood kids must still have been up at the lake, for all the pavements and lawns were empty. There was no one to watch as Emma guided Richie across the street and to the gate of the Sparrow House. Looking back, she felt ashamed, frightening a little boy like that, yet she knew that if Richie were still alive today she wouldn't have given that summer dare a second thought.

Hands on his shoulders, she squared him up to the gate. 'Time to be brave.'

Even if Hiram had never lived inside its walls, the house would always have inspired ghost stories. Emma's mother, a doctor of social history at the university, had taken a special interest in the stories and legends of Milton Lake, and had once told her daughter that the ramshackle ruin over the road had stood there for almost a hundred years. Back then there had been no other houses on Connolly Avenue and the Sparrow House had towered over the Lake, alone and aloof. Built by Hiram's grandfather, it had been a grand place in its day with a face of handsome sandstone bricks, a porch lined with smart Doric columns, and a beautiful rose window gracing the third floor.

Now the once-bright brickwork had turned tobacco-brown and several of the columns had fallen, taking much of the porch roof with them. All the windows were boarded up and the rose eye in the brow of the house was patched with a circle of bloated wood.

Richie licked his lips. ''K. Here goes.'

She had felt a twinge then: this was a cruel game, and if her parents caught wind of it she'd be in serious trouble. No more sleepovers with Chan, no more film nights with her dad. This weekend the Kinema by the Lake was showing a double bill of movies by the legendary Japanese director Akira Kurosawa. Emma had been almost as excited about seeing *Rashomon* and *Seven Samurai* as her film-fanatic father, but this stupid dare could ruin everything. She should take her brother straight home.

'You really want to do this, Rich?'

'Yup.'

'I can't talk you out of it?'

'Nope.'

'Then let me come with you.'

'No way!'

'But—'

'How'm I assupposed to prove I'm braver than you if you come with me?'

He had her there. 'All right, but I'm staying by the gate. You get scared, you run right back and I won't tell anyone,

I swear. Deal?' She spat in her palm and they shook on it. 'And watch where you step, I don't want to have to explain to Mum why there's a rusty nail sticking through her baby boy's big toe.'

'I'm not a baby!'

To prove it, he pushed open the gate and hurried up the overgrown path. While his little boy legs scampered, shadows descended from the hills. They chased Richie down the path, overtook him near the steps and stole under the porch. Suddenly the front door of the Sparrow House looked like a dark rectangular mouth waiting to swallow the little visitor.

'Careful!' Emma called.

Was she telling her brother to watch out for rusty nails and loose floorboards or was it the doorway that unnerved her? Emma had inherited her passion for movies from her father, but whereas Bob Rhodes stuck to art house films Emma's tastes covered all genres. She particularly liked old thriller movies in which shadows and sound effects created atmosphere. Now, as she watched her four-year-old brother grow smaller and smaller against the monstrous bulk of the ruined house, a hundred movie scenes came back to her: whispers in the basement, crazed laughter echoing from locked rooms, wasted fingers reaching for the door handle . . .

'Richie, come back.'

But it was too late. The house had cast its spell over her brother. He had already climbed the porch steps and was picking his way towards the door. *Step on a crack, break your mother's back, step on a nail, boy, you'll wail.* He ducked under a section of sagging roof, climbed over one of the fallen columns, slapped away a curtain of spider webs, and there he stood, a few centimetres from the door, craning onto tiptoes to reach the bell.

Richie, come back now!

Her lips were shaping the first word when the rat poked its head out from under the door. Even from the gate, Emma could make out a powerful body housed in sleek black fur. It squeaked out a warning, enough to push Richie back onto his heels and send him scurrying across the porch. He bounded down the steps and was back at the gate before Emma had a chance to open it.

'Did you see?' he gasped. 'The rat. It was *huuuuge*!'

'I saw.' She took his hand and led him to the roadside. 'That was stupid. I never should've let you do it. Don't tell Mum and Dad, will you?'

When he didn't answer she looked down at her brother. He was gazing back at the Sparrow House, those big green eyes fixed on the shadows that played under the porch. On the big black door that waited like an inviting mouth . . .

Within fourteen months, Richie Rhodes would try to return. Perhaps to complete the dare and ring the bell, perhaps just because the house called to him. It took a long time for the little boy to summon his courage and take his chance. And in the end, it was all for nothing. Richie never made it to the porch and the big black door. He didn't even make it as far as the gate.

2

'Someone's moving into the Sparrow House.'

Bob Rhodes looked up from his marking. 'Mm?'

Emma stacked the last dinner plate on the draining board and wiped her hands. Before turning to the kitchen table, she caught her reflection in the stainless steel cooker hood. A little greasy, her hair hung down to her shoulders; *before* she had kept it short and neat, but she hadn't had it cut since the funeral. She had never been that much into make-up, a bit of lipstick and blusher was her limit, but even that she had let slip. Now her skin was pale as milk and she thought her lips looked grey and ugly. No wonder Miles had lost interest.

'There were men delivering furniture and boxes all afternoon.'

Bob put down his pen. 'Sorry, love, start again.'

Emma gave an exasperated sigh. With his tweed jacket, Einstein hairdo, and that owlish way of blinking whenever someone asked him a question, Bob was the perfect model of an absent-minded professor.

'Final time,' she said. 'The Sparrow House—someone's moving in.'

'Oh. Who?'

'No idea. The delivery guys chucked all the stuff through the front door, locked up and drove off.'

'The Sparrow House?' His frown deepened. 'The *Sparrow House*?'

'Is there an echo in here?'

'But why would anyone want to live *there*? The place is practically derelict. I've told the council numerous times, it's a health hazard. They say it's private land, owned by some distant cousin of Hiram Sparrow, so it's up to her to maintain it. Bloody bureaucrats.'

'Maybe the cousin's come to live here.'

'Unlikely. I remember Margery Glock saying the woman was very wealthy and had her own estate up in Scotland. Can't see a rich woman coming to live in a rundown house at the end of a boring little street like this. She must have sold it.'

Emma turned to the kitchen window. It had started snowing again, a fine flurry glazing the pavement and sugaring the lopsided chimney of the Sparrow House. It had been three days since the first flake and Milton Lake had not yet seen the heavy fall promised by the forecasters. Richie had loved the snow.

'Your aunt Julia called. Said Henry's not been too well.'

'He hasn't been at school for a few days.' Emma's gaze remained fixed on the door beneath the porch. Snow spotted the paintwork, white on black. 'Is he OK?'

'I expect so, you know how my sister frets. Arthur says the boy caught a chill out in the woods.'

'Yeah, right. As if *he* cares.'

'You shouldn't be so quick to judge people, Emma.'

'Arthur Torve is a bully, plain and simple. Just because you're a parent doesn't mean you automatically care about your children.'

They locked eyes for a moment.

'Seems that colossus Henry hangs around with carried him all the way home,' Bob said, his attention returning to the pile of unmarked homework. 'Must've been a very sudden chill to make the boy so poorly.'

'I'll go see him later, bring him some sweets or something.'

'That's kind. You can tell him he got an A for his experiment separating out limonene last week. I had the pleasure of observing sixty students and Henry had by far the best lab technique. I can drop you off at the Torves' on my way into school if you like. Another ruddy departmental meeting, and then a staff meal afterwards. I don't expect to be home until after you've gone to bed.'

Departmental meetings, PTA meetings, head of year meetings. Some of them were probably genuine, but Emma knew that most were just excuses to get out of the house. It had been that way ever since Bob's wife had left him and Emma had started calling him by his Christian name.

It was a little after seven-thirty by the time Emma finished her homework. The barometer in the hall had dropped five degrees so it had to be close to freezing outside. She pulled her parka from the rack, muffled her ears with a scarf, and stepped into the night. The glare of streetlights dazzled the frosty air and tinged the snow-coated pavements a liquid orange. Emma allowed herself a single glance before setting her eyes on the path. First the kerb—she winced—then the gate and the porch and the door. On this bleak December night the other houses on Connolly Avenue were aglow with light and warmth. Only the Sparrow House stood apart, hugging the cold and the darkness to it. For the time being, it remained empty.

Emma crunched along the street, hers the only footprints in the snow. It was very nearly a mile and a half trek to the Torves' but she'd declined Bob's offer of a lift. She enjoyed walking and the chance it gave her to think. Not about Richie or the accident, her thoughts never lingered there, nor about her family, the vanished mother and the father who'd pulled the plug. Her friends, *ex-friends*, she corrected herself, sometimes swam into her mind but just as quickly she ushered them out again. Instead she focused on the future: a time when she could shake off guilt and grief and fly far away from Milton Lake and its ghosts. She was sixteen. In another two years she would go to university, stay in the city during the holidays, and never, ever come back to this miserable little town. After uni, she planned to travel, to see some of the sights from her favourite movies, to breathe exotic air and walk under different stars. She would be free at last.

You'll never be free, bitter and twisted, Richie's voice spoke inside her head. *Wherever you go, I'll be there, reminding you of what you did. How you let me die . . .*

By the time she reached the gates of Arthur Torve's lavish house it was snowing again. In the near distance she could hear the lap of the lake and the lonely cry of a night bird from Black Acre Forest. Emma removed a glove and pressed the intercom.

'Yes?' a voice snapped through the static.

'Uncle Arthur, it's me, Emma.'

She heard a *tsk*. 'What do you want?'

'Just visiting Henry, I heard he's been ill.'

'He has a minor chill. Thanks for your concern, Emma, but it's rather late to come calling.'

The intercom went dead. Emma checked her watch: 7:56. On whose planet was this considered 'rather late'? She thought about trying the intercom again but, much as she'd like to deny it, the bullying Arthur Torve scared her more than a little. She knew he scared Henry too, and her aunt Julia.

'Won't he let you in either?'

The giant crossed the road and joined her at the gate. Sas followed Emma's gaze up the driveway to the mock-Tudor mansion and the life-size stone lions guarding the door.

'How you doing, Ems?'

''M fine. How are *you*, Sas?'

Something was obviously wrong. She'd known Sas almost as long as she'd known Henry. He was a good kid, loyal as a faithful hound and transparent as a pane of glass.

'Bob told me you carried Henry out of the forest.'

Sas ran a hand through his snow-soaked hair. 'Yup.'

'Must've been a pretty bad chill if he couldn't walk.'

'Weren't no chill.'

'Then what?'

'Dunno, do I?'

'What happened, Sas? Truth now . . . Look, I'm gonna get it out of you one way or another, so you might as well spill.'

'It was the Chainers.'

'That stupid gang Freddie Liszt started up?'

''S not stupid.'

'You haven't joined? Oh Sas, next you'll tell me Henry's become a Chainer, too.'

'Nope.'

'Thank God for that!'

'He can't join. He didn't bring back the head.'

'OK,' Emma breathed, 'I want the full story and I want it now.'

There wasn't much to tell. It seemed that to become a member of this infantile gang, Henry had been required to bring back a mannequin's head from the Funland ghost train.

'He was in there a long time,' Sas continued, 'so I says to Freakazoid, rules or no rules, I'm going in to fetch him. You can chuck me out the gang if you want, but he's my best friend.'

Emma felt a surge of affection for the overgrown boy.

'We got over the gate and started running. We're almost at the train when I see Henry staggering down the path. Bloody hell, Ems, he looked . . . '

She glanced up into large, moist eyes. 'What?'

'Scared to death.'

Scared by a couple of dusty old dummies? That didn't sound like her cousin. His mother was a timid creature, frightened of her own shadow, but Henry had inherited some of the daredevil blood that ran through Emma's veins. Something unpleasant must have happened to him amid the shadows of Hiram's Horror House. Something seen? Something felt? Emma shook her head. If she wasn't careful she'd start believing all those stories about the vengeful spirits said to haunt the old amusement park.

'Did he seem ill before you went to Funland?'

'He was on edge, I suppose, we all were, you know how that place can get under your skin. But, Ems, I swear he was fine right up until he walked into the ghost house. I never should've let him go in there on his own. That place . . . '

Sas wiped a runner of snot from his nose and stamped his feet. The barometer in the hall must have dropped another couple of degrees, Emma thought.

'It was where Hiram Sparrow went to set off the bombs. Where he took the rifle and blew his brains out. Eleven years ago . . . Emma, do you think—?'

'Get a grip.' She reached up and slapped the boy's shoulder. 'A big, sensible man-mountain like you believing in ghosts?'

'Something scared him bad,' Sas insisted. 'I could feel him shaking in my arms, trembling like a little kid having the worst kind of nightmare. Didn't seem he blinked once all the way home. Just stared up at me and said the same thing over and over: *Where's the head, Sas? Where's the head?* Me and Mrs Torve took him up to his room, got him into bed. She was gonna call the doctor when his dad comes in, listens to what I had to say, and takes the phone out of Mrs T's hand. Says Henry caught a chill. Weren't no chill, Ems, I swear, and even if it was, why didn't he let us call the doc?'

A good question. Uncle Arthur had always been the kind of man who viewed illness as a test of character. Even so, his only child had been carried home in a trembling delirium. Surely even Arthur Torve would have allowed his wife to call the doctor.

'What happened next?'

'Mr Torve said Henry needed to rest and that I could visit tomorrow. That was three days ago. Every time I press the buzzer he tells me to go home. What're they doing to him in there, Ems?'

'They? What do you mean?'

'I've kept watch. They keep coming and going, half a dozen of them at all hours of the day and night. Mrs Glock was the first. She nearly ran me over as I was heading down the road after leaving Henry. I went back, looked through the gates. At first I thought Mr Torve must've come round and called Dr Glock, but the door opens and it's the doc's *wife* that waddles out. I hardly had time to think before another pair of headlights came flashing down the road. You won't believe who it was.'

Emma hardly noticed the fresh fall of snow, the wind pinching and prickling her face.

'Farter.'

Mr Sidney Carter—'Farter Carter' as he was known to the pupils of Tennyson Academy. The nickname was not entirely based on the fact that 'farter' rhymed with the headmaster's surname, for Mr Carter had an unfortunate problem with gas.

'Torve is president of the PTA, maybe Farter needed to discuss some school stuff,' Emma reasoned.

'He stayed all night.'

'What? How do you know that?'

'Because the cars were still there when I came back at six in the morning. Farter's beat-up old Nissan, Doc Glock's Beamer, and the others. I saw them all arrive within ten minutes of me being thrown out: next to come along, Miss Roper and Miss Worple.'

Roper and Worple? The furrows in Emma's forehead deepened into canyons. The two old ladies who ran the sweetshop by the train station? What on earth were they doing at the Torves'?

'They took the gate so fast I thought that three-wheel granny-mobile of theirs was gonna flip over. Then Mr Merriglass comes flying along on his bike.'

'Who?'

'Oh, maybe you don't know him, your dad being an atheist and all. He's the vicar at St Jerome's. I got a look at him as Henry's dad opened the front door. He had this really excited expression on his face, but seemed kinda worried too.'

'You've got sharp eyes, Sas. You said six people have been coming and going, who was the last?'

'No idea. A woman, I think. She pulled up in an old red Jaguar but the windows were tinted and I couldn't see her face. She parked right by the door and waited for Torve to open it, then rushed in. The others have come and gone but the Jaguar hasn't moved.'

Emma saw it now, stationed under the smooth gaze of the stone lions. While Miss Roper and Miss Worple's Reliant Robin and Mrs Glock's BMW were spotted with fresh snow, the red Jaguar wore a thick mantle over its graceful back. Sas was right, the mystery woman hadn't left the house in days.

'What are we gonna do?'

'What can we do?' Emma shrugged. 'Call the police and say Henry's parents are keeping him wrapped up nice and warm in his bed? Accuse them of inviting a few friends into their own home?'

'These people aren't their friends. I've known the Torves for years and I've never seen Mr Merriglass or those two old sweetshop women visit the house. Something's going on, Emma. You believe me, don't you?'

She did, but for the life of her she couldn't fathom what it all meant: Henry so scared he'd lost his wits; the Torves locking their son away like the mad relative in a gothic novel; and then that mismatched collection of people coming to call.

'I believe you, Sas, but there has to be a logical explanation for all this.'

'That sounds like your dad talking.'

True enough. The ever-rational Bob wouldn't credit for a moment the half-formed ideas swirling around at the back of Emma's mind—ideas inspired by a lifetime living under the shadow of Funland and the memory of Hiram Sparrow's crimes. Her father had once told her that Milton Lake was more prone to 'superstitious nonsense' than most towns because of what had happened here. He said that some tragedies were just too senseless for human beings to get their heads round, and so rather than think about the causes logically, they fell back on old ideas of good and evil. That was why, following the tragedy, ghost stories had taken root in the town.

'I'll speak to Bob,' she said. 'Uncle Arthur might be able to slam the door in our faces but he'll have to talk to his brother-in-law. Don't look so worried, Sas, we'll get to the bottom of this, I promise. Come on, I'll walk you home.'

After a little cajoling, she managed to prise him away from the gate. Between them they tried Henry's mobile a dozen times before reaching Sas's house on Old Chapel Road, every attempt answered by the same polite message: *Sorry, this phone is switched off.*

With a weary goodnight, Sas disappeared through the snug doorway of his mother's cottage and Emma turned her steps homeward. Snow whirled around her in gusts and eddies that seemed to mirror the storm of her thoughts. Before her world had closed down, one of Emma's favourite pastimes had been to curl up on the sofa and watch old black and white mystery movies. Her boyfriend Miles had never understood this passion, anything made before 1990 held no interest for him, but Emma thrilled at the smoky beauty of those classic films. Now it felt as if she had stepped into a detective story of her own. Of course, the truth about Henry's 'imprisonment' wouldn't be half as intriguing as her imaginings, but for now a window had opened and, for the first time in over a year, she found herself interested in the world outside.

By the time she reached Connolly Avenue, the moon was sitting cloudy-eyed above her house and the wind had hushed itself to sleep. Silence in the street, but for the ring of a distant telephone.

She took the key from her pocket.

'*Ems, 's that you?*'

The key dropped from nerveless fingers and made a perfect mould in the snow. She was hearing things: sounds from a TV or radio warped by the snow so that they sounded like . . .

'*Look up, I'm at the big round window! I'm watching you.*'

Her brother.

'Richie . . . '

It was barely more than a whisper on cracked lips . . . but he heard.

'*You didn't forget me! I knew you wouldn't! I've waited so long for you to hear me. Waited and waited and waited for you to look up from the pavement and* see *me.*'

His laugh, just as bright as she remembered it.

'*Look up now, Emma.* Look.'

Every instinct told her to grab the key, get into the house and bolt the door behind her. To leave the dead thing outside, giggling and alone. She felt something inside her mind crack, a hairline fracture in her wall of sanity. If she stayed out here with the voice then the crack would widen and she might never be able to patch it up.

'*Look, look, look.* See me.'

She obeyed.

The stained brickwork of the Sparrow House bled into the night so that the snow capping its roof appeared to float in midair. Beneath that white brow, a light was seeping from under the boarded-up rose window. Had the stranger moved in, Emma wondered? Or was it her little brother moving around in the attic and bringing light to the decade-old darkness of the Sparrow House? She left the key buried in the snow and moved towards the tumbledown gate and the shadows that waited beyond.

3

The house had been Richie's goal. Perhaps, after the plug was pulled, his spirit had flown here, determined to prove itself once and for all. Bob would laugh at such an idea; to him, Richie was gone for ever. Up until thirty seconds ago, Emma would have agreed: 'There's no such thing as a soul,' she had snapped when her cousin Henry tried to comfort her after the funeral. 'What's left of Richie is rotting in a wooden box under the earth, don't go imagining he's anywhere else.'

And yet now: '*Be brave. I'm waiting.*'

Emma moved in a daze along the garden path, a small part of her mind registering the undisturbed snow. At the thump of her boots, mice and rats nesting under the porch scuttled into darker, safer corners. She reached for the handle of the black door.

This afternoon she had watched the deliverymen haul in the last crate and lock the door behind them. Now it swung open with only the faintest of sighs. The air inside was stale and colder than a February dip in the lake. Beyond the door, a huge high-ceilinged hall stretched the entire width of the house, corridors branching off to left and right, the doors to rooms standing slightly ajar, as though there were people inside watching her through the cracks. An uncarpeted staircase carved from oak and silvered with spider webs rose in sections around the walls. Near the summit, moonbeams struggled at the chinks in a boarded window and threw feeble lances of light into the hall.

Dust covered every surface. Dust on the Tiffany lampshades, dust in the elephant's foot umbrella stand, dust circling the twenty or so crates stacked against the walls. In passing, she noticed the words stamped on the sides: **PROPERTY OF HARVEY DOWD ESQ**. The name seemed strangely familiar.

'*I'm up here. Hurry, Ems, hurry.*'

She tilted back her head and followed the staircase through all three storeys of the house. High above, just where the first moonbeams glittered, a pair of small chalk-white hands gripped and flexed around the banisters. Emma took a shuddery breath. Was this really happening or was she curled up on the sofa at home, dreaming dreams of captive cousins and haunted houses? She watched the hands slip back through the bars, heard the bump of bare feet and the creak of the attic door.

The stairs made barely a squeak as Emma rounded the newel post and gained the first floor. Every kid in Milton Lake had, at one time or another, been struck by the desire to investigate their town's tragic past. Emma had ignored the draw longer than most, fearing that if she delved too deeply into Hiram's horrors she'd never be able to open her bedroom curtains and look across the street again. It had been on one of their occasional sleepovers that Chan had convinced her to surrender to curiosity. Among the online newspaper reports they had found a map showing the layout of the Sparrow House. Though Emma saw it from her window every morning, the plan had presented the house as an unfamiliar place full of secret rooms and sprawling corridors, buried basements and cavernous chambers. It had also highlighted the location of Hiram Sparrow's bedroom.

Emma's eyes slid sideways. Under the spears of moonlight, the blue door shone like a pale portal. Breath coiling the air, she hurried past, making for the stairs and the second floor. Here another door confronted her, this time emerald green. The memory of the map reminded her that this room had belonged to Percival Sparrow, Hiram's father, a miserly old man who had met his death on this very staircase.

She reached the third landing. Here the moon-spears threw their full force against the attic door and illuminated the handprints on the knob.

'Richie.'

At the sound of her voice, the door sprang open.

Emma staggered back against a chaos of shrieks and the clatter of wings. A cyclone of black bodies filled the long, low attic. Seconds later, the dust had settled and the storm had vanished. The birds nesting under the tiles had made good their escape through a dozen different holes in the ruined roof. In the stillness that followed, a shower of snow wafted in and settled on the mounds of dung that littered the wooden floor. At the far end of the attic, the darkened glass of the rose window reflected a trembling girl with wide green eyes and an expression frozen halfway between hope and horror. There was no furniture in the attic, no place to hide. Emma was alone.

'*You should've been watching me.*'

She stepped forward. 'Where are you?'

The door slammed shut. Emma turned, grabbed the handle. It was stuck.

'*Watching me. Watching me. You didn't love me enough to save me.*'

'That's not true!'

'*Then why did I die?*' The voice dripped with spite. '*You knew I'd find a way. Knew I was just waiting for my chance—*'

'No!' She wrenched at the handle. 'I never thought—'

'*You wanted them all to yourself. Bob and Rowan and their perfect little girl. You hated me from the minute I was born.*'

The truth stabbed at Emma. When her parents had brought that soft, squirming, squalling bundle home from the hospital, she had resented him. For the first few months of his life she'd even refused to call him by his name, referring to her baby brother as 'the thing'. 'Why won't the thing stop crying?' 'The thing is so stinky.' 'Can't we just take the thing back to the hospital?' But even then, in those childish moments, she had never hated him.

Ice crackled around the handle. Emma snatched back her fingers and folded them against her chest. The Sparrow House had been cold before but now the temperature plummeted to a bone-numbing freeze. A spider web hanging from a rafter fell to the floor and shattered as if it were made of glass.

'*Turn round, sister. Look at what a year under the earth has done. Look, and then you can kiss me goodnight.*'

Emma obeyed.

The little boy stood under the boarded window, his head drooping so that a mop of brown hair masked his face. Richie Rhodes wore the remains of the suit in which he had been buried. After a year of worms and decay, the trousers were full of holes and the miniature jacket hung loose from his wasted shoulders. Stripped to the bone, a pair of powder-pale hands twitched at his sides.

'*You must pay for what you did.*' The voice gargled as if choking on grave dirt. '*You must give your life to me. Your soul, your* flesh . . . '

Step by painful step, the dead child moved towards her. Months under the earth had wasted his muscles, so he came forward like an infant learning how to walk, three clumsy shuffles followed by a sudden lurch.

'*Give me your flesh, Emma.*'

He stood before her now, a barefoot boy in his Sunday best. The stench and coldness that radiated from him made Emma's senses reel.

'*Give me what I ask and you won't have to see my face.*'

'Richie . . . I don't underst—'

'*Give me your flesh . . . and I'll forgive you.*'

Tears fell and froze on her cheeks. He would forgive her. The pain would stop, the darkness fall back.

'Yes,' she whispered, 't-take what you need. I'm here for you, Richie. I love—'

Their names. He had used their parents' names. *Bob and Rowan.* It had only been since they pulled the plug that Emma had started calling them by their first names. To Richie, they had *always* been Mum and Dad.

'You're not him.'

She backed up until her shoulders hit the door. Her hand gripped the frosted knob. Still it wouldn't budge.

'You're not Richie. Not my brother. What are you?'

'*GIVE ME YOUR FLESH!*'

The little boy began to change. His lustrous hair faded into limp grey strands that rustled down to the nape of his neck. His small hands cracked and widened, the fingers lengthening into arthritic claws as a rounded back hunched above his sloping shoulders. The joints of his knees and elbows popped and his legs and arms grew into long, spindly limbs. The rags of Richie's burial suit transformed into striped pyjamas stained with splodges of food and drink. By the time he stopped growing, the old man was eye-level with Emma.

'*We hunger for your flesssshhhhh,*' he slurped. '*You must give it to us. The whole town must surrender its flesh to the unmade.*'

Emma tried not to look into the empty eye sockets, nor at the lipless mouth with its thrashing, frothing tongue. In spite of the decay, she recognized the old man's face from the numerous pictures she had found on the internet. A beetle crawled out of a hole in Percival Sparrow's cheek and disappeared into the hollow of his left eye.

'We are coming out of the empty and friendless darkness. Emerging into the world of flesh.'

Percival placed withered hands against Emma's face. She willed herself to push him away but a kind of hopeless acceptance rooted her to the spot. Whatever was about to happen, it was no more than she deserved. She looked into the hollow suns floating before her, and thought—*an eye for an eye . . .*

Dimly, Emma heard the roar of an engine and the screech of rubber on the wet road outside. Lights flashed through the boarded window and arced over the slanted roof. A blade of illumination shone right through the . . . *Ghost*, her inner voice cracked with madness. *What would Bob say now? Not so easy to call a thing 'superstitious nonsense' when it's sinking its fingers into your flesh.* For that was what the old man was doing—pushing his vaporous hands into Emma's face until his wrists had reached her cheekbones. An icy agony lashed out from the fingers that wriggled at the back of her throat, the pain reaching into every corner of her body, skipping like fire across her mind and draining her strength. She fell like a rag doll, hitting her head hard on the attic floor.

Hiram's father loomed over her, his skinny hands sunk deep into her face and throat. He was searching for something, rooting around like a frantic thief. She could no longer feel her arms and legs. Her skin was cold as stone. Over the rush of blood in her ears, she heard the slam of a door, a hollered curse, the splinter of wood. Then footfalls on the stairs, fast and heavy.

'*Too late*,' the ghost chuckled. '*Whoever is coming, he cannot deny me the flesh. I will be whole again.*'

Percival lowered his face until she could smell the corruption on his breath. A fresh wave of agony, brighter than anything Emma would have thought possible, finally brought a scream to her lips.

'*He polished the stairs with grease, my darling Hiram. Couldn't wait to get his murderous mitts on my money, so he greased the stairs and the banister and watched me fall. But I wasn't ready to die. None of the unmade are, and now we have been called back to the world.*'

Dead fingers began to close around something inside.

Something dear and true and precious.

'*The way has been opened and the way becomes wider. We come to take back what was lost. We return for the fle—*'

Kicked off its hinges, the frozen door flew over Emma's head and ricocheted down the length of the attic. She was lying on her back, body arched onto her heels, pain dancing along her spine. In this bowed position, her head was thrown back and she saw the doorway upside down. He stood there for less than a second, a tall boy silhouetted against the dusty moonlight. There was something in his hand, a stick or length of metal. Then he was moving again.

The ghost of Percival Sparrow still had its fingers in her throat when the blow came. The boy brought the metal pipe—she could see it now, its blue-grey surface shimmering—up behind his right shoulder. He held it there like a baseball bat and, with a gut-deep roar, took the swing. His aim was true. Accompanied by a sound like the ripping of tough canvas, the spirit's head was cleaved from its shoulders. The creature clearly had some substance but it wasn't a thing of skin, blood, and bone. While its soft head splattered against the wall its body remained kneeling. A fountain of viscous fluid spurted from its neck; then the torso collapsed, crumbling and folding until all that remained was a lime green puddle foaming on the floor.

Emma choked. The deep unnatural pain was gone. A hand closed around her wrist and she was drawn gently to her feet.

'It's not over.'

The boy had a warm voice, dry and a little creaky. For some reason, it put her in mind of a sun-scorched road rutted by the passage of wheels and the tread of weary men. *He's American . . .*

'You don't need to see this. No one does. No one *should*.'

Despite his words, he made no attempt to guide her back through the door. He held her by the arm, his grip strong but not uncomfortable. She stole a sideways glance. It was too gloomy in the attic to confirm anything beyond what she already knew—a boy of about her own age, a few centimetres shorter than Sas and, despite the cold, dressed in jeans and a thin white T-shirt. He had raced up three flights of stairs, smashed a door off its hinges and decapitated a ghost with a metal bar that, by the look of it, weighed a tonne, yet he didn't seem to be sweating or even breathing that hard.

'*Strange boy . . .*'

Percival Sparrow echoed Emma's thoughts. She looked down at the smoking puddle and found a face floating on the surface.

'*But you will not deny us. The blind necromancer has opened the way and the more he calls the wider the path becomes. This is only the second summoning, and as yet we come one by one, but soon the calls will multiply and the gates will weaken until the hungry break free in a flood. The flood that comes for the flessshhh—AAARRRRRGGGGGHHHHHH!'*

It was a scream the like of which Emma had never heard. A hellish, hopeless, heart-rending horror. It haunted the attic for a long time after the puddle had finally evaporated.

'Where—?'

'Gone.' The grip around her arm tightened. 'Time you were gone, too.'

Before she could catch her breath, he had pulled her through the door and across the landing. All the gentleness of a moment ago seemed to have left him. He took the stairs three at a time while she stumbled in his wake. Partway down the first flight, her feet slipped on the dusty oak and she fell against him. To stop herself keeling over, Emma pressed one hand against the small of his back and the other against a firm shoulder. He turned and looked at her.

Hazel eyes like sombre pools set into a pale face. Each feature was sharp and prominent: a nose just the right side of hawkish, a strong chin jutting from a hard jaw, cheekbones like curved blades. The dark hair that fell into his eyes was cropped short at the back, resulting in a peculiar, uneven cut. Emma supposed he was handsome, but not in any obvious or conventional way.

'I can carry you if you want.' His voice was soft again. 'I guess I'm sorry, for the rough stuff.'

'I don't need to be carried,' she said, a little harder than she'd meant.

'OK.'

He guided her down to the second floor, then the first. A hundred questions rattled inside her head; earth-shattering questions about life and death, souls and spirits, gates and necromancers, whatever the hell they were. Questions so huge that every time she tried to frame them the words seemed to crumble on her lips. By the time they reached the ground floor she had fallen back on something simple.

'Who are you?'

He stopped and let go of her hand. 'Best you don't know, miss.'

'*Miss?*' she almost laughed. 'Who says "miss"?'

'I do. Now if you please, it's late and I have a lot of unpacking to do.'

She looked around at the crates. One had been broken open, its heavy lid tossed against a wall. Before coming to her rescue he had rifled through the packing cases, but for what? The metal bar . . . She shook her head. Why would anyone pack such a thing?

'Harvey Dowd. You're the new owner of the Sparrow House.'

'Goodnight, Miss Rhodes.'

Strong fingers locked around her wrist.

'How d'you know my name?' she demanded. 'How did you know I was in trouble?'

He moved her to the front door, opened it, and deposited her on the porch.

'Watch your step, the floorboards are treacherous.'

'What's going on in this house . . . ?'

And then she made the connection. She ought to have seen it right away but her mind had been clouded with fear and pain. Her cousin Henry was involved in this somehow. Strange things did not often happen in the sleepy town of Milton Lake (not since Hiram Sparrow's massacre eleven years ago) and now two inexplicable events had occurred within a few days.

'Please, you have to tell me. My brother—'

'The spirit read your mind, showed you what it wanted you to see. That wasn't your brother.'

'I know, it was an "unmade", but what are they?'

He reached out and held her by the shoulders. Hazel eyes bored into hers.

'Listen to me, Miss Rhodes, and listen well: you are to go home, you are to sleep, you are to forget everything that happened here. It was a bad dream, understand?'

'No!' She shook herself free. 'Are you nuts? How can I forget?'

He blinked. His brow furrowed.

Harvey Dowd slammed the door in her face.

4

'You look tired, didn't you sleep last night?'

Usually Bob was out of the house before she stirred but today he had found her at the breakfast table, nursing a cup of strong black tea. Had she slept? No. In fact, she hadn't even gone to bed. After being ejected from the Sparrow House, she had spent half an hour hammering on the front door while Harvey Dowd played deaf to her pleas and threats.

Back home, she sat at her bedroom window and stared across the street. The house looked as it always did, cold and cemetery-still. Was she going mad? Perhaps her friends had been right that day they confronted her in the school gym. Miss Langley, the girls' PE teacher, had asked if Emma would mind staying behind to tidy up after the netball match. That was where they found her, Chantelle, Miles, Madeleine, and Lola. They felt sorry for her, of course, Miles had said, and God knows they'd been patient, but it had been almost six months since Richie's death, and they all had to get on with their lives. Anyway, it was just weird, Madeleine added, how Emma didn't even cry. Lola said it was like she was carved from stone. Chan had just stood there, holding Miles's hand and avoiding Emma's gaze. When she didn't respond to anything they said, Miles suggested his girlfriend (*ex*-girlfriend) should 'get some help', and the four of them left her alone in the gymnasium.

Bob took his bowl to the sink. She watched him rinse and stack. Then something seemed to catch his eye and he leant forward and used the cuff of his blazer to wipe a spyhole in the misted window.

'I see your stranger's moved in.'

'What?'

She joined him at the sink. Through her own spyhole, the Sparrow House presented its blind and lifeless face. It had all been a crazed dream—the ghost, the boy, perhaps even Sas and his story about Henry and the amusement park.

'There's no one there.'

'*Someone's* there all right,' Bob insisted. 'And whoever he is, he has superb taste. That thing's a classic.'

He pointed down the side of the house. Half hidden in shadows, a powder-blue motorcycle stood balanced on its kickstand. It was a beautiful machine, muscular around the wide eye of its headlamp and with sleek chrome piping lending it lean and stylish lines. Emma remembered the roar of the engine, the headlight beam splashing into the attic darkness.

'What I wouldn't give to ride one of those.' Bob whistled 'You recognize it, Ems?'

She stared at him. Did Bob know Harvey Dowd?

'The fifties double bill at the Kinema? We went together, don't you remember?' She saw the hurt in his eyes. '*Sunset Boulevard* followed by *The Wild One*? That was the bike Marlon Brando rode in the movie, a Triumph Thunderbird 6T . . . ' He turned away. 'I should be getting to work. Bloody meeting went on for hours last night, I've got stacks of marking to catch up on. Do you want a lift?'

'I'd rather walk.'

'Suit yourself.' He scooped up an armful of papers from the table. At the kitchen door, Bob paused. 'You're all right, aren't you, Ems? If there's anything—'

'I'm fine.'

He nodded and disappeared into the hall.

Before she left for school, Emma crossed the road and tried the black door again. There was no answer and, after a moment's hesitation, she descended the porch steps and started the long march to Tennyson Academy.

Go home. Forget everything. And in the attic: *You don't need to see this.* That's what he'd said, yet the boy had allowed her to watch as the face in the pool spoke its cryptic words and screamed its terrible scream. Maybe he hadn't had time to drag her away. Maybe he needed to hear the message the spirit delivered. Yet something told her this wasn't right—the boy had experience, knowledge, and nothing the ghost said seemed to surprise him, so why had he kept her there, by his side?

Halfway down Connolly Avenue, Emma saw Mrs Glock shuffling her big behind into the driving seat of her BMW. Damn! With everything that had happened, she'd forgotten to speak to Bob about Henry. It all had to be connected, didn't it? Harvey Dowd and the apparitions, Henry and the mysterious comings and goings at the Torves'?

Before Mrs Glock could pull out of the driveway, Emma slapped a hand on the bonnet of her car. The doctor's wife blinked and wound down her window.

'My dear, you did give me a start!'

'How's Henry?'

The directness of the question caught Margery off-guard. 'Henry?'

'My cousin, Henry Torve.'

'Ah, yes . . . Is there something wrong with him?'

'You know there's something wrong with him.' Emma flashed a cheery smile. 'Haven't you been visiting my aunt and uncle? Henry's friend says he's seen your car in the drive a lot over the past few days.'

Bejewelled fingers gripped the steering wheel. 'Of course, so silly of me. Arthur and I are co-presidents of the Milton Lake Historical Society and we're planning to expand the visitor centre by the lake. There's so much work involved that I seem to spend more time at the Torves' than I do in my own home! Your cousin, now. Yes, I'm told he's caught a bit of a ch—'

'A chill, right. And all the others? Miss Roper and Miss Worple, Mr Carter?'

'All committee members, devoted to the cause of keeping Milton Lake's rich heritage alive.'

'All of it?' Emma raised an eyebrow. 'What about the Sparrow House? That's the oldest house in the Lake and it's falling to pieces. Why doesn't the Historical Society look into that?

Maybe because it's a private residence you don't have the power. You could always contact the new owner, though.'

A flicker behind the pink-rimmed spectacles. 'New owner?'

'Moved in last night. I'm surprised you didn't notice the delivery trucks—something wrong with your binoculars, Mrs Glock?'

'Now, Emma, you shouldn't tease.' She smiled mischievously. 'But I must confess I'm curious. Who is our new neighbour?'

'I don't know his name,' Emma lied. 'He's just a kid. His parents'll probably turn up today . . . '

There had to be an adult in the picture, didn't there? If he could ride a motorbike, the boy was probably seventeen, he certainly didn't look much older. What seventeen year old could afford to buy a house, even one as rotten as the Sparrow place?

'Away with the faeries, Emma?'

'The ghosts.'

'I beg your pardon?'

'Ghosts.' She eyed the woman closely. 'Spirits.'

Mrs Glock's jaw went slack. For a moment, Emma thought that she was about to say something. Then the guarded expression returned and Margery Glock wound up her window and drove the BMW into the churned slush of the road.

Emma barely had time to catch her breath before she heard the growl of the motorbike. Clad in jeans and a black leather jacket, Harvey Dowd raced past without so much as a glance in her direction. She watched him weave the

Thunderbird along the line of early morning traffic already crowding Connolly Avenue. A breakneck slalom around buses, wing mirrors, and cyclists brought him to the junction where he turned into the main road that led out of Milton Lake.

It was only when she reached the end of the road that Emma realized she had not kept her eyes fixed on the pavement. For the first time in over a year, she had walked the street of memories and been untroubled by dark thoughts. Filling her lungs with icy air, she continued on her way. The miles passed, the wet snow slurped at her boots, and the keen, pale face of the boy stayed fixed in her mind's eye until she reached the eastern edge of town and the gates of Tennyson Academy.

There they stood, as they did every morning. Madeleine and Lola exchanged mobile phones and laughed hysterically at some online video while Chantelle, decked out in a skimpy outfit that only approximated their school uniform, smoothed down Miles's collar and stared adoringly into his cool blue eyes.

Madeleine spied her from the gate. 'Weirdo alert!'

'Mads, don't be mean!' Lola gasped, then fell into another fit of hysterics.

Chan gave Emma a sheepish glance and returned to her role as chief priestess at the shrine of Miles. Passing through the gate, Emma was stunned when Miles caught hold of her hand and pulled her into their cliquey circle.

'We need to talk.'

It was the first time any of them had spoken to her since the confrontation in the gym. Since then it had all been sly looks and whispered jokes on the girls' side while Chan tried to hide her blushes. Meanwhile Miles behaved as if she had simply ceased to exist. Looking back, it was all so obvious—the way Chan had laughed at his jokes, the glances thrown when she thought no one was looking. It must have been very easy after the accident for her to convince the neglected Miles that he might have a lot more fun with the kind of girl who hung on his every word.

Now Chan looked thunderstruck as Miles brushed her away and took Emma's hand.

'What are you doing, babe?'

'I just need a minute with Ems.'

'But you're supposed to be with Chan,' Lola gawped. 'This is not cool.'

'Agreed,' Emma said. She tried to pull away but he held her fast. 'You let me go or I'll kick you where you don't want to be kicked.'

'OK. 'S cool.' Hands raised, he backed up. 'It's just . . . Your mum, she knew about stuff, right? Freaky stuff. I remember coming over when she was still around and her talking about souls and auras, crap like that.'

'You've been acting weird all morning.' Chan frowned. 'What's going on with you, M-Tag?'

She called him 'M-Tag' now? Emma wanted to burst out laughing.

Miles bent down and tried to lock eyes with Emma. It was then that she noticed how his hands were shaking.

'What's happened?' she asked.

'She believed it, didn't she? Your mum.'

'Believed what?'

'Souls. Spirits. Your dad thought it was rubbish, but she . . . ' He licked his lips. 'My grandad. I've seen . . . '

Her heart lurched. 'What?'

The school bell shook the frosted air and the last stragglers dawdled through the gate.

'What's she talking about?' Chantelle demanded. Then, for the first time in months, she addressed Emma. 'He's *my* boyfriend. Mine. He doesn't need you—'

Miles swallowed hard. He tried his best to smile. 'Got you!' He pointed a still trembling finger at Emma. 'It was a trick. I wanted to get her to say she believed in ghosts, just like that crazy mother of hers. I almost got her to say it too, then you had to start flapping that pretty mouth.' He grabbed hold of Chantelle and planted a kiss on her glossy lips.

Lola and Madeleine cackled as if they had been in on the joke from the start.

'Oh my gosh, she is *such* a freak,' Madeleine marvelled. 'Gonna get lost now, freak?'

'Happy to.'

At the school entrance, she looked back. Chantelle and the girls were collecting their bags ready to saunter into class while Miles stood at the fence, fingers tight around the chain-link. Emma was surprised by the concern that flickered in her heart. Craving attention, he had left her for her best friend but even now she couldn't deny the good times they'd enjoyed together. Beneath that vain exterior, she had discovered a boy who helped his little brother with his homework and a devoted son who spent his weekends mucking in at the Oxfam shop managed by his mother. Now something was haunting Miles Taggart and, much as it might rankle, Emma found that she still cared.

It wasn't until lunchtime when she was crossing the playing fields towards the library that she saw Miles again. Propped against a goalpost, he was staring down at his muddied football boots. A game had just finished and his teammates were clapping him on the back before heading off to the shower block. He didn't move a muscle, just stood there like a waxwork. There was no sign of Chantelle. Emma was about to call out to him when Sas lumbered into view. When she glanced back, Miles was a speck in the distance. He seemed to be making for the thick arm of Black Acre Forest which curled protectively around the school.

'Did you speak to your dad?'

'Sas, I'm sorry, I didn't get a chance.'

His face fell. 'You promised. We have to find out what they're doing to Henry—his folks, Farter Carter, and the rest.'

'I know. Listen, something happened last night and I didn't have time—'

'He was there for *you*, Ems. When Richie died and your mum left, Henry was there. You shut him out, just like you shut everyone out, but he was there. All I asked you to do was talk to your dad.'

'Sas, wait!'

He shook his head and stalked back to the main school building. Emma wanted to go after him, to explain her experiences in the Sparrow House and how it might all be connected to what had happened to Henry at Funland, but how could she without frightening Sas away? Sure, he knew something odd was going on at the Torves', but ghosts? Before she went any further, she needed some evidence that her crackpot story was true.

The Smedley Memorial Library was a separate building to the modern Tennyson Academy. A single-storey structure, it stood on the site of a primary school that had burned to the ground in 1903. Every pupil at Tennyson knew the date because the old redbrick building that had replaced the school, and which now served as their second library, sported a plaque outside the door. Etched on the grey slate was the date and the name of the teacher who had perished in the fire—Miss Evelyn Alberta Smedley.

Most of her classmates favoured the stylish chrome and glass library of the main school, but to Emma that was a soulless place. She much preferred the cosiness of Smedley with its aroma of damp plaster and dusty books. There were corners in which you could hide away for hours and heavy oak tables into which four generations of children had carved their initials. Patched beanbags lay scattered on the floor while a quiet study area with half a dozen computers occupied the rear.

'Emma, how lovely to see you.'

Perched on her seat behind the issue desk, the librarian blinked over her half-moon spectacles. No one knew how old Miss Lucas really was, but kind estimates put her at sixty-five. Emma smiled and gestured towards the study area.

'Feel free, dear. You're my only visitor today.'

She dumped her bag under the desk and fired up one of the almost obsolete PCs. Connecting to the internet, she typed 'Hiram Sparrow' into Google. Start at the beginning, she thought. The beginning for her had been in the attic of the Sparrow House.

After a few minutes she realized that she was already aware of all the online material relating to the Funland massacre. In any case, the mystery seemed larger than the pathetic figure of Hiram Sparrow and his grubby crimes. True, his father Percival had returned from the dead, and Henry's encounter had taken place in the Funland ghost train, but what if these hauntings weren't restricted to the Sparrow family? She now felt sure that her ex-boyfriend had seen something too. Like it or not, she needed to talk to Miles.

For now, it was time to widen her gaze. She typed 'ghost' into the search engine. Six hundred and ten million hits. She blew a strand of hair from her forehead and tried the first entry from an online encyclopedia: here was the noisy poltergeist and the ominous fetch, phantom trains and ghost ships, spirit guides and psychopomps. Amid the hundreds of ghostly variations one nugget of information caught her eye—since ancient times it had been reported that iron had the power to repel cursed spirits. Emma thought of the metal pipe Harvey had used on the ghost in the attic . . .

She entered 'the unmade'. A few results, none relevant. Then, prefacing the terms with 'ghost' she typed 'the gates', 'the hungry', 'the empty wastelands'. Nothing significant.

She tapped out 'Harvey Dowd' and clicked. The page loaded and Emma sat up arrow-straight in her chair. Of course!

She knew the name had sounded familiar. Another double bill of old movies at the Kinema by the Lake flashed into her mind. An afternoon spent with her father under the flickering projector light, munching popcorn and sharing sweets. One of the films had been a black and white comedy starring James Stewart as a man whose best friend was an invisible six-foot rabbit. Taking its name from the rabbit, the movie was called *Harvey*, and the eccentric man, Elwood P. *Dowd.*

It was an alias.

A made-up name.

Harvey Dowd was a lie.

5

Emma was almost at the classroom door when she realized she had left her bag in the library. The afternoon bell echoed through the corridors and students swarmed inside, droning and buzzing as they hovered by their lockers. She was about to take off when she saw Bob sidestepping through the swarm.

'Hey! Can we have a word?'

He checked his watch. 'Sorry, running late.'

'But you don't teach Thursday afternoons.'

'Departmental meeting.'

'It's about Henry. I need you to call Uncle Arthur—'

But he had already vanished, swallowed up by the crowd.

Emma gave the door of the language lab a savage kick and set off in the direction of Smedley Library. En route, she saw Sas shambling into one of his classes. He turned away when she waved.

There wasn't a soul to be seen in the playing fields. Emma's gaze moved to the road beyond the school fence. She half-expected to see him there, sitting astride the Thunderbird, a visored helmet turned towards her; this strange boy with a false name who understood the secrets of the dead. Harvey Dowd. An odd alias for a seventeen year old to have chosen—the name of an imaginary bunny from a film that most kids their age would never have heard of.

The sun was already dipping in the midwinter sky when Emma stepped into the snug warmth of the library. She found the issue desk unmanned and no sign of the librarian among the bookcases. Miss Lucas had been warned by Farter Carter that, if she had to abandon her post, she must lock the door behind her. Computer equipment had been stolen from Smedley on more than one occasion. Emma didn't like to skip class but decided she had no choice but to wait until Miss Lucas returned. She dropped into her old chair, stirred the dozing computer and entered her student login.

Had there been anything she'd missed in her earlier researches? A clue from the Sparrow House? A sight, a sound, a word . . . *The blind necromancer.* That odd phrase of Percival Sparrow's popped into her head. She typed and clicked. An encyclopedia entry immediately redirected her to 'Necromancy':

An ancient form of magic in which a sorcerer attempts to call forth the soul of a deceased person. Sometimes the goal of the necromancer is simply to reawaken the dead, more often it is for the purpose of divination. Spirits might be invoked to provide messages from the other side, to speak of past times and foretell the future, or to guide the living to some secret knowledge or hidden treasure. The dangers of necromancy were once considered very real. The dead might break free of the necromancer's control, especially if the magician was unskilled or—

The library door slammed shut. Emma looked up from the screen.

'Miss Lucas?'

The lights flickered and went out. The computer blipped to black and the electric heaters whirred to a stop. It was still quite bright in the library; the golden sun poured through the slatted blinds and laid bumblebee stripes across the cramped shelves and empty tables. From somewhere close by a small bell started to *tring*. A telephone demanding to be answered. Emma rose from her seat and moved towards the issue desk. Her breath began to steam the air and gooseflesh puckered her skin. The heaters had only just switched off, how could it have already turned so cold?

She leant over the desk and picked up the phone. 'Hello?'

The line was dead, but the ringing continued.

Necromancer. She gripped the desk. *Caller of the dead . . .*

'*C'uurrrrg.*'

The sound came from the study area at the back of the library where Emma had been sitting. A horrible rasping noise accompanied by a smell reminiscent of a Sunday roast burned to a crisp. Wherever it was, the telephone ceased its ringing and Emma turned and looked over her shoulder.

A small woman stood with her face turned to the wall. She was about the size of Miss Lucas and, for a moment, Emma breathed easy. The librarian must have slipped in without her noticing. With a greeting on her lips, Emma took several steps forward before the figure came suddenly and dreadfully into focus. It was *not* Miss Lucas.

Dead for more than a century, Evelyn Alberta Smedley ran her hand over the wall. '*Solid. S-solid at last.*'

She wore the smoky tatters of a schoolmistress's frock, a few shreds of lace at the collar and a blackened bow at the back. Evelyn Smedley shuffled on the burned sticks that were her legs and began to turn her hairless head towards Emma.

'*Flesh.*' Words choked from smoke-scarred lungs. '*I need y-your f-flesh.*'

Emma ran to the library door and yanked the handle. Just like in the attic, the knob was coated with ice and would not budge. From behind came the creak of charred bones and the crackle of roasted skin. Miss Smedley was making her painful way through the library.

Emma couldn't rely on the pale-faced boy rescuing her again. She had to *think* . . . Iron! Yes! She spun round, eyes raking the room. There were scraps of metal lying everywhere: staples and paper clips, chair legs and heater panels, but all too small to use as a weapon or too difficult to detach in a hurry, and none of it definitely made of iron. Taking on the ghost would mean close-quarters combat. If she attacked with the wrong weapon? Well, all Evelyn had to do was reach out with her cold hand.

The spirit had reached the issue desk, not twenty paces from where Emma stood. She could now see the sensible black shoes that had melted into Evelyn's legs, making it difficult to tell where leather stopped and skin started. Emma tried to look away. It was a hopeless effort. She caught sight of an egg-shaped head with little holes where the ears had been; goggle eyes staring out of lidless sockets; skin ridged white and scarlet, like the contours left by lava on the face of a volcano.

'*Must have y-your flesh!*'

She ducked under the reaching hand and slammed into the issue desk. Piles of uncatalogued books and Miss Lucas's 'Keep Calm And Carry On' coffee mug went crashing to the floor. A shadow told her to duck again as the spirit's hand swiped through the air. This time, Emma stayed low. She crawled under the desk, scuttled into Miss Lucas's domain, and regained her feet.

A metre of oak separated Evelyn from her prey. The ghost threw back its head and screamed, an ear-splitting shriek that shattered the window in the office door and sent loose papers skirling around the library. Evelyn leant over the desk and grasped the edge on Emma's side. The ease with which Percival Sparrow's head had left its shoulders should have told her that these spirits were not completely solid, yet still Emma stood amazed as Evelyn began to pull her body *through* the table. While her legs moved under the desk and her upper body floated towards Emma, the same feverish word scraped through Evelyn's lips—*Flesh, flesh, fl-fl-flesh!*

Emma eyed the windows. Set high into the walls, they were probably sealed like the door—these spirits seemed able to lockdown their hunting grounds—still, it was worth a try. She was about to push a desk against the wall and clamber up when a blaze of sunlight flickered through the frosted glass.

The ghost screamed again. Bathed in the flame-red light of the setting sun, Evelyn Smedley clutched at what remained of her face.

An idea. A chance. Emma bolted for the little back office behind the issue desk. It meant passing within arm's reach of the spectre, but Evelyn was still shrieking, trapped inside an imaginary hell of pain and fire. For the moment, she was unaware of her prey.

Emma pulled open the door . . . and groaned. Miss Lucas might be a sweet old lady but she was also the most scatterbrained person Emma knew. Her office was a chaos of chipped mugs and broken kettles, box files and board games, yellowing calendars and cardboard boxes full of rubber bands, paperclips, staplers, and Post-it notes.

The screaming from the library had stopped. A shadow gathered in the doorway.

Emma started throwing books and boxes over her shoulder. It had to be here. She had seen Miss Lucas confiscate it from a group of Year Nines only a few days ago. Unless she'd binned it, of course. *If that's true, then I'm lost . . .*

'*Flessshhh!*'

'Yeah, so you said.' Her back to the ghost, Emma kept searching. 'Don't you know any other tunes? That one's getting pretty old.'

'*Fl-fl—*'

'—esh? You know, I'm starting to miss Percival. At least you could have a proper conversation with him.'

A hand landed on her shoulder. A second grasped her hair and pulled back her head. Skinless lips touched Emma's ear.

She felt a spray of spittle as the dead teacher repeated her favourite chant. Then the hand on her shoulder transferred to her cheek and she felt a familiar pain as the ghost's fingers pressed into her face. She was about to cry out when she saw the lighter. It sat in a box of confiscated property on the shelf to her right. She stretched, fingers fumbling for the box and the tiny hope that rested inside . . .

An icy agony lurched into her throat, a spasm jolted her body, and Evelyn's grasp slipped just enough for Emma to make up that last crucial inch. She hooked the box with her middle finger. It teetered on the edge of the shelf. For a heart-stopping second, she thought it would come crashing down and spill its contents across the floor. She made a desperate grab. Among a fistful of mischief-making material—a laser pen, a permanent marker, a pocketknife—she retrieved the lighter. The pain made her movements clumsy, but she managed to drop the other items while keeping hold of her prize.

The unmade woman chuckled. She sensed that her own prize was close at hand . . .

Emma thrust the lighter over her shoulder and felt it touch the paper-dry flesh of Evelyn's face.

'Scared yet?' Emma gasped, and flicked the wheel.

She heard the whisper of the little flame. Then the hideous scream. Those lips had been so close that the cry pierced her eardrum like a hot pin and set stars dancing before her eyes. Emma felt the fingers withdraw from her face and throat, leaving the precious something safe. Shivering, she turned, lighter still in hand. Evelyn's skin had been as parched as dead tree bark, all it had taken was a single spark. Now the schoolteacher's head was wreathed in a red and orange cowl, the flames spreading downwards, skipping across her shoulders and engulfing the rest of her body. Emma looked on, pity in her heart. To have died in such a terrible way, and now to have to relive it in death . . .

Still screaming, Evelyn tottered forward into the office. Emma jumped out of the way as the ghost landed in a pile of paperbacks. Her writhing form had started to melt into that same lime-green ooze into which Percival Sparrow had disintegrated. It seemed that iron wasn't the only way to kill a ghost. Before the decay was complete, the flames around Evelyn began to catch at the paperbacks. The fire spread quickly, jumping from book to book. Embers floated into the air and smouldered at the edges of calendars and box files. By the time Evelyn had formed a bubbling puddle on the floor, the fire had mounted every shelf and was pushing Emma out of the office.

Within a few seconds, the windows had clouded over and flames were lashing into the library. Emma vaulted the issue desk and headed straight for the door. Before she had a chance to try the handle, the door burst open.

She stared at the stranger. 'Better late than never.'

The boy from the Sparrow House glanced over her shoulder. She could feel the heat of the conflagration pressing at her back.

'An unmade?'

'I dealt with it. Now are you going to move or shall we just stand here chatting?'

He took her hand, gently this time, and guided her from the building.

'We should get out of here,' he said. 'Too many awkward questions otherwise.'

'Yeah, I've got a few of my own.' She pulled her hand free. 'And this time you're going to answer them. You've been a very naughty rabbit, *Mr Dowd.*'

A furious look darkened his features. And then he smiled, his eyes lighting up.

'You've got guts. Brains, too, if you handled an unmade all by yourself. Maybe I—'

BOOM. Punched out by flames, the windows of the Smedley Memorial Library shattered and a fire alarm sounded from the main school. In a few seconds, teachers and pupils would come flooding into the playground.

'What were you saying about getting out of here?'

He took her hand again and together they raced across the fields. When they reached the shelter of the forest, Emma looked back and saw smoke billowing like a huge black claw, its talons scratching at the colourless sky. She turned to the boy.

'It's bad, isn't it? Whatever's coming.'

'Yes,' he murmured. 'Very bad . . . Worse than anything you can imagine.'

His smile died and, with it, the setting sun.

6

It was weird, being back in the Sparrow House. Just last night these walls had echoed to the sound of a child's voice, familiar and yet full of malice. Now, with a few battery-powered lamps burning in the hall, the atmosphere of evil seemed to have lifted.

'What are these?'

Emma reached out to touch the jingling chimes that hung from every doorway.

'They're something my . . . my grandpa helped invent,' he said, drawing her hand away. 'You've heard of dream-catchers?'

'American Indians made them, right?'

He nodded. 'The dreamcatchers of the Ojibwe hung over the places where they slept. Good dreams filtered through while nightmares were snared in the net. This is based on the same principle. After Percival Sparrow's spirit departed—'

'Departed? That's one way of putting it. Another might be that you cut off his head and sent him screaming back to his grave.'

The boy's chuckle was sunny and dry, and again Emma was struck by an image floating at the back of her mind. It flickered there, as if thrown by a projector: a long dirt road raised above the level of a glistening lake or wetland and, in the distance, an old clapboard farmhouse. She saw fresh tyre marks on the road, but no sign of a car.

'Are you OK?'

She shook her head. 'Go on, you were talking about Percival.'

He looked at her for a moment, his gaze focusing on the spaces around her. 'After the spirit departed I wanted to make sure the house stayed clean. My grandpa called his invention "soul-catchers". The loop is made of iron, the net is finely worked silver, another metal with supernatural properties. Instead of nightmares the nets catch any malevolent ghost that might try to enter the house.'

'How do you know all this stuff? Did your grandad teach you?'

'Yes. My grandpa.'

'Is he the one who sent you? Did he buy the house? Is he coming here, too?'

'Whoa,' he chuckled again, 'you could give Ed Murrow a run for his money! Come on, I'll answer a few of your questions and then I need you to answer some of mine.'

He led the way down one of the shadow-cloaked corridors and into a large room at the back of the house. There were more lamps set up here, positioned on half a dozen unopened crates. Streetlight played at the gaps in the boarded window while the lamps poured yellow puddles onto the ceiling. Emma guessed that this might once have been a sitting room or parlour. An enormous marble fireplace took up most of one wall, its columns decorated with carved vines and flowers. Covered in decades of dust, an expensive-looking rug stretched out over the bare wood floor.

Entering the room, Emma saw that one of the crates had been opened. She couldn't resist a quick peek inside. Typical of a boy's packing, the box was a jumble of unwashed clothes and personal possessions. What weren't typical were the contents: a bundle of faded magazines called *Boy's Life* tied up with string; stacks of records by artists with names like Muddy Waters, Howlin' Wolf, and John Lee Hooker; a pair of cardboard glasses with the bold promise 'GENUINE X-RAY SPECS!' printed on the arms. Before she could see any more, the boy stepped round her and replaced the wooden lid.

'Sorry, but my grandpa doesn't like people rooting through his stuff.'

'I was hardly "rooting".' Emma hoisted herself onto another crate. 'Nostalgic, is he? My mum was like that. Kept all the toys and junk from when she was a kid.'

'Dr Rowan Rhodes.' He took a seat next to Emma. 'She left just over a year ago, when your brother died. I'm sorry for your loss.'

'How do you know so much about me?'

'I made it my business to find out about you. About most of the folks in Milton Lake, come to that.'

The boy tucked his legs beneath him. He had taken off his jacket, and now Emma could make out the span of his broad shoulders and the v-shaped torso that tapered down to a narrow waist. His long arms were wired with muscle and the bruise on Emma's wrist attested to the strength in those big hands.

'Most of us?' she echoed. 'That's something like twenty thousand people.'

'I'm thorough. Where I come from there aren't the kind of distractions you and your schoolmates have to deal with. Boredom makes a man patient and careful.'

'Even so, that's a hell of a lot of research.'

'I focused on some people more than others; those who seemed likely suspects.'

'Suspects for what? And why focus on me? I'm nothing special.'

'I thought so, too. Then I met you. I made a mistake last night, throwing you out. You're smart and I could use someone with your local knowledge. As much as I could gather from newspaper reports and information from the census, these people are strangers to me. To you, they're friends and neighbours. Will you help?'

'Help how?'

The boy's face darkened. 'Help me stop the dead from rising. If we don't act then Milton Lake could become the first staging post.'

'For what?'

'A war against the living.'

'You're not serious.'

'You've seen what they're like, these hungry souls. Countless more wait behind the gates, and now a path has been opened to them. Presently, it's a narrow gap, only a few spirits with a close connection to Milton Lake can come through. But as Percival Sparrow said, with every call the way is widening.'

'You knew it was going to start here,' Emma said. 'How?'

'For some months now I've been tracking this . . . *machine*. It used to belong to my grandpa and an associate of his, a man called Randall Wolfe. Randall lived in an old manor house just outside London. A few months back, the house was broken into and the machine was stolen. It seemed to have been a carefully planned burglary—whoever the thief was, he knew what he was looking for. The only hope we had of getting it back was to wait until it was activated. The machine gives off an energy signature each time it's used. I can track the signature with this.'

He took a handheld device from his pocket. It looked something like a Geiger counter with retractable antennae on the top and a small window behind which sat a needle and a scale of numbers.

'Randall Wolfe's spirit detector.'

'That's how you found me last night,' Emma said, 'and today at the library.'

The boy nodded. 'The signature is two-way. One burst when the machine is activated and calls through to the unmade—that signature is so powerful the detector has trouble locking on to it. The return signal indicates where the ghost has materialized and is weaker and easier to trace.'

'Doesn't the spirit show up in the same place as the machine?'

'It should. In fact, the first time it was used, the ghost probably did manifest close to the machine—the readings at the site showed that to be the case. But I think that was a case of sheer dumb luck. The machine is being used by someone who doesn't know how to operate it properly. If he did then the danger facing this town might not be so grave. The problem is, I can only pick up the return signature. That's why I tend to show up a little late.'

'You're forgiven,' Emma smiled. 'So what you're saying is that this machine operates like a kind of summoning tool for a necromancer, and that after it was stolen from Randall Wolfe it was brought here, to the Lake.'

The boy looked at her curiously. 'That's exactly what I'm saying. After the burglary, I kept an eye on the spirit detector day and night. It was strange, the theft had been so carefully staged I assumed whoever was responsible must be a skilled necromancer, and that it wouldn't be long until he or she activated the machine. But months passed without any sign of the unmade coming through. There were explanations, of course: maybe the thief had died before he could use the machine; perhaps he was sick or injured; maybe a rival necromancer had in turn stolen it from him—there's not much honour among dark magicians. And then, just four days ago, the detector goes off the scale. Someone had made a call and the unmade had answered.'

Made a call. Something scratched at the back of Emma's mind, but she was too enthralled by the boy's story to pay it much attention.

'Now it's your turn, what do you know about necromancers?'

He listened as she recited the bits and pieces from her supernatural researches.

'You got all this from the internet? There sure is some dangerous stuff stored in all those wires. But I gotta admit, you've grasped the basics.' He shook his head. 'All this spirit activity in Milton Lake points to the machine being here. A single necromancer, or possibly a group of black magicians, are opening up pathways. But the evidence also indicates that these people have no idea how to work the machine.'

'You keep saying that. What makes you think it's being used by newbie necromancers?'

'Newbie?' he frowned.

'Never heard of "newbie"? Where are you from, exactly? OK, "unskilled necromancers", then.'

'A learned magician would be able to focus the summoning power of the machine on the specific spirit he or she wanted, then draw that spirit directly to him. But the summonings in Milton Lake are haphazard. I've traced four different ghosts so far: the first arrived at the old amusement park; the second came yesterday evening—that was Percival Sparrow who you encountered in the attic; the third I traced to St Jerome's graveyard. That ghost came through at three this morning but I arrived too late to observe it. The fourth was this afternoon at Smedley Library. Up until the third ghost, I'd seriously considered this was all related to the Sparrow family. This house, Percival, the Funland ghost—who might well have been Hiram Sparrow . . . '

The thought of the dead murderer returning to the scene of his crime made Emma sick to her stomach.

'But since then we've had Evelyn and this third spectre at the graveyard.'

'Maybe that was Hiram again,' Emma suggested. 'He is buried up there.'

'No, I made a thorough investigation of Funland the day I arrived. Somehow the spirit there was vanquished. After a ghost is returned to the gates it takes a long time for it to find its way back. Whoever came through at St Jerome's, it wasn't Hiram. The point is, these necromancers aren't focused. They're pulling in spirits from different points in Milton Lake's history, and when the spirit arrives there's no sense that they're there to greet it or have any control over it. It's like the machine's being operated by a desperate lunatic.'

'OK, so what is this "machine"?'

'Long story. I'll tell it to you soon, I promise, but consider tonight more of an introduction to the subject of ghosts.'

'Then what exactly are "ghosts"?'

'The kind we're dealing with? They're the unmade.'

The boy hesitated, his gaze fixed on the boarded windows. A car passed along the street outside, its headlights beading the cracks.

'Are you OK?'

'Yeah.' He sighed. 'It's a sad thing to think about, that's all. These spirits, the way they are, it's not really their fault.'

'How can you say that? They're evil, cruel. They want to . . . ' What was it they wanted? Emma thought of those fingers pressing into her face, searching for the precious something hidden inside.

'They were people once,' the boy said. 'Bad people like Hiram Sparrow, good people like Evelyn Smedley. Good or bad, once they become the unmade their spirits are corrupted until every shred of human sympathy is crushed out of them.'

'How can that happen?'

'Some people die in such a way that they can't accept their deaths. There are many reasons: maybe they met a sudden or violent end—murder, suicide, a tragic accident. Unfinished business might keep other ghosts fixed on our world. But these spirits do not remain on Earth. At the point of death they are pulled from this reality and trapped in a dimension that sits adjacent to our own. Think of it like a prison located between the worlds of the living and the truly dead. There they linger, year after year, decade after decade, century after century, until at last they forget what it was that stopped them from moving on. Inside the walls of their shadow prison, they can see our world going about its business. See people who can feel and touch and taste and exist as they never can. They begin to look at the flesh, as they call it, with envious eyes. These unmade people in bodies no more solid than air . . . they wish to be whole again.'

Emma shuddered. 'How?'

'If they're lucky enough to be summoned by a necromancer, the spirit will offer a deal. Knowledge and prophecy in return for a body they can call their own. The necromancer will usually abduct some suitable vessel—a homeless person, someone who won't be missed. The unmade will then press its hands into the vessel's face until it finds the unfortunate person's soul. It then begins to crush that soul and implant its own.'

'You're talking about possession.'

'And by then it's too late. I can deal with summoned spirits—iron hurts them, and, as you discovered today, they're vulnerable to the things that killed them. These methods destroy their ectoplasmic bodies.'

'Their what?'

'When a spirit is called into this reality then, for a short time, the necromancer's spell gives it a certain substance so that it can speak, touch, move about. The material that makes up this form is called ectoplasm. It's not completely solid, the ghost can vanish and reappear at will, pass through walls and doors. The upside is that it gives me something to attack. But it's a temporary state until the spirit can find a body to possess. Once that's achieved, well, that's a proper human life. To end it would be murder.'

'Don't they deserve to die? They destroyed a person's soul, stole their life.'

'They deserve death, yes,' the boy said slowly, 'but what would become of me if I gave it to them?'

Emma remained quiet for a moment. Then she said, 'So each time this necromancer uses Randall Wolfe's machine the gates are weakened. More and more spirits will start coming through. How many?'

The boy shrugged. 'Their numbers are untold. If this foolish magician continues making calls then, within a week or two, the entire town could be possessed. So you need to tell me, has anything unusual been happening in Milton Lake?'

'Until yesterday I'd have said that this was just about the most boring town in existence. But then I met Sas at the Torves', and since then . . . Well, let's just say I think we might have a witness to the first summoning.'

Emma told the tale of Henry's initiation into the Chainsaw Gang, the Torves locking their child away, and the mismatched collection of people sighted by Sas.

'If this is true then Henry could have seen the necromancer,' the boy pondered. 'Like I told you, there was evidence in the ghost train that whoever operated the machine was there when the first spirit came through.'

'And that's why they're keeping him out of sight,' Emma nodded. 'Henry saw them: a group of necromancers that included his own father.'

'Run those names by me again.'

She counted them off on her fingers while he upturned the lid of a crate and started rummaging among sheaves of paper.

'Got 'em.' He held out a list of names and pointed to six with red asterisks beside them. 'Torve, Glock, Worple, Roper, Merriglass, Carter. Already among my prime suspects.'

'But they're all so . . . '

'Ordinary? What did you expect? Swirling capes, pointy hats, and pentagram pendants? This isn't the Middle Ages. People studying black magic hold down regular jobs, they run their kids to football practice, volunteer at church fetes, pay their taxes, and crash out in front of their TVs. True, not too many little old ladies, doctors' wives, lawyers, and vicars are necromancers, but there are a few in every town and city.'

'You're telling me that all across the country people are conjuring the dead!'

'I'm saying that there are lots of people *trying* to conjure the dead. Thankfully, most haven't the first idea how to do it. What we have here in Milton Lake is a group of people who've studied the dark arts for years only to meet with failure after failure. Until now. Somehow, they stole Randall Wolfe's machine—a device that gave them the shortcut they needed to make contact with the other side.'

'But how do you know that Torve and the rest are interested in this stuff?'

'The world of necromancy is a small one. I hear things: who has purchased what spell book, where in the country certain occult artefacts have been spotted. The Milton Lake Circle, as it's known, has been in existence for five or six years. Seven members, all of whom have had dealings with the supernatural before. Mr Merriglass used to be a well-respected exorcist; Roper and Worple have been casting silly little spells for years. Mrs Glock and Mr Carter have some weak psychic powers and Arthur Torve dabbled in necromancy at university.'

'And the seventh member?'

'Mrs Nugent. She seems to be a friend of Arthur Torve from his university days.'

Emma felt relieved. An uncomfortable suspicion about the identity of this woman had been growing in her mind. Now it seemed that suspicion was unfounded.

'So it looks like the Circle is behind all this.'

'Perhaps.' The boy placed the papers back into the crate. 'To be sure, I'll need to speak to your cousin.'

'A trip to the Torves'.' Emma nodded. 'I'm down with that.'

'Down with it? Does that mean you're coming?'

'You're starting to sound like my dad.' Emma jumped down from the crate. 'So I can't keep calling you Harvey. Time to fess up, what's your real name?'

'Redway.'

The boy went delving in another of the wooden boxes. After a quick search, he withdrew a black motorcycle helmet, which he tossed to Emma.

'My name's Nicholas Redway. Time to hit the road.'

7

The blue and silver body of the Triumph Thunderbird finned its way through a screaming white ocean. With her arms tight round Nick's waist, Emma could feel the throb of its mechanical heart and the rhythmic judder of its tread on the slush-slick road. With a twist of his wrist they jolted forward, the belly of the bike roaring as it ate up the tarmac. For the first time in a year, Emma's heart quickened, not through fear or distress, but from the exhilaration of being alive.

Nick swerved to a stop and killed the engine. Emma was about to clamber down from the saddle when a pair of strong hands gripped her by the waist and lifted her onto the pavement. The same gloved hands slid the helmet from her head.

'Seems ages since I last saw snow,' he murmured.

Emma thought of the sun-scorched road. 'Don't you get snow where you come from?'

He looked away. 'Come on, show me the house.'

Leaving their helmets hanging from the bike's handlebars, they walked together under the flickering streetlights.

'There's something I forgot to mention,' Emma said. 'Something else that happened today.' She told him about the encounter with Miles.

'He asked about souls?'

'He was frightened, shaking, I've never seen him like that. He said something about his grandad. Mr Taggart died five years ago, a heart attack.'

'Where's he buried?'

'St Jerome's.' Emma whirled round. 'Do you think it's him? The third ghost?'

'It's possible. Listen, I don't want you talking to Miles about any of this until I have time to think it through. Promise?'

'You think he's in danger?'

'I think he *was* in danger, that's what's worrying me.'

A muffled voice called out from the snow shadows. 'Ems, 's that you?'

Sas came lumbering through the night, his billowing coat and hooded head mantled white. 'Who's this?'

'A friend. Jesus, Sas, how long have you been out here?'

'Since school finished early. People have been looking for you, Ems. After the fire they took a register and you weren't there.'

'Oh God, I didn't think . . . I should call Bob.' She fished out her mobile. 'Damn it! Nineteen missed calls. I had my phone on silent. And now I can't get a signal.'

'Must be the storm.' Sas eyed the stranger. 'And what do they call you?'

Nick glanced at Emma. 'It's OK, you can trust him.'

'My name's Redway.' He held out his hand. 'And you're Brandon Lorne, Henry's best friend. I've been hearing all about you. So, do you want to do something a bit more useful than stand around in the cold?'

Sas's nostrils flared. He fronted up to the American.

'Take it easy, boys.' Emma stood between them. 'Sas, I'm sorry I didn't speak to my dad about Henry, but Nick's here to help.'

'All right, Yank,' Sas growled, 'what do you want me to do?'

'I want you to think about your pal, locked up there in his room. I want you to show me how angry that makes you, and then I want you to show *them*.' Nick gestured at the house behind the gates. 'Think you can do that?'

'You need a distraction.' Sas grinned. 'You just watch.'

A three metre high wall surrounded the Torve house on all sides; a tricky prospect if it hadn't been for Sas. Two energetic boosts and Nick and Emma scaled the wall with ease. Nick dropped down into the snow-capped shrubs on the other side, then reached up for Emma. As she descended, they heard the buzz of the intercom and the peevish snap of Arthur Torve's voice.

'What is it?'

'I'm not going away this time,' Sas bellowed. 'I want to see him, and if you don't let me in I'm going to ring every doorbell on this street and tell your neighbours that you're keeping Henry locked in his room.'

'Don't be ridiculous, I'll call the police!'

'Good, I want you to. I want them to check Henry's OK.'

A pause, filled by the howling snowstorm.

'Brandon, be reasonable,' Arthur said, his voice thick with oily charm.

'I want to see him.'

'He's asleep.'

'Let me see him or I swear—'

'I'll come down and we can talk this over.'

The line went dead. Nick hurried to the gate and spoke through the bars.

'Good work. Keep him talking as long as you can.'

'What about the others?' Sas pointed to the cars in the drive.

'When he gets down here you just start shouting and ranting,' Nick instructed. 'These people don't want to attract attention, so my bet is they'll all be listening in at the intercom. Keep their focus on you and Torve.'

'Are you going to rescue him?' Sas asked bluntly.

'I'll do what I can.'

Nick rejoined Emma under the cover of the shrubs.

'What if they do something to Sas? You say the Circle doesn't want to attract attention, wouldn't it be easier just to drag him into the house and lock him up?'

'Have you seen the size of that kid?' Nick boggled. 'No one's going to be dragging him anywhere . . . OK, here comes Torve.'

Emma's uncle stepped out from the warm rectangle of the door and stalked off down the driveway. Dark against the snow, his shadow lurched like the silhouette of some gigantic stick insect.

'Time to move,' Nick whispered.

He indicated a narrow path around the back of the shrubs. They had only gone a few paces but already Sas's voice was muffled by the wind. Emma caught the last words—*I mean it, I'll call the cops*—and thought, *Don't overplay your hand, Sas. Just keep him there as long as you can.* As they slipped out from the shrubbery and made for the side of the house, Emma gasped—

'Back door. It's not far. Keep going.'

The house provided some shelter from the wind, enough for Emma to clear the snow from her eyes. She saw Nick caught for a moment in the feeble glow of the curtained moon. The tousled locks that covered his forehead had been whipped back, revealing a livid scar running from his right temple into the fringe of his hair. An old injury by the look of it, left to heal without stitching. She wondered who this boy really was. Where were his parents? His grandfather? How had he entered this life of necromancy and ghost hunting? And why did she keep getting flashes of that rutted road with its glistening wetland and worn-out farmhouse? There was something wrong with Nicholas Redway, a secret hiding behind that inscrutable face, a mystery that had reawakened Emma's slumbering consciousness.

'This the door?' Nick asked, pulling Emma from her thoughts.

She nodded and tried the handle. Locked. Ferreting in the pocket of her parka, she withdrew the Swiss Army knife given to her by Bob on her twelfth birthday and slipped it between the door and the jamb. While she prised, a grip from her hair went to work on the lock. After a few seconds, tumblers rolled, the mechanism clicked, and she pushed open the door.

Nick grinned. 'Pretty neat bit of house-breaking, Miss Rhodes.' He looked ahead into the darkness of the house and the smile faltered. 'Let's see what these amateur necromancers are up to.'

His voice had lost its dry warmth, and now Emma pictured a cold New England night, icy waters beneath frost-haloed stars, the farmhouse grim and forsaken. *New England* . . . Where had that come from?

The back door opened into a laundry room tangy with the smell of detergent and sweaty trainers. Emma crossed to a second door that led, via a corridor, to the reception hall and the stairs. They had reached the end of the corridor, melted snow dripping from their coats, when Nick drew her back into the shadows. She heard the bump of slippered feet overhead. Then one of the doors off the hall opened and the headmaster of Tennyson Academy stepped out. Entering the hall with its gaudy chandelier and gleaming marble floor, Mr Carter turned to the stairs.

'The boy?'

'Sleeping.'

Miss Worple and Miss Roper descended the last step. Wrapped in identical fluffy pink dressing gowns, the sweetshop owners smiled toothlessly at the headmaster.

'We had to use a potion to calm him.'

'He's still afraid? Well, I suppose seeing Hiram Sparrow raised from the dead would be enough to scare anyone,' Carter grimaced. 'Unfortunate, the boy being there.'

'Only if he forgets what he saw.'

'Hmm. I suppose you know his friend is at the gate again?'

'*Tut*,' said Miss Roper. 'And then there's this business with Emma Rhodes.'

'What about her?'

'Didn't Margery tell you? The girl confronted her this morning. Started asking questions about Henry. She seemed to know Margery had been spending time here.'

'Seemed to know about *all of us*, come to that.'

'You can't mean the Circle!' Carter said, aghast.

'Oh no, I'm sure not. Margery made up some story about the Historical Society.'

'But the girl did mention something else quite startling. She spoke of ghosts.'

'And of a boy who's moved into the Sparrow House.'

'Who is he?' Carter asked.

'Arthur has made enquiries. His name is Dowd, Harvey Dowd.'

Carter grunted. 'Doesn't ring a bell.'

'We've spoken to certain friends,' Miss Roper said. 'No one has heard of him.'

'What can a boy know of necromancy?' Carter snorted. 'No, I'm sure he can't be involved. As for Emma Rhodes, she's been weird ever since the death of her brother. We mustn't let a mere coincidence distract us. We're close, ladies. Within a few days we should be able to locate our prize. Come on, let's join the others.'

As the door of the sitting room closed behind them, Emma ran through the to-and-fro of the conversation. Something in those words had jarred, but for the life of her she couldn't put her finger on exactly what.

'You told them about me,' Nick whispered.

'I'm sorry, I didn't think.'

'No, you didn't. This isn't a game, Emma, you have to be more careful.'

He led the way to the stairs. This was where they would be most exposed. Lit by the glare of the chandelier, they could be seen by anyone entering the front door, leaving the sitting room, or from any of the bedrooms at the top of the landing. Although the carpet muffled their boots they left behind a trail of telltale marks. Emma prayed that the damp footprints would dry before anyone noticed.

At the top of the stairs, they froze. One of the doors at the end of the corridor had opened and a woman in a black silk kimono emerged. The corridor light was turned off and the woman's face was thick with shadow. Only her eyes could be seen, two circles of white without pupil or iris, both as large as goose eggs. She groped her way along the corridor like some poor creature recently blinded. Turning into the upstairs bathroom, the chandelier snatched her from shadows and Emma recognized her at once. Not a spectre returned from the grave, but Henry's flesh and blood mother, her eyes covered with wads of cotton wool. All part of Aunt Julia's nightly beauty regime.

As her aunt closed the bathroom door behind her, Emma breathed again. At least the encounter had proved one thing: Julia wasn't part of the Circle.

Henry's bedroom was located at the end of two garishly wallpapered corridors. The door opened at her touch and Emma stumbled into the darkened room.

Even with the lights off, she could make out the shape of familiar objects—TV and Playstation in one corner; Mr Potato Head perched on the windowsill; a model of the solar system hanging by wire from the ceiling, the planets stationary around a football-sized sun. It had been a long time since she had visited her cousin—not since they pulled the plug—but aside from the odd poster nothing seemed to have changed. The curtains were drawn and the half-hidden moon cast an uncertain spotlight over the boy in the bed.

Nick drew back one of Henry's eyelids and examined the dilated pupil.

'They've given him a sedative.' He sniffed Henry's lips. 'A mix of belladonna, monkshood, and something I can't quite put my finger on.'

'They've been keeping him drugged.'

'Not all the time.' He pulled back the sheets. 'See?'

Angry red welts marked the skin where Henry's wrist was handcuffed to the bed. Emma started searching her pockets for her mobile phone.

'That's it, I'm calling the police.'

'If we involve the authorities now we'll never have a chance to question him.'

'Is that all you care about?' she snapped. 'I'm not going to leave him like this.'

'We have no choice. I could probably carry him out of here, but I don't think your lock picking skills extend to handcuffs. The best we can do is get whatever information we can, then call the police.'

For all the anger that simmered inside, Emma could see the sense in Nick's plan. Time was running out and they needed to get at the knowledge locked inside Henry's head.

'So how do we talk to him if he's drugged?'

'Bring me one of those pens from the desk.'

She handed him a blue felt tip and he flicked off the lid. Then, positioning pillows under Henry's shoulders so that his head was tilted back, he drew a rough symbol over the apple of the sleeping boy's throat:

'His conscious mind is dreaming, but the soul never sleeps. You've probably wondered why the unmade reach through their victim's faces and into their throats? The soul, the spirit, whatever you choose to call that essence that makes us what we are, it sits here.' He indicated the drawing.

'But what is it?'

'An ancient symbol used by the alchemists.'

'Those nutters who thought they could turn base metal into gold?'

'Those are the guys, but not all their knowledge was at fault. This was the alchemical symbol for the element phosphorous. They saw light as representing the spirit, and phosphorous intrigued them because it was light trapped within solid rock. Just as Henry's light is trapped within this sleeping shell.'

Nick took a lighter from his pocket, struck the wheel and drew a flame up and down the boy's throat.

'What the hell are you doing?'

'Shhh. Look.'

The skin around Henry's Adam's apple didn't burn or blister, in fact there wasn't so much as a reddening of the flesh. What did appear to burn brighter was the symbol. It started as a faint bluish glow, seared into a brilliant indigo and then faded to a bruised purple until at last the symbol itself vanished. In the same instant, Henry's mouth fell open and a spectral light shone from the back of his throat. Henry was still limp, eyes closed, arms hanging at his sides. His lips did not move, yet still he spoke.

'*The head! Where's the head? Where's the—*'

'You're all right,' Nick soothed. 'You're safe.'

'*S-safe?*'

'Yes. Your cousin Emma is here.'

'It's me.' She took his hand. 'I'll make sure you're safe.'

The lie stuck in her throat. How could she guarantee his safety? After they had learned what they could they would leave him here, chained up like an animal. The beautiful light strengthened, bathing the room in an iridescent glow. He believed them.

'We need to ask you some questions,' Nick said, 'and we need you to be brave. I want you to think back to that afternoon at the amusement park. The ghost train—'

'No.' The voice whimpered from the cavern of Henry's mouth. 'I can't.'

'You can. You must . . . You walked in the darkness, alone.'

'To prove my guts. Sas wanted me to join the Chainers.'

'That's right. And you showed them, didn't you? You saw the ghost.'

'Hiram Sparrow. He didn't have a head. He—' Henry shuddered. 'I thought he was going to kill me, just like he killed all the others. But then he stepped onto the track . . . and he screamed. *Screamed.*'

'The track was iron . . . ' Nick murmured. 'Henry, I need you to stay calm and focus. Do you remember hearing a sound just before the ghost appeared? A bell.'

'An old-fashioned phone. *Brrring, brrring, brrringing the dead,*' Henry laughed.

Emma nodded. 'I heard it too, in the library. And then outside the Sparrow House before I heard Richie's voice.'

'It's the machine,' Nick confirmed. 'Henry, do you remember anyone else being in the ghost train with you?'

'Someone was moving about in the next room, I thought it was a tramp.'

'The Circle,' Emma said. 'Or one of them at least. Uncle Arthur?'

'Maybe he didn't know his son was there.' Nick frowned. 'Henry, did you notice anything else? Noises? A voice? A smell, a feeling, anything?'

'Oranges . . . The tramp smelt of oranges.'

Footsteps in the corridor outside. A voice raised in anger:

'Oaf of a boy kept me talking till my lips were blue. We can't keep this up much longer, Miss Worple. If we can't shake Henry out of this terror and get him to talk, then perhaps it would be better to wipe his memory of the ghost train altogether. I won't have my boy chained up like this for ever. Yes, I'm going to check on him now.'

The handle turned . . .

'Henry? Are you awake?'

. . . and Arthur Torve stepped into the room.

8

'It's freezing in here! Who left this window open?'

Emma was still clinging to the sill when her uncle slammed down the sash and drew the curtains. In the time it had taken Arthur to stalk the corridor, Nick and Emma had rearranged Henry's pillows, slipped his manacled arm under the sheets, and clambered out of the window. Heedless of a broken neck, Nick had jumped straight into the bank of snow four metres below. Emma of the Milton Lake diving board days would never have had a problem with such a measly drop, yet now she hesitated.

'I'll catch you,' he hissed. 'You trust me, don't you?'

Trust you? I hardly know you! All the same, she let go of the sill.

The hood of her parka snapped over her head and she was lost in a snowy cyclone. Then came the jolt of gravity denied. She felt those strong arms again, catching, clutching, cradling before he set her down on her feet. Together, they raced through the ankle-deep snow, clambered over the wall and dropped down into the street.

They found Sas rubbing his hands and stamping his feet. 'Where is he?'

'We couldn't get him out,' Emma panted. 'He was handcuffed to the bed.'

'Handcuffed!'

'They haven't hurt him,' Nick said. 'Not really. He seems to be suffering from some kind of shellshock. His father, the others, they just want him to keep quiet about whatever he saw in the ghost train.'

Something about that explanation didn't ring true for Emma. Arthur had spoken of getting Henry to *talk* when surely what they really wanted was for him to *forget*. They had summoned the ghost themselves, so what could Henry possibly know that they didn't?

'They're holding him prisoner,' Sas said. 'Cuffs prove it. I'm calling the police.'

Nick stepped forward. 'I don't think so.'

'What are you talking about?' Emma protested. 'You said that after we got the information from Henry we could report what was happening.'

'If we tell the police that we saw Henry handcuffed then the Circle will know someone was in the house. I don't want to put them on their guard.'

'We'll call anonymously, they'll never know it was us.'

'Whatever,' Sas grunted, 'I'm doing this.'

He had barely removed the phone from his pocket when

fingers a shade whiter than the snow snatched it from him. Sas's hand closed into a meaty fist.

'Give it back.'

'Sorry, kid, but if you don't stand down you're gonna get hurt.'

'You think you can beat me up just because you're a couple of years older?'

'Pretty much.' Nick sighed. 'You're big for your age, but you're soft as butter. Back home I'd spend three hours every morning before school lugging bales and shovelling horse shit. Then I'd work at the burger joint in town till closing time. Whenever a greaser got fresh with one of the carhops, I'd be sent out by the manager to kick his ass. I kicked *a lot* of ass. So I know I can put you down, I just don't want to.'

A cold glint shone in Nick's eyes, and suddenly Emma saw the ruthlessness that lurked inside. For the sake of the town, he would beat Sas to the ground and leave Henry imprisoned. What kind of life had he known that could harden him so?

'Give him the phone.'

'Emma, stay out of this.'

'But Sas is right. We can't leave Henry chained up like that. You want to help people? Then start with him.'

She ran her hand down the snow-soaked sleeve of his leather jacket. The muscles in his arm were like wrought-iron, his fingers strong as soldered steel. Troubled hazel eyes held her gaze for a moment . . . then he threw the phone to Sas.

'What if they trace the call?' Sas asked, his voice still thick with anger.

'This is the Milton Lake police we're talking about, not the goddamn CIA.' When he saw he'd touched a nerve, Nick held up his hands. 'Just don't use any names.'

Sas dialled and made his report, putting on an accent that seemed to travel from Cornwall to Scotland via Newcastle and Belfast. Meanwhile, Nick looked back over the wall to the curtained window from which they had escaped.

'This was a bad idea.'

'Come on,' Emma cajoled, 'what can they really do to hurt us? That lot are about as intimidating as a church jumble sale committee.'

'They only seem that way because you think you know them: the funny old women who run the sweetshop, the bullying principal, the gossipy doctor's wife. But there *is* a secret side to them. A ruthless drive for influence, wealth, dominion over others. The kind of lust for power that can lead an otherwise loving father to chain his child to a bed. Believe me, there's nothing more dangerous than a Circle that's strived for the secret of necromancy and always fallen short.'

'What the hell are you two talking about?' Sas looked from one to the other. 'Circles? Necromancy? Has this entire town gone stark raving mad?'

'Something like that,' Emma said. 'Honestly, it's best you don't know. Just get yourself home, there's nothing more we can do here.'

It was true. The police would come to the Torves', find Henry, and take him to some safe place far from the influence of the Circle. Neither Emma nor Sas could be there when they arrived. That had been the price for Nick handing over the phone: anonymity. Of course, Uncle Arthur would put two and two together: Sas's performance at the gate, the open window, the police knowing about the handcuffs, and he'd know that Henry's best friend hadn't acted alone. Who else cared about his son? Who else had spoken that very day of ghosts? In spite of Nick's wishes, anonymity was a distant hope.

With a final forlorn glance at the house, Sas lurched off into the night.

'Sorry if I was hard on the kid,' Nick said. 'He didn't deserve that.'

'No, he didn't.' Emma took her helmet from the handlebars. 'He's the most caring, loyal person I know, and you made his loyalty sound . . . I don't know, *weak*. Like his love for Henry was something to be laughed at.'

Nick's hand went to his forehead, his fingers tracing that livid scar.

'Love is just about the most dangerous thing in the world,' he said. 'Worse than any black magic. It makes people selfish, eats up their lives.'

'You've never loved anyone?'

'I loved my father. Loved him fierce, just like he loved me.'

'You mentioned a grandfather but not your dad. Is he—?'

'Dead. They both are. My pop was a soldier, served in the Eighth Army Rangers. He died years ago, in battle. My grandpa brought me up after that.'

'I'm sorry . . . Your grandad must have died recently, you talked as though he was still alive when the machine was stolen.'

'He was old. So old he said it didn't matter.' Nick's features tightened. From some nearby place in the night-drowned town came a wail of sirens and a scratch of blue light. 'We need to get out of here.'

They left by the lake road, a wide arc of crumbling blacktop that skirted the lake's southern shore. There were no houses here, just a rind of trees that appeared to have peeled off from the skin of Black Acre Forest. Turning left, the Thunderbird glided downhill until it reached the junction of Connolly Avenue. The wind had fallen and the snow lay still. When Nick cut the engine outside the Sparrow House, it felt to Emma as if the world had frozen around them and that they were the only two beings still in motion.

'Guess I'll see you soon,' she said. 'Maybe.'

'Are you quitting on me, Miss Rhodes?' he smiled.

'No. I . . . I just thought I'd annoyed you, standing up for Sas like that.'

He looked at her for a moment, those amber eyes seeming to flash in the spaces around her. 'Don't you see?' he said at last. 'That's why I need you. To remind me to listen to people like Sas. Now go home, get some rest, I've got a surprise for you in the morning.'

Twirling the keys of the Thunderbird, he stepped over the tumbledown fence, his long legs clearing the picket with ease. He didn't look back, not even when he reached the porch and disappeared into the house, yet Emma had the uncanny feeling that he remained watchful. Maybe he . . .

She turned to the kerb and saw the stain peeking out from under the snow. The pale pink blemish no scrubbing could remove. Emma wrenched her eyes away and marched across the road, the crump of snow drowning out the voice inside her head. *I might not be a ghost, Ems, but I'm still here, always with you, always near.*

Her latchkey was in the lock when the door opened and she was dragged into the house. At first she thought it must be the Circle—they had made the connection and decided on drastic action. Rough hands shook her by the shoulders. Then, to her surprise, Emma found herself crushed into a hug.

'Where the hell have you been?' Bob struggled to control his voice.

'Just out. It's not that late, is it?'

They separated, and she was stunned to see him cuff a spill of tears from his cheeks. Bob hadn't cried since the funeral. He looked beaten down, his teacherly tweed hanging from his thin shoulders. She hadn't noticed how much weight he'd lost.

'I've been calling your mobile.'

'It was on silent.'

'I had the police out looking for you, friends, neighbours—'

'It's ten-thirty! What's the big deal?' Then she remembered the fire. 'Oh . . . I'm sorry, I didn't think.'

'I know that, Emma,' Bob muttered. 'God knows, I do. Miss Lucas said you were the last person in the library before the fire started.'

'That's not true. I left, she saw me.' No need to mention that she'd sneaked back in after Miss Lucas had gone walkabout.

'They found your bag in the ashes.' Bob put weight on every word. 'Jesus, I've already lost one child, I don't ever want to think that I could lose another.'

Her fingers twitched. The instinct was there, to reach out, to hold, to hug, to comfort, but *he* had been the one to pull the plug.

'You didn't lose Richie, you gave up on him.'

Bob blinked at her through his owlish glasses. 'He was dead, Emma. It was all just machines and lights and wires and pumps. Even your mum saw that, in the end.'

'His soul—'

'When Richie stopped breathing for himself, when his brainstem died, he was gone.' Bob sighed. 'It was cruel to keep him trapped inside that shell.'

Emma frowned. 'What do you mean, "trapped"? If you really thought he was no more than meat and brains then what was there to be *trapped*? Do you even believe what you're saying?'

Bob managed a few steps towards the kitchen before slumping against the wall.

'I don't care if you think it was my fault, Emma, but I want you to know one thing. Now you listen to me, because the way you've been this past year, it's breaking my heart. It wasn't *your* fault. It just wasn't, OK?'

It was, the little voice insisted, and the little voice was stronger than Bob's.

Emma headed straight upstairs and into the bathroom. The boiler in the airing cupboard gave an throaty groan as hot water belched from the taps. She added a handful of bath salts, peeled off her wet clothing, and sank into the tub. Downstairs she could hear Bob on the phone, thanking neighbours and making apologies to the police. As she slipped her aching shoulders under the water, Emma wondered what was happening at the Torves'. Had the police found Henry? Had they arrested Uncle Arthur and Aunt Julia?

Dee-dah-dee-dah, dee-dah-dee-dah, dee-dah-dee-dah-dah.

She jolted upright. A ringing phone. The stolen necromancy machine somewhere nearby . . . Then she realized that the sound was coming from the jeans she had dropped on the bathroom floor. Maybe it was Nick calling—the spirit detector had sparked into life and he needed her help. She reeled in the jeans and plunged a damp hand into the pocket. The screen on her phone displayed a familiar caller ID.

'Miles?' she breathed. 'Are you all—'

'Ems, you gotta help me.'

His voice was different: a breathless wheezing, the pitch fluttery and high.

'What's wrong? Talk to me.'

'Last night. He-he was here . . . And th-this morning, I found his handprints on the window. That's how I know it wasn't a dream. I saw them in the moonlight, hands on the window like two brown spiders. Hands smeared with dirt from the graveyard. Do you think he clawed his way out?' There was the wheeze again, a weak hiss like a deflating balloon. 'Did he smash through the lid and claw his way through the earth?'

'Your grandfather . . . ?'

'No,' he whimpered. 'It can't be. Grandad Pete's been dead for five years. *Five years.*'

'But you've seen him again, last night at your window. I believe you, Miles, just tell me what happened.'

'*Tap-tap-atap-tap—TAP-TAP.* When I was little and I heard that knock, God, I used to get so excited. Grandad Pete had come to take me out for the day—a kick about in the park, a movie at the Kinema, helping out at his allotment. I loved him, Ems, so why . . . ' A desperate fit of coughing, not the kind of sound you would expect from the healthy lungs of Tennyson's star midfielder. 'Why has he done this t-to me?'

Emma remembered Peter Taggart very well; a kind, courteous old man who had cherished his grandson above all things.

'What happened?'

'I was in bed. Heard the tapping. Opened the curtains. The moon was behind him, so I couldn't see his face at first. Just his eyes, y-yellow and gleaming. His hands were flat on the glass as if he was pushing. *Let me in, sonny boy.* That was his name for me. *Open the window and let your old grandad in. I've been so cold up at St Jerome's, I need to feel warm again. You have to let me* in.'

'You didn't.'

'No. But he came in anyway. Pushed and pushed until he sank right through. I couldn't move, c-couldn't speak, was s-so scared. And then Grandad . . . ' She could almost hear the shudder. 'His fingers pressing into my face. Searching. What was it your mum used to say? We all have an essence hidden inside. It was only when he found mine that I felt it. My soul, Ems. He's crushing my soul.'

Emma's heart responded to Miles's fear and panic while her logical mind turned over a new mystery. Based on her experience in the Sparrow House, she had assumed that possession by an unmade was the work of moments. Now she wondered if the process was more gradual. Peter Taggart's attack on his grandson had begun last night and, although his speech had started to resemble that of an old man, Miles was still in command of his body.

'You've got to hold on,' she told him. 'Fight as best you can.'

'But he's so *huh-huh-hungry*.'

Despite the heat of the bathwater, Emma shivered.

'I can feel myself fading, drifting. Your mum, she studied this stuff, right? Folklore, the supernatural. You've got to tell her what's happening.'

'I don't know where she is. We haven't spoken since Richie—'

'Richie's dead,' his words came hot and fast. 'Can't you get that into your head? He's dead and he's not coming back . . . I loved you, Ems, I really did, but you sh-shut me out, p-pushed me away, made me feel . . . Doesn't matter now. *Please*, you just have to help me.'

'I can't get hold of my mum,' Emma insisted, her voice shaking, 'but there's someone else who might be able to help. He—'

'J-just hurry.'

The line went dead.

Emma jumped out of the tub. The air swirled like an Amazonian mist as she pulled on a robe and stared at the phone in her hand. Everything this evening had happened so fast she had forgotten to ask for Nick's number. Only one thing for it.

Steam billowed into the corridor as she ran to her room. Downstairs Bob was still on the phone, his voice muffled. She hurried to the wardrobe, pulling out armfuls of jeans and vest tops, blouses and sweaters. She hadn't bought any new clothes in over a year and, after twelve months' growth, the Kings of Leon T-shirt she selected was a little tight. She was just pulling on a pair of skinny jeans when the engine's roar sent her stumbling to the window.

Emma hammered on the glass but there was no hope of him hearing. Like a sprinter in the starting block, Nick craned over the handlebars and sent the Thunderbird hurtling out of Connolly Avenue.

9

She was caught in the riptide between waking and dreaming, the real and the unreal colliding around her. Images, words, thoughts and feelings: X-ray specs and muddy waters; the cruel jokes of the living and the dead; bloodstains on pavements; wooden crates filled with oranges falling from a storm-tossed sky; the trill of an old telephone; the croak of an old man . . .

A farmhouse, the rutted track leading to it scored with fresh tyre marks. A wooden shack at the roadside, vegetable boxes stacked outside. A patrol car with black and white panels, its driver's door swung wide, a radio mouthpiece dangling in the dirt. *Sheriff, come in—Sheriff, do you read me?* The slosh of the sheriff in the water . . .

Emma sat up in bed. She closed her eyes against the pale sun and kneaded her temples. Too many images, too many mysteries. The fractured sights and sounds associated with recent events in Milton Lake she could understand, but why the farmhouse and the road? She guessed it had something to do with Nick, but what? And why was *she* seeing it?

She blinked at her clock radio: 8:03. How could she have slept through *three* alarms? Tearing back the sheets, she bounded to the window. No sign of the Thunderbird outside the Sparrow House. Had Nick returned and left again before dawn? Maybe he hadn't come home at all last night. Maybe an unmade had reached inside him, taken his soul and claimed his body. A knot of anxiety tightened in Emma's stomach.

She ran to the bathroom, showered, brushed her teeth, and pulled on a fresh set of clothes. Moments later, the front door slammed behind her. Kicking open the Sparrow House gate, she tried both Henry's and Miles's numbers. Henry's went to messages but Miles answered. He spoke just two words—*Too late*—and hung up. Shaken, Emma crossed the porch and hammered on the flaking black door.

'Come on . . . Where are you?'

'Is your new friend not at home? Never mind, I'll just leave this on the step.'

Emma had to hand it to Margery Glock, for a big woman she was light on her feet. There hadn't been so much as a squeak from the rotten floorboards, and yet there she stood, muffled up in a fake fur coat, a steaming apple pie in her hands.

'I hope the rats don't get at it,' she chuckled, depositing the covered dish on an upturned flowerpot. 'I saw him this morning, you know, tearing up the road on that awful motorcycle. How do you know him, dear?'

'I have to get to school.'

She was at the porch steps when Margery called after her. 'I thought I ought to warn you, in my capacity as chairman of the Neighbourhood Watch, hoax calls are taken *very* seriously by the police . . . Now, you have a lovely day, sweetheart.'

Emma didn't breathe again until she reached the road. The smug arrogance in Margery's voice told the story very clearly. Somehow, the Circle had fooled the police. That meant Henry was still being held prisoner, handcuffed and drugged. Apart from gathering a few bits and pieces of information their night-time break-in had achieved nothing. Nick was right—she had underestimated the Circle.

Part of her wanted to go back home and keep watch at the window. Another impelled her to hurry round to the Torves' and find out what had gone wrong. On reflection, neither plan made much sense. Who knew when (*if* . . . she shuddered) Nick would return, and what could she do at the Torves' except confirm the Circle's suspicions? Better to get to school and try to find Miles.

There was no one at the gates when she arrived. Out across the football field, the blackened shell of the Smedley Library stood gaunt against the boiling white sky. Emma hurried through the main entrance and signed in at the reception desk. She had taken the corridor into the humanities block, and was hurrying towards first period history, when Mr Carter stepped into her path. The second Circle member to surprise her that morning.

'Not so fast, Miss Rhodes.'

He looked her up and down, tongue clucking against the roof of his mouth. School legend insisted that Farter had once been a PE teacher, and the barrel chest, stocky legs, and tree-trunk arms seemed to bear this out.

'And where were you yesterday when the police arrived?' He *knew*. 'Come on, out with it.'

'I don't know what you mean, sir.'

'Don't know what I mean, sir? Do you have many run-ins with the law? I *mean* after the fire, of course.'

She relaxed. Too quickly. Carter clucked again.

'You're aware that your bag was found in the ashes? I suppose you're going to tell me that you left it in the library by mistake?'

'Yes.'

'And that you decided to skip school for the afternoon without ever knowing about the fire? Right, well the police will want to hear all about it. My office, lunchtime.'

He began to march away. Then stopped and gestured with his finger.

'Come. There's something I want to show you.'

She followed him down a corridor decorated with Year Seven art projects. It was the last day of school before the Christmas holidays and every wall was a collage of winter landscapes and holly bushes, painted robins and sugar paper Santas. Richie had loved Christmas. Even when Rowan had lectured them about the Pagan winter festival that Christianity had hijacked, and Bob had rolled his eyes at the irrational spirituality of it all, Emma's brother had enjoyed every corny moment. This year would be different, of course. This year there would be no Christmas at the Rhodes' house.

Carter tapped the window in the door of classroom 6G. Geography teacher Miss Hemmel and a sea of Year Nine heads turned to the glass. One belonged to Henry Torve. Emma shouldered her way into the room.

'Sorry to intrude, Miss Hemmel, this'll just take a moment.'

Emma hardly heard Carter's announcement. She marched straight up to Henry's desk.

'Are you OK? Henry, answer me.'

'Um. Err. OK. Hi.' The rest of the class started to giggle. Henry leant forward and whispered, 'Ems, have you gone completely mental?'

Gone was the terrified boy of last night. In his place, the old Henry—a smart, fun-loving kid without a care in the world. Emma's phone bleeped. A message: *Doesn't remember anything. Seems to buy the 'chill' story. Check his wrist.* She looked across the classroom and found a thunder-faced Sas slipping his mobile into his blazer pocket. Emma grabbed Henry's hand and pulled up his sleeve.

'Ems, come on!'

There was no bruising to show where the handcuff had been. What had Arthur Torve said to Miss Worple last night? *If we can't shake Henry out of this terror and get him to talk, then perhaps it would be better to wipe his memory of the ghost train altogether.* And that's precisely what they'd done. Emma imagined the scene: the vicar Mr Merriglass, solicitor Arthur Torve, doctor's wife Margery Glock, all the respectable and upright members of the Circle stalling the police downstairs while Miss Worple and Miss Roper cast their spells. One to wipe Henry's memory, another to heal his wrist. Then it was just a matter of hiding the cuffs and repeating the story of a chill.

'That's Henry's cousin, Emma Rhodes,' a boy at the back whispered. 'Her little brother died last year and she went proper crazy.'

Henry twisted round in his seat. 'Shut your mouth, Kyle, or I'll shut it for you.' He turned back to Emma. 'Are you all right?'

'Yeah.' She squeezed his hand. 'I'm sorry.'

Carter stepped aside to let her pass. She was halfway down the corridor when he called after her.

'Wonderful to see the boy so fully recovered, eh? Mr Torve would never allow any harm to come to his son . . . My friends and I are much less squeamish, however. You would do well not to test our patience.'

The threat was clear: the Circle might not know *how* she knew about them and their hopes for the stolen necromancy machine, but they clearly suspected her interference. The knot of anxiety in her stomach pulled tighter than ever. They had seen fit to warn her off. Anything more drastic would risk drawing attention to themselves; Emma had lived in Milton Lake all her life. But a friendless boy new to the town? If Nick Redway were to disappear who would miss him?

She kept her head down all the way to 3H. When she opened the classroom door, Mr Meadow was calling for quiet.

'All right, you lot, enough giggling . . . Emma, there you are. Please find a seat, we're already running late.'

Still lost in thought, she took her place near the back of the class. She was shuffling through her satchel for a pad and pen when Mr Meadow demanded silence for the last time. Emma flipped open her pad and turned her gaze to the front.

The swear word that burst from her lips caused an immediate eruption. Goggle-eyed girls covered their mouths and exchanged '*Oh my Gods!*' while the boys brayed like a pack of hyenas.

'Miss Rhodes! I ought to send you straight to the head,' Mr Meadow fumed, 'but you've already missed enough school for one week. *If* you could manage to keep your disgusting language under control, we will begin again.' He surrendered the floor to the new boy. 'Apologies for the interruption, Mr Bleeker.'

At the front of the class, Nicholas Redway grinned. 'No problem, Mr Meadow.'

Sitting together in the third row, Chantelle, Madeleine, and Lola stared up at the pale-faced boy with expressions that varied between fascination, flirtatiousness, and outright lust.

'Well, as I was saying, my name's Johnny Bleeker and I'm from a little town in Maine, New England called Mearsville,' Nick said. 'I was born and grew up on my pop's farm. We kept cows, hogs, chickens, turkeys, raised corn, potatoes, beets, dry beans. When I was little I helped my grandpa sell sweetcorn at our roadside stall. I went to high school one town over, had a weekend job flipping burgers at a fast food joint. Then, last month, my family moved back to the old country, as my grandpa calls it. My pop got a job not far from Milton Lake, and that's just about it.'

He's lying, Emma thought, *and, like all the best lies, most of it's probably based on truth.* She thought back to those dreamlike flashes—the farm, the track, the roadside stall, the sheriff's car. That she was catching glimpses of his life in America was clear, but what did those glimpses mean and why was *she* seeing them? Perhaps more importantly, should she tell him? She decided against it. It seemed unlikely that the visions had anything to do with the necromancy machine and the Circle's plans, and might only serve to distract Nick from his work. In any case, she would like to know more about him before she revealed this mysterious insight into his old life.

Chan raised her hand. 'Do you work out? It's just you look pretty buff. Maybe it's all that sweaty labouring you had to do on the farm?'

Lola and Madeleine giggled. Emma looked around for Miles; he certainly wouldn't appreciate his girlfriend flirting with the new guy. Then she remembered that he didn't take history. And if he were here, would he even recognize Chantelle, let alone feel any jealousy? Was Miles still Miles?

While 'Johnny Bleeker' batted aside questions about college football, US TV shows (about which he appeared to know nothing), and American high school proms (much more glamorous than their UK counterparts, Lola sighed), Emma had her phone under the desk and was surfing the net. Now she had a name *and* a location. A search for 'Nicholas

Redway, Mearsville' produced no clear result. Was it possible that, like Harvey Dowd and Johnny Bleeker, Nick Redway was an alias? Emma didn't like to think that he had lied to her again.

Mearsville at least was a real place, a four mile square patch of nothing in Cumberland County. From the tiny write-up on Wikipedia it appeared that the town had never amounted to much, and that during the 1960s the last residents had abandoned it to wolves and weeds. Was this a further attempt by Nick to cover up his identity or was there something more to his story of long-forgotten Mearsville?

One last search confirmed something she already knew. 'Johnny Bleeker' was another mixed-up name stolen from the movies. The 'Johnny' part came from the rebellious leader of a motorcycle gang in the 1950s film *The Wild One* while 'Bleeker' was the name of a lawman from the same film. Bob had only mentioned the movie yesterday in connection with Nick's Triumph Thunderbird.

'OK, interrogation over.' Mr Meadow held up his hand for hush. 'As this is the last day of term we don't expect you to take an active part in class, Mr Bleeker. We will, however, expect a proper school uniform come January.'

Meadow cast a disapproving glance over Nick's buckled biker boots, black jeans, and open neck shirt.

'I think he looks cute,' Madeleine said.

Nick flashed a smile and the girls swooned. Emma rolled her eyes; surely he wasn't being serious? Mr Meadow invited him to take a seat and Madeleine pulled a chair from an empty desk across the aisle and fluttered her fake lashes.

'Got a place at the back,' Nick said. 'Thanks anyway.'

The girls watched open-mouthed as the new boy took a seat next to Emma. There might as well have been cartoon thought bubbles floating above Lola's and Madeleine's heads: *He chose* her *over me? Look at her, not a scrap of make-up and that wiry hair hasn't been cut in months. And he's soooo hot.* Chan's expression was a little more difficult to read—a strange mix of anger, bewilderment, and, could it be, shame?

'May I borrow a pen and some of your paper?'

She tore two sheets from her pad and handed him a ballpoint.

'What are you doing here?'

'Said I'd surprise you, didn't I?'

'You could've given me a heart attack.'

'Glad I didn't. I've got enough trouble with ghosts without you coming back to haunt my sorry ass.'

While Mr Meadow droned on about cotton manufacture in nineteenth century mill towns, Emma made a show of taking notes.

'I wanted to get a good look at this old boyfriend of yours,' Nick whispered. 'And it was about time I started to blend in a bit. A boy lurking about in the town's most haunted house was gonna start attracting attention.'

'Yeah, well I'm not convinced you've succeeded in keeping a low profile.'

It wasn't just Chan and the other girls, several of her classmates kept looking over their shoulders at the swaggering American.

'It's not about keeping a low profile exactly, the Circle are already aware of me,' Nick explained. 'It's more about keeping them guessing. "The Mysterious Boy in the Sparrow House" might confirm their vague suspicions that I've something to do with the machine. "The Cocky New Kid on the Block" might wrong-foot them for a couple of days.'

Mr Meadow glanced at his watch, then at the window where fresh snow pattered the glass like soft white moths.

'Ladies and gentlemen, the hour is upon us. I suppose I ought to wish you all a Happy Chris—'

The break-time bell rang through the school—and Nick thrust his head under the desk. The rest of his body was almost out of sight when Emma reached down and grabbed the collar of his jacket. A second later, he reemerged, ballpoint clasped in his fist. He held it up to the class, all of whom had turned at the violent scrape of his chair. A rather melodramatic way to retrieve a pen, but they bought the unspoken explanation. Only Emma knew that he had been holding the pen all along.

He'd made a slip. He couldn't help it, some kind of instinct or training had kicked in and his body had responded. Another lie, another mystery.

Emma filed it away with the rest.

10

Miles sat on the low wall that ran between the football field and Black Acre Forest. Beside him, Chan would occasionally glance at her boyfriend through a screen of honey-coloured hair, then drop her eyes again. Even from their bench on the opposite side of the field, Emma could see that the girl was worried.

'Notice any change?' Nick asked.

Emma sank into the folds of her parka. It was cold, bitterly so, but it wasn't the wind and snow that made her shudder. 'He . . . he looks the same,' she said. 'A bit paler, I guess, and tired, like he hasn't slept in a few nights, but I thought he'd be—'

'Walking with a cane? Wrinkled skin, grey hair, and bladder trouble?'

'I guess it was the voice,' she nodded. 'He sounded old on the phone, so I wondered if he might have changed physically. Is that stupid?'

'Not at all, in fact it could well have turned out like that. Possession doesn't happen right away. The human soul is just about the strongest thing in existence and it takes an invading spirit a while to crush it. During that time the body is a battleground over which the rival souls will fight. Sometimes the resident spirit will have control, like last night when Miles managed to call you, other times the possessor will take over.'

'Will the soul always be crushed?' Emma asked. 'Do possessing spirits always win?'

'Almost always. The unmade have a hunger that the living cannot match. And once the possessing ghost takes full control, it has the chance to shape its new body.'

'You mean Peter Taggart could really change the way Miles looks?'

'Easy as switching clothes,' Nick nodded. 'But the choice is limited. A spirit like Peter can either keep his vessel's appearance or transform so that he appears as he did just prior to death.'

'Healthy seventeen year old or frail old geezer? Somehow, I don't think he'll go for option two.'

Miles's clear blue eyes stayed focused on Emma. That the grandfather was in control and winning the battle for possession seemed obvious. The words that had answered her phone call this morning—*too late*—all but confirmed it.

'What are we going to do?'

'We need to get him alone, and soon.' Nick eased the spirit detector from his pocket and extended the antennae. The device gave off a high-pitched squeal while the needle flicked across the dial. 'Your friend is cooking around the low to medium level.'

'Is that good?'

'That is *not* good. It means there's an invading spirit inside and that the ghost is settling in very nicely. If the readings were high it would suggest a fully detached spirit, much easier to pull out.' The detector squealed again and Nick slapped it with the flat of his palm. 'This isn't going to be pleasant.'

'What isn't? What can we do?'

'I need you to send him a textual message.'

'A text? Saying what?'

'You know his secret: he's not Miles any more. Say you know of a group called the Circle—'

'Are you crazy?'

'Lies always work better when there's a pinch of truth to flavour them.'

Emma suppressed a shiver. It was unnerving, hearing the same idea she had had about Nick's story from the classroom repeated back to her.

'The Circle are friends of yours, talented necromancers with the power to force Peter's spirit out of his grandson's body. Say you'll get them to do this unless he agrees to meet you.'

'But what do I want in return?' There had to be a motive for the threat, a reason to get Peter alone. She had it: 'I'll say that if he agrees to dump Chantelle and go out with me, I'll keep quiet. I want revenge for her treating me like crap, public humiliation, he might buy that. Where shall I say to meet?'

'Somewhere nearby. A building that won't be in use this afternoon.'

'The swimming pool.'

'No, not there.' His voice was cold as he thrust the detector back into his pocket. 'What's that place over in the trees?'

Emma followed his finger into the thicket of the forest. Between the trees, she glimpsed the red bricks and broken windows of the roofless cottage, and a summer walk from years ago came back to her: little Richie snug and sleeping in the papoose slung from Rowan's shoulders, Emma trailing behind, picking wild flowers and half-listening to her mother's stories. Those had been the days when Dr Rowan Rhodes had taught history at the university. Long ago days before a fascination with the supernatural had driven a wedge between her and her sceptical husband.

'It's the old forester's cottage,' Emma murmured. 'Years ago the town used to employ a man to tend Black Acre. No one's lived there for a long time.'

'It's far enough from the school,' Nick nodded, 'but we'll need to gag him.'

'What?'

'Wrenching a spirit from a body is just about the most painful thing you can imagine, for both host soul and invading ghost.'

'Will Miles be OK . . . afterwards?'

'If he survives.'

'If?'

'We may already be too late.'

Nick cast a look at the boy on the wall. Summoned by the end of break bell, Chan had left him there and was hurrying back to the main school building. Emma noticed how her old friend ploughed through the churned up mud of the football field, heedless of the mess she was making of her high heels.

'Leave it half an hour and send the message,' Nick said. 'It won't look good if I'm here when he receives it. Say you want to meet at two o'clock in the forester's cottage.'

He got up to leave.

'Wait a minute,' Emma protested, 'there are things we need to talk about.'

'Sorry, I have an induction session: "Effective use of the school library". I guess if I don't burn it down then I'm already ahead of the game. I'll meet you at the cottage at half one.'

He waved to her over his shoulder as he strode off, the swaggering Yank back in character.

A few minutes later, Emma was settling into her seat at the back of higher maths. She enjoyed the subject and had read ahead, so didn't feel compelled to listen as Miss Chala revised their quadratic equations homework. Instead, she took a moment to refine the text dictated by Nick and send it on its way. She had just started to pay attention again when she noticed the face at the window. He stood behind the glass, his hands pressed flat against the pane. Emma remembered Miles's words from last night: *hands on the window like two brown spiders*. Peter Taggart smiled and nodded.

When the lunchtime bell rang, Emma surveyed an almost blank notebook. Grabbing her satchel, she squeezed into the bustling corridor, and was almost within sight of Carter's office when Lola and Madeleine ambushed her by the girls' toilets. Physically the two friends were exact opposites—Madeleine doll-like with her tiny stature, flawless skin and jet-black hair; Lola just the right side of gangly with long runner's legs and a bushel of lustrous brown curls.

'Oh *hiiiiii*, Ems,' Lola cooed.

Freak, weirdo, nutter, psycho: Emma had heard it all, but this was the first time since the confrontation in the gym that they had called her by her name.

'Oh my God, you look totally cute in your parka.' Eyes saucer-wide, Mads shook her head. 'You could always pull off that tomboy look.'

'Totally,' Lola agreed.

'What do you want?' Emma asked guardedly.

As if rehearsed, both girls screwed up their eyes and wrung their hands.

'We've been total bitches.'

'Total. But it wasn't our fault.' Lola shook her head so vigorously Emma thought the bushel might come loose and topple off her shoulders. 'It was Chan, she's such a bully. She said we couldn't talk to you any more because she was going out with Miles, and we felt like we didn't have a choice because we've known Chan the *looongest* out of anyone. But Mads and me, we've been talking all morning. We didn't mean to be so horrible and, well, we want to be friends again.'

'Yay!' Madeleine clapped her hands.

'The old gang back together. Except Chan, of course.'

'Why not Chan?' Emma smiled.

'Because she's gone totally weird.'

'Like I did, you mean?'

The girls exchanged an uncomfortable glance.

'You were upset about your brother,' Lola said. 'And that was totally understandable.'

'Tota—'

Emma closed her eyes. 'If I hear that word again I may have to totally slap both of you.'

Madeleine giggled. 'Chan is so boring these days, just follows Miles around like a big dumb dog. Anyway, we've had it with both of them and we want to be friends with you again. Please say yes.'

'Please, please, please.'

'Has this got anything to do with my new boyfriend?'

A small lie, but it achieved the reaction she'd hoped for. Lola and Madeleine did double takes—the kind of thing Emma had only ever seen in movies—and proceeded to let rip with shrieks so shrill they could shatter glass.

'He. Is. *Soooo.* Cute!' Lola cried. 'How long have you guys been going out? Is he a good kisser?'

'Has he got a brother, Ems? I so totally would—'

'You so *totally* wouldn't.' Emma's tone cut the excitement dead.

She hadn't realized how much anger had been brewing inside. All those sly looks and cruel jibes had been added to a simmering pot stored somewhere so deep barely a fume had escaped. She had shut herself down, made herself cold and untouchable, yet now Emma understood that the outside world had still managed to penetrate.

'Do you know why you totally wouldn't?' Her smile turned into a grimace. 'Because he's clever and kind and, unlike you two . . . *things,* he has a soul. He would look at you and his gaze would pass right through. Know why?'

'No,' Lola squeaked.

'No,' Madeleine bleated.

'Because you're not there. You're just two venomous puffs of air. So he'd turn up his nose and walk away, like I'm walking away right now.'

Anger and resentment had boiled and vaporized into nothing. Another ghost vanquished, she thought, another step through the door and into the world beyond.

The police were waiting when she reached Carter's office. The headmaster was nowhere to be seen although his framed photograph glowered down from the wall. The two uniformed officers sitting behind his desk seemed friendly enough. They asked what time she'd left the library; whether there had been any students or strangers hanging around the building; why she'd left her bag behind (she claimed straightforward forgetfulness); and why she hadn't assembled after the fire alarm (she admitted skipping afternoon lessons to meet her boyfriend. The policeman with the moustache smiled indulgently).

'Do you know how it started?' she asked.

'Old building like that? Probably faulty wiring,' the moustachioed officer said. 'We might get something from the CCTV cameras.'

Emma froze. 'Cameras?'

'There was one in the entrance, so if it was started deliberately we could get a look at the arsonist on his way out.'

'Or hers,' his colleague added.

'Only problem is the camera didn't transmit to a remote recorder. The video was stored on a DVD player in Miss Lucas's office and the system looks pretty fried. We've got the tech boys working their magic but they don't hold out much hope.'

Emma cursed inwardly. She'd never noticed the camera. Dangerous as it had been with the library burning down around her, it would have been the work of moments to eject the DVD and destroy the only evidence that might connect her to the fire. Now she just had to pray that the tech boys' sorcery wasn't up to the job.

By the time she left Carter's office it was one twenty-three. Outside, the snow was falling thick and steady. She pulled up her collar and made her way around the wind-whipped police cordon that looped the ashy remnants of the library. At the forest edge, she glanced back and saw that hers were the only tracks in the freshly laid snow. Should she wait for Nick or move on to the cottage? In the end, the decision was made for her.

One of the side doors of the school opened and the possessed boy stepped out. Emma backed up into the trees. She watched through fat flakes as he rolled a cigarette, tamped, and lit. Even from this distance she could see the pleasure he took from that first deep breath of nicotine. Miles Taggart had never smoked . . .

She couldn't go back without him seeing her. Only one option, then: continue to the cottage and trust that Nick would notice the boy and cut around the back of the school, entering the forest at a point invisible to Peter.

A slope began near the first trees and inclined gradually upwards to a bank that overlooked the school and the town beyond. This was the foot of Summer Rise, one of the three forested hills that made up the valley into which Milton Lake nestled. On the opposite edge of town stood Spring Fell, the western hill that rose above Connolly Avenue. To the south was the largest of the hills, Winter Heights, with its steep main road plunging down into the vale.

Patches of moss struggled through the December-hard earth, but otherwise Black Acre was still and sleeping. Emma left the beaten path and made a beeline for the cottage. It did not sit deep in the forest, but she was confident it was far enough from the school for Nick's purposes. The forester's home stood in a little clearing, its shattered windows curtained with the husks of dead vines. Its door had been stolen long ago, probably to provide timber for a tree house. Of the roof, only a few tiles remained, strewn on the ground like the broken teeth of some forgotten dragon.

Emma decided to scale the bank behind the cottage. A cluster of trees clinging to the hillside provided excellent cover from which she could keep watch on the clearing below. It wasn't an easy scramble, the frozen slope offered few footholds and old roots came away in her hands. Bruised and breathless, she eventually reached the shelter of a gnarled oak and hauled herself round so that her back rested against the trunk.

She had just settled when the boy dropped down beside her.

'Jesus! What is it with you and dramatic entrances?' She closed her eyes, composing herself after the shock. 'Did you see Miles?'

Nick nodded. 'I cut around the back of the school.'

'Great minds.'

'What time do you make it?'

'Twenty minutes to. You're late.'

'Sorry, I had a run in with Carter.'

Emma stiffened. 'And?'

'He welcomed me to the school. He's suspicious as hell, but what could he say?'

'He threatened me this morning.'

'What?' The anger in his voice was like a scorpion sting.

'My knight in faded leather,' Emma joked, but to see his anger roused like that was oddly comforting. 'He made it clear that he thinks I was involved in calling the police. Then he hinted that if I didn't keep my nose out of the Circle's business Henry might suffer.'

'I see.'

'And he's not the only one. This morning Mrs Glock had a few things to say. She left an apple pie outside your door, by the way. A welcome-to-the-neighbourhood gift.'

'Never take an apple from a necromancer,' Nick said, 'I've read my fairytales. By the way, I bumped into your friend Sas on my way out. He told me about Henry. Seems they found a way to wipe his memory of whatever happened in the ghost train.'

'There's something odd about all that,' Emma said. 'Remember when Carter was talking to Worple and Roper?

He said it was unfortunate, Henry being there when Hiram was summoned.'

'Because he might have inadvertently seen members of the Circle there, too. That was why they had to keep him locked away until they could safely remove the memory.'

'OK, except one of the old ladies agreed that it *was* unfortunate, but only if he *forgot* what he saw.' Emma paused to let her meaning sink in. 'Do you see? Surely if the Circle were afraid of Henry revealing the secret of their necromancy she would have said "only if he *remembers* what he saw".'

Nick nodded. 'So they wanted him to remember something.'

'But he couldn't, and then they ran out of time. The police arrived and the Circle had no choice but to wipe his memory, including whatever information they were after.'

'But they were there at the ghost train,' Nick protested. 'What could he have seen or heard that they didn't?'

Emma had no answers and so left the question hanging.

'So where did you go last night?' she asked. 'After Miles called I saw you speeding off on your bike.'

'The spirit detector activated. More unmade coming through.'

'Why didn't you come and get me?'

'You looked tired. I could handle it on my own.'

'How many?'

'Three.'

'*Three?*' Those words of Percival Sparrow came back to her: *The blind necromancer has opened the way and the more he calls, the wider the path becomes.* 'Who were they?'

'Children. I found them in the woods to the west of town. They claimed to have been dead for a hundred and sixty years. Back then a travelling circus was passing through Milton Lake and one of the brown bears got loose and went on the rampage. It found the kids playing in the forest and, well, they weren't very pretty to look at. I used iron to . . . ' He sighed, unable or unwilling to go on.

Emma laid a hand on his arm. 'They summoned more spirits last night,' she murmured. 'Only hours after the police came to the house.'

'Like I said, they're desperate. They have the means to summon but their luck isn't holding. The first ghost was accidentally sent back when Hiram stood on the ghost train's iron rail. Since then every spirit they've called forth has been banished before they had a chance to locate it. We're the banishers, in case you were wondering.'

'I think I'm keeping up,' Emma said sarcastically. 'But isn't this really dangerous? If we keep getting in their way the Circle will have to stop us.'

'What choice do we have? If we stand aside and let them continue using the machine then the gates will fall and the unmade will overwhelm Milton Lake.'

'So what do we do?'

'We wait and we watch. They won't be keeping the machine at the Torve residence, it's too risky when they know someone's on their tail. We have to try and find it. In the meantime, we stay ahead of them, putting down as many spirits as we can.'

The crack of a branch ricocheted through the forest. It seemed to come from far away but with the snow muffling every sound it was difficult to pinpoint the direction. The clearing below remained empty.

Emma had turned back to Nick, a careless word forming on her lips, when she saw the shadow loom behind him and the word fractured and reformed into a broken, garbled warning. In the next second, he was gone, falling away from her, rolling and spilling head over heels, neck and arms twisting beneath him. His body cut a path through the thin coat of snow that the clouds had draped over the hillside. Scattered in dots and splashes, he left a crimson trail behind. He missed the edge of the cottage wall by an inch and rolled unconscious into the clearing, his blood-smattered face turned to the sky. From this distance it was difficult to tell if he was breathing.

Peter Taggart used his grandson's strong hand to wrench Emma to her feet. He dropped a bloodstained rock to the ground and kicked it down the slope. Emma struggled against him but his grip was like iron.

'Stop squirming or I'll throw you down too,' he barked. 'Now, I believe we had an appointment.'

11

'So you know my secret, do you? Clever girl.'

The laughter wasn't quite right, too deep and gravelly. The same went for the way he worked the muscles in his grandson's face, how he cocked his head to one side and the way he stood. Little differences all adding up to one clear message: this wasn't Miles Taggart.

He held the phone to her face. 'What is this "Circle"? Was the kid one of them?'

Emma glanced over her shoulder. Nick remained where he had fallen, silent and still.

'He can't help you. He's dead. When you've been around death as long as I have you develop a nose for it. Was he an exorcist? Some of the unmade who've been sent back talk about exorcism.'

He pushed her against the tree and Emma bit down into her bottom lip. The pain was there but she felt it at a distance.

'I know you, don't I . . . ?' Peter frowned. 'Yes, you're Bob Rhodes's girl. You courted our Miles.'

Emma spat back. '*Courted?* You're gonna have to update your slang if you want people to believe you're a twenty-first century teenager.' Something clicked in her head, an idea flickering like a moth in the dimness. Then it was gone again.

'And now you want to court me?' Peter laughed. 'Your ex's grandfather. I believe that's what the young people call "gross".'

'That was just a lie to get you here.'

With one hand pinning her to the tree, those strong fingers caught Emma by the throat. 'This is so strange,' he said, his smile faltering. 'I have all his memories, you see? All these thoughts that aren't my own. It's like sorting through a stranger's attic—you open random boxes and a jumble of different sights and sounds come tumbling out. I've heard his mother, my daughter, singing in the garden. I remember how his young heart hammered when he stole sweets from Roper and Worple's shop. I've tasted the victory of the football field and I've sensed the loneliness that he hides from everyone. And there, right at the heart of him, I see the girl he loves . . . '

'You're in his body,' Emma said, holding his gaze, 'so I guess you'll feel this.'

A swift kick to the groin and he went down shrieking. A moment later, Emma was skidding and slipping down the bank. The image of Nick on the ground juddered through a haze of tears: left leg bent awkwardly beneath him, his chest unmoving and a dark red jewel glistening against the side of his head. The sight of blood caught her like a blow. It dragged her back to a scream of brakes, to clouded eyes and a little broken body, to a scarlet stain spreading over the kerb outside the Sparrow House. Richie . . . She imagined the voice, the one that sounded so like his: *Your friend is gone and now we're alone again. Just you, me, and the darkness . . .*

She dropped to her knees, cradled his head, felt for a pulse. Nothing. Maybe her hands were too cold. She put an ear to his lips. Was that a creak of air moving deep inside? It was too small a sound to be sure. Clogged with dirt and hair, the ragged gash above his ear had at least stopped bleeding. She laid his head on the ground, and was about to push air into his lungs when a hand caught her hood and she was dragged backwards.

'I told you, he's dead.'

Peter pulled her through the open doorway and into the derelict shell of the forester's cottage. They entered what might once have been a parlour, the whitewashed walls tattooed with decades of graffiti. Then his hands were at her throat again and he slammed her into the wall, the impact sparking stars inside her skull.

'I want to know about this Circle. Who are they?'

She could only just hear him over the thump of blood in her ears.

'C-can't breathe . . . '

He loosened his grip a little. 'Better? Now answer.'

'You wuh-weren't like this,' she gasped. 'I remember Miles's gr-grandad, he was a kind, l-loving man. He'd never hurt anyone, l-least of all h-his grandson. But now you're killing him, c-crushing his soul.'

Got to buy some time. The horror she felt at Nick's death was like a cold hand around her heart but a sense of self-preservation had kicked in. Only two days ago, in the attic of the Sparrow House, she had almost welcomed death; had seen the sacrifice as a kind of justice. But now some of that darkness had retreated, and Emma found herself stepping back into the world. She didn't want to leave it yet.

Peter's fingers flexed around her throat.

'Do you have any idea what it's like behind the gates?' he whispered. 'We watch in silence, see all the things we took for granted: a sudden breeze, the feel of a friendly hand, a hug, a caress, a kiss. Can you imagine what it's like to live without those things? To exist in nothingness with sight as your only sense? We see all of this . . . ' He looked around the ruined cottage. 'Beauty. Men and women moving blindly through the world, hardly noticing the sounds that teem in the stillness, the thousand textures in every beam of light. What would you do if you existed behind the gates, robbed of all these small and wonderful things?'

Tears coursed down his cheeks. 'I'm killing my grandson, but he is of my blood and possession is always easier when that is so. I have to taste this world again. I cannot go back. I will not.'

'You want a human life,' Emma murmured.

Peter closed his eyes, as if receiving a blessing. 'Yes.'

'And everything that goes with it.'

'All of it. The abundance, the beauty.'

'The pain?'

An idea. What if she could use his hunger against the old man? Unlike with Evelyn Smedley, she had no tool with which to recreate his final moments, but maybe she didn't need one. *They are vulnerable to the things that killed them.*

Peter stared at her. 'What are you talking about?'

'The tingle in your arm. Pain growing, turning into white-hot agony. Agony lashing out from your chest, striking into your jaw, your neck, your back, your stomach.' She remembered the symptoms from a first aid class taken years ago. 'You're sweating like a marathon runner but you haven't moved a muscle. You're dizzy, stumbling, and all the time that vice in your chest is tightening and tightening . . . '

It was like a kind of sorcery: as she conjured them with words so the symptoms appeared. The pain began to bite and Peter's gaze became unfocused. Sweat sprang out on his brow and ran in torrents down his face. The hand around her throat trembled. Finally, he snatched it away, clutched his chest and stumbled to his knees.

'Stop,' the plea sizzled between his teeth. 'I w-won't hurt you.'

'Tightening around your heart . . . '

She hesitated. Behind the crinkled eyes she thought she could see a glimpse of the man as he had been in life. That kindly grandfather who would have readily sacrificed himself for his beloved Miles. Years in the empty wastelands beyond the gates had twisted his mind and left behind this ravenous shadow. She remembered Nick's words: *They were people once* . . . But Miles was a person, too.

'Bands of metal,' Emma continued. 'Bands of *iron* getting tighter and tighter.'

Both hands were now pressed to his chest. His head rolled back and he whimpered into the weeping sky. Emma forced herself to complete the spell.

'You remember it, don't you? All the pain and fear and sorrow. Miles told me you were alone when you died.'

He looked at her with such anguish her own heart trembled.

'Remember . . . yes. I wanted to say goodbye to Miles and my daughter. Hold their hands and say goodbye. That's why I stayed when the light came to take me . . . As soon as it faded, *they* arrived from behind the gates. The Night Watchmen in their dark cloaks and hoods. They said I couldn't stay with the living because I had no latch to the world, so I must go with them. I asked if I could come back and they laughed. *Such a sound* . . . A necromancer might summon you, they said, but there are billions of souls behind the gates and only a handful of skilled necromancers in the world. You might wait a thousand years. They dragged me away, screaming out of this life and through the gates.'

There was movement in the open doorway, a figure slumping against the frame. Emma felt the darkness lift as Nick posed the question—

'Are you ready to go back?'

'There's no other way?' Peter asked without turning.

'None . . . that I know of.'

Nick's skin was paler than ever, his features drawn with a pain that hardly seemed physical. He steadied himself against the door before coming into the parlour. A sudden wind crested the hilltop and plunged down into the roofless cottage, scattering ash from the fireplace and raking back his hair. The dark stain above his ear glimmered like a gunshot. Emma was about to go to him when he held up his hand, a gesture for her to stay by the wall.

'Will the Watchmen come again?' Peter sobbed.

Nick knelt in front of the possessed boy, his back turned to Emma. When he spoke again, his voice was as soft as mercy. 'Ready?'

'I thought you were dead. I was sure.' No longer insane, the tears of an old man stained Peter's cheeks. 'I'll forget, won't I? I'll watch the world and grow jealous and hungry.'

'Are you ready?' Nick repeated. 'Then let me in.'

Peter thrust his arms out at his sides and threw back his head. The wind whipped up and seemed to focus in a cyclone around the two figures. Pressed against the wall, Emma watched as Nick pulled back his shirtsleeve and flexed his long fingers. Over the cyclone's howl, she heard Peter call out—

'Do it! Do it NOW!'

A vortex of snow whirled around them until they seemed little more than shadows. Then it happened. Nick's shoulder rolled forward and he plunged his hand through the boy's face and deep into his throat. Emma had seen the pliable bodies of ghosts pass through dense structures but this was different. This was solid matter penetrating solid matter without the slightest resistance.

Just like Percival Sparrow, Nick searched for that deep and secret treasure, except this time there were two souls to find. Only seconds passed, yet outside the cyclone it seemed like hours. Emma could do nothing but stand and watch, a strange mix of joy and sorrow, relief and anxiety ebbing and flowing. Nick had prepared her for the terrible scream, but when it came she still had to hide her face against the wall.

When she looked back, the vortex had vanished and Miles was sprawled unconscious on the ground. Standing over him, Nicholas Redway and Peter Taggart. The old man was just as Emma remembered—silver-haired and stooped, dressed in what could only be the memory of a smart blue suit.

'I'm sorry, sonny.' He bent down and touched his grandson's golden hair. Then he looked over at Emma. 'Thank you for helping me remember.'

Nick took a short length of iron pipe from the pocket of his jacket.

'The worst part's over. Now I just have to send you back.'

'Why?' Peter panicked. 'Can't I stay like this? I won't hurt anyone, I promise.'

'I'm sorry. If you'd succeeded in possessing Miles then the path you opened would have closed up behind you. Now it stands wide—a crack in the gates. More unmade could come through, they wouldn't even need to be summoned. The only way to close up the breach is to send you back.'

'Can't you save us?' Peter cried. 'Can't anyone?'

The man's hopelessness made Emma want to weep.

'For God's sake, have pity.'

Nick lifted the bar behind his shoulder. 'I do.'

And with that, he swung.

Peter's body collapsed into that now familiar bright green stew. It bubbled on the concrete floor, growing ever smaller as the ghost lost its form and returned to the gates. Meanwhile, Nick grabbed Miles by the collar and propped him in a sitting position against the wall. A twitch. A groan. Miles took a startled look around the cottage.

'Where am I? What are you doing to me? Ems? Are you really . . . ?'

Suddenly the memories came back and terror flared in his eyes. Emma guessed that it was like emerging from a nightmare only to discover that every dark dream had followed you into the waking world. Ghosts were real, but the true horror was infinitely more disturbing: the dead we mourn could come back and claim our lives as their own. Emma knew that Miles could not live with such memories. He simply wasn't strong enough. Luckily, Nick seemed to know it too.

'Listen to me: you are to go home, you are to sleep, you are to forget everything that happened here. It was all just a bad dream.'

'My grandad . . . ' Miles's voice came out slurred, as if he was drunk or very tired. 'Hands like spiders on the window. He tried to—'

'Your grandfather's dead, understand?' It sounded more like a command than a question. 'These last few days, you've been unwell, but now you're better and you *know* that all the weird things you've heard and seen, it was just a fever.'

'But—'

'None of it was real.'

'Y-yeah . . . ' Miles managed a weak smile. 'Just bad dreams.'

'Even us talking now, even this is a dream.'

'Even Emma?'

'Even Emma.'

Nick pulled him to his feet. With a big dopey grin plastered across his face, Miles zipped his jacket and zigzagged out of the cottage.

Emma joined Nick in the doorway. 'Will he be OK?'

'I hope so,' he shrugged. 'It'd be a real shame if he walked under a bus.'

'That's what you tried to do to me, isn't it?' she said. 'After the attic, you tried to hypnotize me, force me to forget. Why didn't it work?'

'Because you're remarkable.'

'Don't make me slap you.'

'You—are—remarkable,' Nick insisted. 'Some people are resistant to hypnotism, that's just a fact, but just now you reached through the madness of an unmade and reminded him who he used to be. In my experience, that's pretty special.'

'You're the one who pulled his spirit out. How did you manage it?'

'During the process of possession the human and ghost bodies get jumbled up. Ectoplasm infects and weakens the host just enough to allow me to reach in and find the unmade. It would've been much more difficult if Peter had resisted, maybe even impossible. Miles has a lot to thank you for.'

They stood in silence for a moment while the snow fell around them.

'I thought you were dead.'

'Dead? *Pfft!*' he snorted. 'It'd take more than a bump on the head to—'

He stumbled against her. His face was drawn and the clotted blood glistened darkly around his ear.

'Are you OK?' Emma tutted at her own question. 'Of course you're not. Come on, I'm taking you to hospital.'

'It's just a scratch. I just nee—'

He reeled again. This time she caught him. He felt like a dead weight but the local Accident & Emergency was only a stone's throw from the school gate.

'No arguments.' She pulled his arm round her shoulder. 'It's about time this town gave something back to its mysterious saviour, even if your reward turns out to be a few painkillers and a dozen stitches.'

His dry chuckle wafted against the side of her face. Together, they tramped away from the forester's cottage and into the fading light beyond the trees.

12

Stitches were not required. A nurse cleaned the wound and then knitted it together with surgical glue. Earlier, a doctor had shone a light into Nick's eyes, turning the hazel pigment a shade of autumn green, and seemed satisfied with the results.

'It looked worse than it really was,' the nurse said, dropping latex gloves into a medical waste bin. 'But we don't want you running off just yet. Anyone at home to look after you?'

'My dad,' Nick lied. 'He'll be back later.'

'*Such* a gorgeous accent.'

It was the second time she had made this comment. She was probably only a few years out of school herself, and it was difficult not to notice the appreciative glances she kept throwing at Nick.

'You must promise you won't be alone tonight. You might've sustained a concussion and, well, I don't want to see you back here. Not under those circumstances anyway.' She used her index finger to make a parting in the black mane that covered his brow. 'But I guess you must know all about head injuries. Such a nasty scar.'

Nick's fingers locked around the nurse's wrist and pulled her hand away.

'Thank you for all you've done,' he said coldly, 'now you must have a lot of other patients who need your help.'

Up until that point Emma could have sworn that he had been enjoying the woman's playful flirting. Now a guarded expression had settled over his features. He let go of her hand and the nurse, massaging her wrist, left without a word. They were alone in the cubicle, Nick sitting on the high bed, Emma on a plastic chair.

'Did you hypnotize her?'

'What?'

'She left pretty quickly.'

He shook his head. 'I think I scared her . . . It's important people don't know too much about me. Safer they don't.'

Does that include me? Emma thought.

'How's it done?' she asked. 'Hypnotism? Is it a gift you're born with or did someone teach you?'

'My pop.' He closed his eyes. 'My grandpa. I learned it through him.'

'Were you very close?'

'Real close.'

'You said in school today that you moved over to England last month.'

'I came here last month.'

'And your dad, he died many years ago.'

'Yes. In battle.'

'Your grandad died recently, too.'

'He died the night the necromancy machine was taken. This Circle, or whoever stole the machine and sold it to the Circle, they killed him. Killed Randall Wolfe, too.'

'I'm sorry.' She started to reach for him, a gesture of sympathy, but something held her back. This wasn't the whole truth, she could feel it. 'How were they killed?'

'Please, Emma. I can't think about it.'

She sat forward in her chair. This was needling at a raw wound but the urge to know was too great. 'He left you money, enough to support yourself and buy the Sparrow House.' Nick nodded. 'You told me that your grandpa raised you, that you were close. But hadn't he been studying the supernatural under Randall Wolfe for years? Wolfe lived just outside London, right? So how could he have brought you up if you only came to England last month and he was here all that time? It's a lie, isn't it? Your dad was dead, your grandpa was in England, so who raised you?'

Unable to meet her gaze, he turned away.

'What about your mother? Grandmother?'

'Mom died when I was little. Never knew my grandma.'

She thought of the old clapboard house and the rutted track.

'Nick, what happened that winter on the farm?'

He jolted forward and a terrible dread washed over his face.

'You're so close to it you *see* . . . ' Despite all the terrors they had witnessed together, this was the first time his voice shook. 'Never ask me about the farm, Emma. You must promise or I'll walk out of here and you'll never see me again.'

His fear was infectious. 'But why do *I* see it? The farmhouse, the sheriff's car.'

He snatched his jacket from the chair back and grabbed the cubicle curtain.

'I don't want to go,' he said, fist closed around the drape. 'Do you want me to stay, Emma?'

Nick's friendship and the mystery he trailed in his wake had opened up the world to her again, but Emma knew she was only halfway into the light. What would happen if he left now? The darkness would surely swallow her and she would return to her world of pain and pavements. And yet it wasn't just to save herself that she slipped her hand into his and drew him back into the cubicle. This haunted boy was like her mirror-self—a cold and lonely thing looking for salvation.

'Stay.'

'Only if you promise not to ask me about these things. I can't stop you seeing what you see, Emma, that has to be your choice—'

'I don't have any control over it.'

'You *do*. The reason is all around you, only I can't tell you how to look for it.' His gaze passed on to something invisible to Emma. 'So you'll catch glimpses of that time, and you'll want to ask me about it, but you mustn't. Not ever.'

Suddenly he was shivering like a drowning man. She pulled him into a hug.

'I promise, OK? I promise.'

Gradually, the fear seeped out of him and he became calm and still.

'Come on,' she said, forcing a smile, 'when was the last time you ate? Let's grab some food and then we can—'

A shape moved against the cubicle's papery curtain and a familiar voice called from the other side.

'Emma my dear, is that you?'

Nick pulled back the drape and found the scatter-brained Miss Lucas blinking under the glare of the hospital's harsh fluorescent lights.

'Oh my dear, I didn't know you were already here,' the librarian flustered. 'And your friend, I-I don't believe we've been introduced.'

Nick said he was honoured to meet Miss Lucas and called her 'ma'am' in that overly polite way of his.

'Creep,' Emma said out of the side of her mouth.

Still, she was pleased to see Miss Lucas blushing like a schoolgirl. The loss of her beloved library had clearly been a terrible blow. Thoughts of Smedley brought back worries about what the tech guys might find if they managed to salvage the CCTV footage. She wondered whether she ought to tell Nick, but decided that it was something beyond their control. All she could do was hope and pray.

Miss Lucas was nattering away when she caught sight of the dried blood in Nick's hair. 'Goodness, what have you done to yourself?'

'Fell from my motorbike,' he shrugged, 'it's nothing.'

'Well, I'm glad you have Emma to look after you and . . . Oh!' Miss Lucas blinked. 'But that means you're not here for your father!'

'Bob?' Emma felt a flutter of panic. 'What's happened?'

'He's had a rather nasty accident, I'm afraid. Slipped on a patch of ice outside the science block. Broke his left arm and all the fingers of his right hand, poor soul.'

'Where is he? Can I see him?'

'They're just plastering his arm and resetting his fingers. Now I've given you a horrid shock, blurting it all out like that; come to the canteen and I'll buy you a strong cup of tea.'

Apart from a table of nurses nodding wearily over their coffees, the hospital cafeteria was empty. Despite her objections, Nick told Miss Lucas to put her purse away and went off to purchase their drinks. Emma pulled back a chair from the tea-stained table and took a seat next to her favourite librarian.

'Was he in a lot of pain?'

'I'm afraid so. It was a horrible break and, what with his fingers, I suppose he'll be quite incapacitated for a while. You and your mother will have to take good care of—Oh my dear, I'm so sorry.'

Emma patted her hand. 'Don't worry.'

'It really was too awful, the way she left you,' Miss Lucas sighed. 'I blame all that silly nonsense she started filling her head with. Such an intelligent woman, too. Doctor of history, wasn't she? Until they kicked her out of the university.'

'She wasn't kicked out,' Emma bristled. 'She left.'

'Emma, I didn't mean to—'

'Your drinks.' Nick placed the cardboard cups on the table. 'Sorry if they're not brewed to your liking, us Yanks aren't big on tea.'

Emma stood up. 'I'm going to see if they'll let me visit Bob.'

'Do you want me to come?' Nick asked.

'No, you keep Miss Lucas company. I won't be long.'

As she walked away she heard the librarian whisper, *I do hope I haven't upset her. I happened to mention her mother . . .* It was strange, but that lovable old ninny *had* upset her, just by making a few observations with which Emma herself very much agreed. Rowan had acted entirely selfishly after Richie's death. That very night she had packed up her things and left the family home. Bob had let her go without a fight, and so it had been left to Emma to tug the suitcase from her mother's hand and block her path to the door. It was only a year ago but, in her mind's eye, that hysterical girl seemed like a little child.

'*Please, Mum,* please *don't go. I'm sorry about Richie. It was all my fault, I know, but Dad and me, we can't . . .*'

No more words would come. The grief was thick in her throat, choking every sound. Gently, her mother had taken back the suitcase.

'*Emma . . . No matter how much I tell you that it* wasn't *your fault, you won't ever believe me. So I have to go. If I can't make it better then I can't stay.*'

'*So you'll just leave. What about Dad?*'

'Your father and I haven't loved each other for a long time. I care about him very much, and I think he cares about me, but that's all.'

'If Richie were still here—'

'If Richie were here then it might be different. But not much.'

'Will you come back and visit?'

'Maybe. But not until I've done what I can to save you.'

'Save me from what?'

Her mother opened the door. *'Yourself.'*

That was the last time she had seen Rowan. It was nonsense, of course, all that talk of forgiveness and saving her. Just the excuses of a woman who wanted to wrench away the hands of a clinging child. In her darkest moments, Emma wondered if Richie's death had come as something of a relief. Rowan had loved her little boy, but he was the only thing that kept her tied to the family she had clearly outgrown. Ever since her involvement with the mystic Lysanna faith of white witchcraft, Rowan had begun to distance herself from her family. For the rigidly rational Bob this empty-headed claptrap soon became unbearable and the arguments between them had been furious. Looking back, Emma knew that only one thing had kept Rowan in Connolly Avenue—her beloved boy.

She asked after Bob at the nurses' station and was taken to a cubicle identical to the one in which Nick had been treated. Outside the curtain, the prim middle-aged nurse whispered—

'It's a clean break to the left arm, but it snapped quite low down on the radius, here.' She pointed to a place on the inside of her arm just above the wrist. 'And again higher up on the ulna. It'll make any movement very painful. The right fingers are all shattered so there'll be no piano playing for a while.'

'I'll have to teach him the kazoo,' Emma deadpanned.

'He was in some discomfort during the X-ray, men are such babies, so we gave him something for the pain.'

'Is that dreadful woman still making fun of me?' Bob's voice came from behind the curtain. He sounded a little slurred.

The nurse pursed her lips and trotted away. Emma pulled back the drape. To her surprise, the sight of Bob dishevelled on the bed brought tears to her eyes. She had often thought of him as a wise old owl with his little blinking eyes behind his big round glasses. Now he looked like a frail, broken-winged bird.

'You've been in the wars.'

'It's a bloody nuisance. These sawbones—' Bob's favourite slang for doctors; for a man committed to science he had never thought much of the medical profession, 'they say I won't be able to use my hands for months! And I'd hoped to do a little planning for next year's end of term tests. Extracting limonene really is much too easy.'

Emma studied the temporary plaster cast on Bob's left arm. The nurse had told her that a more permanent cast would be fitted once the swelling went down.

'How'd you manage to get in such a state?'

'I thought . . . ' his eyes glazed over for a moment, 'thought I saw someone I knew. I was teaching 7H biology—photosynthesis, reaction centres, chlorophylls—when out of the window, I saw this boy walking into the sixth form common room. He wasn't a pupil. Not any more. He'd left Tennyson years ago.'

'And?'

It wasn't unusual for Bob's old students to pay him a visit; he was the kind of teacher who seemed to leave a mark on the lives he touched.

'He was a boy.' Bob's eyes flickered. '*Still* a boy . . . Adam Carmichael. I remember him well. He dropped out of school and joined the army. Came to me the day he left, asked if I thought he was doing the right thing. I told him a military career was a noble path. Six months later he was dead.'

Forgetful of his injuries, Bob made a movement to straighten his glasses. He had barely shifted his shattered fingers before a jolt of pain blinded him. Emma adjusted the arms so that his spectacles sat square on his nose.

'I saw him as plainly as I'm seeing you now. He stood at the common room door and looked up at me. His clothing was a strange mixture of school and army uniform, and all of it was . . . God, it was *ragged*. Ragged with gunshot. And the left side of his face. Gone. It was terrible, Emma, terrible. I ought never to have started . . . ' He closed his eyes. 'Never to have started running after him. When I got outside, he'd vanished. That's when I slipped.' Bob laughed. 'Can you imagine a more unlikely person than me to start seeing ghosts?'

'You don't think there's a chance—?'

'A chance of ghosts? Of the dead returning to us . . . ?' Bob looked troubled, haunted. 'Emma, I think—Oh hello, young man.'

Nick stepped into the cubicle. 'Sorry to disturb you, sir, I wonder if I could speak with Emma.'

Bob frowned. 'I know you, don't I?'

'This is N—' Emma stood up sharply, the true name crumbling on her lips. 'Johnny. Johnny Bleeker. He's just moved into the Sparrow House.'

'Of course! You're the owner of that fine motorcycle.'

'Pleasure to meet you, sir. In other circumstances I'd shake you by the hand.'

'I wouldn't thank you for it just now. But of course, I should have realized by your accent, you're the new boy at Tennyson. Looks like you've had a rough first day.'

Nick touched the crusted glue around his ear. 'Slipped and hit my head.'

'Well, we're a fine pair. So how do you two know each other?'

'We met in the street. You were taking out the garbage, weren't you, Emma?'

'Yeah, that's right.'

Bob's gaze slipped between them. He managed a lopsided smile. 'You're friends. That's good. I'm very pleased to meet you, Johnny.'

'Thank you, sir. Emma, if we could have a quick word.'

Bob nodded enthusiastically. 'Take all the time you need.'

A little way down the corridor, they turned to each other and spoke in unison.

'Another spirit's come through.'

Nick's eyebrows pinched together. 'How did you know?'

'My dad saw something at school—the ghost of a boy he used to teach. He thinks he was seeing things, but it certainly sounds like an unmade: a violent death, a spirit linked to Milton Lake.'

'The detector must have activated while I was knocked out. I've only just checked it—a single ghost somewhere nearby. I'd better go.'

'I'll get my coat.'

'You should stay here with your dad, he needs you.'

'You need me. I'll just go and tell him—'

A cracked but youthful voice cut her short.

'Excuse me, I'm looking for Mr Rhodes, the science teacher.'

Emma wrinkled her nose. It surely wasn't unusual for the aroma of blood to salt the air of a hospital, but there was something different about the smell of this blood. It had the curdled stink of decay.

'Could you say Adam Carmichael is here to see him?'

Sweat, smoke, diesel fumes, the stench of flesh rotting under a hot sun. Emma looked down at the sand-dusted school shoes, then the khaki trousers, and the Tennyson tie poking out from behind the army-issue flak jacket. A confusion of clothing conjured by a disturbed spirit, and all of it mottled with black-brown stains. The first bullet hole started at the spirit's stomach, a hideous tear that was repeated a dozen times across the boy's chest, arms, and shoulders. Through some of the larger holes she could see needles of splintered bone and secret gleam of organs.

'He was such a good guy, you know? I can't think of anyone I'd rather be. And Mr Rhodes will understand, because I've been waiting so long and I'm so *hungry*.'

'Lower your eyes,' Nick whispered. 'Don't look at the face.'

She saw his hand come to rest on Adam Carmichael's sloping shoulders.

'Follow me, soldier, I'll take you to Mr Rhodes.'

The ward was quiet, all the patients tucked away in their little cubicles. There was no one to witness the two figures turn into the corridor that ran between A & E and the canteen. Emma lifted her eyes in time to see Nick open a door and usher Adam inside.

'But this is just a store cupboard. What are you do—?'

The scream was muffled by the closed door and, she guessed, by Nick. What horrors he lived through, this boy from Mearsville, this man of shadows who had forbidden her to look into the smoke that billowed in his wake. The things he did to keep strangers safe were enough to torture the dreams of the strongest soul, yet he faced them with a smile, brave and alone.

The cupboard door opened. He came towards her, the iron bar disappearing back into his jacket. Emma took his hand.

13

While Nick returned to collect his bike from school, Miss Lucas gave Emma and Bob a lift home in her gruesomely brown Morris Marina. Right hand strapped to his chest and plaster cast in his lap, Bob winced as the car bounced over speed humps and potholes. By the time they reached home, night had planted its long black roots into Connolly Avenue and the street was empty. Emma helped Bob from the car, they said their goodbyes to Miss Lucas and started a slow and careful progress up the icy path.

'What on earth is that?' Bob frowned.

A symbol had been drawn in chalk on the front door of their house:

Emma followed the pattern's swirl and saw the suggestion

of a gate enclosed within the whole. Its meaning was obvious: another less than subtle warning from the Circle.

'Probably just kids mucking about,' she said, and pushed open the door.

While Bob settled himself in front of the TV, Emma bustled about in the kitchen, brewing tea and cutting rounds of corned beef sandwiches. Returning to the lounge, it soon became obvious that life in the Rhodes house was going to become somewhat tricky, at least for the next couple of weeks. Emma had to hold the teacup to Bob's lips and feed him his sandwich. He couldn't even operate the TV remote.

'Not much fun waiting on your old dad, eh? Not when there's a handsome young man just across the street.'

She placed the empty cup in its saucer. 'We're just friends.'

'Good,' Bob nodded, 'that's wonderful. Look, you don't have to worry about me, you go off and enjoy yourself.'

'Last night you were screaming at me for being out with him.'

'So that's where you were, was it?' he smiled.

'We're just friends,' Emma repeated.

The grumble of the Thunderbird's engine sounded from the road and the headlight swept across the lounge window.

'He seems like a nice boy, that's all I'm saying. Most kids today live at a hundred miles an hour, but he has a quieter way about him.'

'Just leave it.'

'Emma, he could be exactly what you need—an interest outside your schoolwork and this house. Even if he is just a friend, well, that's a start.' He looked down at his swollen fingers. 'There's not much I can do for you now. This boy, he could open up the world for you again.'

Wasn't that exactly what Emma had been telling herself? That Nick had opened a door and shown her something of the world outside. Hearing those same hopes repeated back to her, they seemed frail and somehow ridiculous.

'I don't need anyone,' she snapped. 'Why can't you understand?'

'All right, Emma,' Bob murmured. 'All right.'

They sat in silence, the TV burbling on in the background. In spite of what she had said, the urge to run across to the Sparrow House was almost irresistible. But how could she? Bob was completely dependent upon her, and so her investigations into the necromancy machine would simply have to stop.

The doorbell rang.

Emma put aside her untouched sandwich and headed into the hall. Outside she found all three members of the Torve family perched on the step: hawk-faced Arthur, bird-brained Julia, and her cousin Henry, the daredevil sparrow nestled between them. Arthur looked at the chalk symbol and gave a knowing smile while Henry cast a concerned glance over his cousin.

'We heard about your father's accident,' Julia squeaked. 'Is Bob all right?'

'He's pretty bashed up.'

'Then I'm sure he'd appreciate some visitors.' Arthur winged his way into the house. 'Come along, Julia.'

Henry remained on the step, toeing a hole in the snow.

'So what was all that about at school today?' he mumbled. 'You know, Sas has been acting pretty weird too, asking questions about Funland.'

'Do you remember anything?'

'You as well? All I did was run into the ghost train then leg it back out again. Doc Glock says I caught a chill and was a dribbling mess for a few days. The way Sas talks you'd think there'd been some massive conspiracy to give me a cold! Look, I get it, he's never liked my dad, not many people do, but it's as if Sas thinks the old git is trying to hurt me somehow. My dad loves me, Ems.'

Much as she distrusted Arthur Torve, Emma thought Henry was probably right. But as Carter had reminded her this morning, the rest of the Circle had no affection for the boy. They might harm him if they thought Emma was standing in their way.

'There is one thing that's a bit odd,' Henry admitted. 'Sas kept on about all these random people visiting when I was ill. I thought he was making it up, but when I got home this afternoon I heard Dad speaking to Mrs Glock and the two old women from the sweetshop.'

'What did they say?'

'Dad mentioned a meeting at the lake on Christmas Eve. At first I thought it was just one of their Historical Society things, but then he said they were going to try to get hold of a *terrenus phasmatis*.'

'That's definitely the words he used?'

Henry nodded. 'I kinda liked the sound of it, so it stuck in my head.'

'Did he say when this was happening?'

'Half seven at the visitor centre.'

The lounge door swung open and Arthur came striding out.

'Now, Bob, it's all been arranged. It's not fair to expect Emma to look after you all by herself, and Henry and I can easily make do.'

'What's going on?' Emma asked.

'Your aunt's going to stay with you until your father's back on his feet.' Arthur towered over Emma like some malevolent scarecrow. 'You shouldn't have to miss out on the season's frivolities just because that clumsy old fool took a tumble.'

'I heard that!' Bob shouted good-humouredly.

Arthur smiled. 'Your aunt can keep a close eye on you both. Should you need anything, she'll be able to tell me right away.'

So that was it: Julia was being installed as a spy. As if on cue, the little woman poked her head into the corridor and gave Emma a moist-eyed smile.

'I think we'll set up a bedroom down here for your father. Perhaps you could help with sheets and blankets while Henry and Arthur bring down a mattress.'

It was all arranged with her aunt's fussy efficiency. When they were finished Emma had to admit that the converted lounge looked just as snug as Bob's bedroom upstairs. At seven o'clock, Julia ushered them all out of the room, insisting that her brother needed his rest. Emma saw Henry and Arthur to the door.

Leaning in for a kiss, she whispered in Henry's ear: 'I'll call.'

Arthur took his son by the shoulder and marched him to the kerb where the Torves' gleaming Mercedes waited. When the car turned out of Connolly Avenue, Emma let go of a long breath. She felt trapped and a little lost.

Across the street, the Thunderbird stood in the grounds of the Sparrow House like a mute, metallic guard dog, its huge eye seemingly trained upon her. She took a step forward.

'Going somewhere, dear?'

Aunt Julia lurked in the corridor, her hands worrying at a tea towel.

'My friend came with me to the hospital. I thought I'd pop over and say thanks.'

'Is this the young American I've heard so much about? Perhaps you could both come along to a little party we're throwing on Christmas Eve? Seven o'clock sharp at the Torves'.'

A ruse to keep her and Nick away from the Circle's lakeside meeting. Although she wasn't a member of the necromancers' assembly, Julia was obviously their puppet. Emma managed a tight smile and set off across the road where she found the front door of the Sparrow House unlocked. From one of the upstairs rooms came the sound of singing and the steady drum of a shower.

I had my heart in your hand

You broke my heart, ain't that a shame?

What can I do

When somethin's wrong with you?

She smiled at the thought of catching him off guard like this, but as she listened to the lyrics, her smile faltered. He had a pleasant husky tone that added to the sadness of the song. Plans broken, hearts crushed, a simple question—*what's wrong with you . . . ?*

She was no longer in the Edwardian house on Connolly Avenue. No longer in the forest-cradled town of Milton Lake. She was standing on a track of beaten earth under a blazing blue New England sky. In the distance, a black bird circled the smoking chimney of a clapboard farmhouse. For mile after mile there was nothing to be seen except a few stray evergreens and a lone scarecrow keeping watch over winter fields.

Nothing except the house, the track, the roadside stall with its stacked crates . . . and the sheriff's black and white patrol car. Hanging from the door, the radio mouthpiece twisted on its wire: *Sheriff, come in*—crrruuuk—*Sheriff, do you read me?* Emma was within ten paces of the car. She made to step forward, a vague idea in her head that she would answer the dispatcher's call, and found herself rooted to the spot. This was, after all, a vision of the past; all she could do was watch and listen.

Away to her right she heard a ripple and slosh—the sheriff wading into the wetlands that lapped on either side of the track. She tried to find him but her head would not turn and her eyes straining sideways could pick out only smoke and shadows on the water. Then came a sudden screech of metal. The bird circling the chimney gave an uncanny imitation and fluttered away towards the evergreens. Emma heard the sheriff swear. A pause. Then the slosh of the policeman returning. Before he could pull himself onto the track, the door of the farmhouse creaked open.

A middle-aged man in bib overalls braced over one shoulder came out onto the porch. From this distance it was difficult to read his expression. He called to the sheriff in a cracked, wavering voice:

'Both?'

'One certainly. The other . . . I best put in a call.'

The man nodded, almost as if he had foretold the sheriff's answer.

'That's as good as both, *damn him* . . . '

The past broke up around her, fracturing into flakes that blew away and disintegrated like snow. Emma found herself in the parlour of the Sparrow House. A fire was roaring in the grate, flames of yellow and orange warming the bare walls. Some of the crates from the night before had been taken away. One of the few that remained had its lid removed, and Emma was surprised to find her hands rifling through the contents.

Something crackled at her touch. She pulled out a newspaper, yellowed with age: **THE CUMBERLAND CHRONICLE**. She barely had time to read the banner headline—***Mearsville Tragedy Latest***—before the paper was snatched away.

'I asked you not to.'

Nick glared from under a veil of dripping black hair. Apart from the towel around his waist, he was naked. Droplets of water sprang from his hard pale body as he threw the newspaper into the crate and slammed down the lid.

'I-I'm sorry,' Emma stammered. 'I was out in the hall and the next thing I knew—'

Back turned to her, the big muscles in his arms and shoulders relaxed.

'It's not your fault. You were brought here.'

'Brought here? What do you mean?'

'I can't tell you, Emma, it's not my place.' He went to the door, hesitated. 'You'll have seen more of the farmhouse, I guess. The deal still stands. Don't ask.'

He vanished into the hall, reappearing a couple of minutes later dressed in frayed jeans and a white T-shirt. Emma sat cross-legged on the rug while Nick dropped down beside her and stretched his long legs towards the fire.

'So,' he said at last, 'what's been happening at the Rhodes' residence?'

She made short work of the explanations before asking, 'Do you think we should tell Henry the truth?'

'You said yourself there are members of the Circle that might hurt him. Better for Henry if he knows as little as possible.'

'I said I'd call him later.'

'You can't. It's possible they have him under a state of hypnotic suggestion. Anything you say would be reported back to them, he wouldn't even know he was doing it.'

'Then what are we going to do?'

'Like I said, wait and watch.' He placed the silent spirit detector at his side. 'By the way, that pie Mrs Glock so kindly dropped off this morning? Laced with sodium amytal—a truth drug. She popped her head in just after I got back. I told her I had an apple allergy.'

'Do people have apple allergies?'

Nick shrugged. 'We both knew it was a lie. She rattled on about the church bake sale until I shut the door in her face.'

'So what should we do about the Christmas party at the Torves'?'

'Politely decline. We've got an appointment with the Circle.' Nick stared perplexedly into the flames. 'Henry said they were going to summon a *terrenus phasmatis* . . . ? Makes no sense. Why summon an earthbound spirit when you could take your time, study the machine, and call up an unmade?'

'In English?'

'There are three avenues after you die.' He counted them off on his fingers. 'First and most common, you take the light. No one knows what happens after that, no spirit has ever returned. Second, you linger and are claimed by the Night Watchmen.'

'Those are the hooded guys Peter Taggart was so afraid of.'

'There are a hundred theories about the Watchmen,' Nick nodded. 'All we know is that they take the souls of the unlatched and imprison them behind the gates. They keep them from breaking free but they cannot intervene when one is summoned by a necromancer.'

'Why not?'

Nick shrugged. 'These laws were created eons before the written word was invented. A lot of ancient knowledge has been lost.'

'OK, what about the third avenue?'

'A spirit refuses the light, probably for the same reasons an unmade might—revenge, unfinished business—but near the moment of death, they find a latch. Someone dear to them that keeps them bound to this world. They stay safe within the living aura of that person and the Watchmen cannot touch them.'

'Peter couldn't find a latch because he died alone.'

'Right. But here's the thing with these latched or earth-bound spirits, or *terrenus phasmatis* if you want to sound fancy: unlike the unmade, they have very limited vision and powers of prophecy. So why, when the Circle has the machine, do they go backwards and start summoning *terrenus* ghosts?'

'Maybe a *terrenus* could tell them how to work the machine better.'

'Possible, but unlikely. Look, if I hadn't been here then the Circle would've tracked down one of the unmade. They have no need of a *terrenus*.'

Emma frowned. 'Wait a minute, if it's that easy why don't we just let them have their unmade? It's their continual use of the machine that's weakening the gates, isn't it?'

'If we allowed that then we'd be sacrificing a mortal life. Don't forget the unmade's price is a human body to possess.'

'Right.' Emma shook her head. It had been a long day.

'And do you really think one ghost would be enough? There are seven members of the Circle, they'd each want a spirit. And then, when their ghosts all have bodies and trot away to live new lives, what then?'

'They'd summon replacements.'

'A wise necromancer calls three or four spirits in a lifetime. This foolish Circle will use the machine again and again until—'

'They destroy the gates. OK, so I've just got one more question for you, Mr Redway.'

'Shoot.'

Emma held his gaze. 'I think it's about time you told me the story of the ghost machine.'

14

'You've heard of Thomas Edison?'

'Developed the light bulb, the movie camera, the telephone; just about the greatest inventor in the history of the world.' Emma nodded. 'Yup, the name rings a bell. My dad's a science teacher, remember—Edison was one of his childhood heroes, I know all his greatest hits.'

Nick smiled. 'Maybe not all.'

Jumping to his feet, he set about rummaging in one of the open crates and returned with a thin manila envelope, which he handed to Emma. Inside, she found a pair of dog-eared newspaper clippings. 'From The American Magazine, October 1920' was written in a bold hand above the first article. The title of the piece, which took the form of a lengthy interview with the inventor, caused Emma's heart to skip a beat: EDISON WORKING ON HOW TO COMMUNICATE WITH THE NEXT WORLD.

'Look at the second.'

The same bold writing flowed across the top of the page: 'From Scientific American, October 30th 1920'. This time the title of the interview was less sensational—**Edison's Views on Life and Death**—but the inventor's claims were no less shocking. Heavily underlined was the following statement: 'I have been thinking for some time of a machine which could be operated by personalities which have passed on to another existence or sphere.' In other words, Emma thought, ghosts.

'Are these for real?'

'Absolutely genuine,' Nick confirmed.

'But if Edison had really invented something like that then everyone would've known about it.'

'Everyone did. Newspapers all over the world took up the story.'

'And people believed it?'

'Most of them probably did. Don't forget, this was an age of miracles. Within living memory the human race had emerged from the gloom of candles into a world where you could press a switch and be bathed in the constant glow of electric light. Astonishing scientific marvels had been achieved in a few short decades, and many of them seemed to stem from the efforts of one man. It wasn't for nothing that they called Thomas Edison the Wizard of Menlo Park.'

'So they believed it, doesn't mean it was true.' Emma thought back to the stories her father had told about the inventor. 'Wasn't Edison a bit of a practical joker?'

Nick nodded. 'He did have that reputation, especially among journalists. So yeah, in the end everyone thought he'd been pulling their leg. After his death in 1931, these reports were pretty much forgotten. There was only one man who knew the true story of Edison and the ghost machine.'

Opening another crate, he lifted out an old-fashioned record player housed in a beautiful mahogany case. Emma noticed the plaque attached to the side—'Edison Disc Phonograph'. Setting the machine on the floor, Nick retrieved a wax record, removed its paper sleeve and slotted it onto the turntable.

'The man was called Oliver Redway. My great-grandfather.' He tapped a finger against the disc. 'This is Oliver's story, but before I play it, I want to show you what the ghost machine looks like.'

He searched again among the crates, this time finding another relic from a bygone age. He passed the candlestick telephone to Emma who turned it over in her hands. Its upright shaft of black enamel ended in a hornlike mouthpiece while the base sported a stiff rotary dial. As she turned it upside down the bell housed inside gave a tiny jingle.

'The old-fashioned ring,' she murmured. 'But this isn't—?'

'No. There's only one ghost machine. This is just an ordinary telephone made around 1918. But "ordinary" was exactly what the ghost machine started out as, until that night in Menlo Park.'

Nick turned the handle on the phonograph and placed the needle against the spinning disc. A crackle like burning wood came through the brass horn. Then a voice, its accent similar to Nick's, though the words were spoken with a deeper drawl:

'The Old Man is dead, and it seems that the whole country from the President down is in mourning. Five days ago, I read in the newspaper the details of how he died. By the end, so they say, Mr Edison had lost his sight and hearing and just lay there, moanin'. It's a cold October day here in Mearsville, but it is not the chill wind that makes me shiver. It's the words of Mary Edison. Eleven Octobers ago she spoke them, and she has been proved right—*You will know darkness and silence before the end.*'

A pause filled only with the crackle of the fire and the phonograph.

'And so my story must be told. I will state the case formally, as I would have in my Pinkerton days, even if only you, Grady my son, ever hear it. I learned a deal from those West Orange boys, so have set up my own little recording studio here in the barn, for I cannot quite bring myself to tell you the tale face to face . . . '

'My name is Oliver—' the needle skipped, '—dway.' I am thirty-six years old and this is the twenty-third day of October, 1931. It so happens that it is also the day I received a letter from Mina Edison, the Old Man's widow.

'Edison himself had dictated the note. Knowing himself to be dying, he had enclosed what he called "a memento of that dreadful adventure we once shared". He goes on, "That I have done my best to deny what I know to be true—the survival of the soul after death—has been the result of the terror which has haunted me since that night in Menlo Park. I did not want it to be true. That is why I treated you so roughly, Oliver. You were the only one whose voice

I could not deny. Now, as silence and darkness nears, I beg your forgiveness. Your friend, TAE." '

There was a rustle of paper, as of a letter being folded.

'I had been working for the world-famous Pinkerton Detective Agency in Chicago for only a couple of months when the job came my way. I'd joined the agency in the hope of escaping the life of a New England farmer that my folks had mapped out for me. After serving in the Great War, I'd come home with a taste for danger, and chasing down gangsters in the Windy City seemed to satisfy that strange hunger just fine.

'It was the spring of 1920 when my boss handed me a train ticket to New Jersey and requested I take my revolver along for the ride. I was to report to Thomas Edison at his laboratory in West Orange. I stood slack-jawed. Surely he didn't mean *the* Thomas Edison? He assured me he did. For some years, there'd been threats against the Old Man's life and so I was to act as Edison's personal bodyguard.

'I travelled to West Orange giddy with excitement, for there I was to meet one of the greatest men of the age! On arrival at the huge facility, I was taken direct to the library. I've never been much of a reader myself, but even I could appreciate the wonder of the place. In every alcove on the ground floor and gallery, more books than a man could count. At the far end of the room was a big old fireplace with a handsome wooden clock on the mantel, and sitting at his desk by the fire, the Old Man himself.

'Wisps of white hair stood out at crazy angles across his broad head and a week's worth of bristle girdled his jaw.

His clothes hung awkwardly from his sloping shoulders and his fingers were stained with chemicals. All in all he looked more like a decently dressed hobo than one of the richest men in America.

'"Eh?" Edison cupped his right ear. "Speak up, young man."

'I repeated my name and said I was from Pinkerton's. He grunted and waved me to a chair in one of the alcoves. And there I stayed. For six months. More or less. I acted as bodyguard whenever he attended public events and wherever his business took him. It was dull work, following around a man whose best days lay behind him.

'Then, one morning in early October, the letter came.

'"Here's the damnedest thing, Ollie," he said, calling me over.

'In time we had discovered a shared love of fly-fishing and fine Havana cigars, things that in the brotherly world of the laboratory were enough to create a bond between two men. I glanced over the letter he held out.

'"Sounds like another crank."

'The lab received dozens of lunatic letters a week, most claiming Edison had stolen inventions.

'"As you say. Yet there are things here the writer could not . . . " he trailed off.

'This letter is the memento the Old Man left me. I'll read it to you now—'

More crackling paper sounded through the phonograph horn.

'"*My Fellow Wizard—I have been watching you with interest these past sixty years, ever since your days selling newspapers and candy bars on the Grand Trunk Railroad. Indeed, knowing what a glittering life lay ahead of you, I paid a visit to your baggage car laboratory. You may remember me, I was the Englishman with the violet eyes . . .* "

'"Damnedest thing," the Old Man said, "but I *do* remember him. At just fifteen, I was already obsessed with invention and had set up a small lab in an old railroad baggage car. Well, one day there was an accident with my chemicals and I burned the carriage down. The baggage master decided to give my ears a boxing (I still say that's what started this deafness of mine). The man was on the point of killing me when this English gent rolls up and tells him to stop. If this is the same fella, he must be nudging eighty."

'The letter continues—

'"*It saddens me to see that, after all your triumphs, you have fallen on fallow days. Let me help you now as I did then. Meet me at Menlo Park on October 10th at 9.30 p.m. and I will show you an invention the like of which the world has never seen.*

'"*This is what I propose: a machine for speaking with the dead.*

'"*If you suspect my motives you may bring a friend. Indeed, I have foreseen that the Pinkerton man will come. I ask only this of you, Thomas—bring with you an ordinary telephone with rotary dial and ensure that the lines at Menlo are connected. Your friend through the years—R.W.*"

'I expected Edison to throw the letter straight in the trash. He did not. It sat on his desk for several days, and I often saw him take it up and re-read those bizarre words.

'I was soon reassured, however. Around that time he was due to give a couple of magazine interviews. I was present for both, and delighted when he made reference to some apparatus he'd been thinking of to communicate with the dead. It showed he did not take the letter seriously.

'Then came the morning of the tenth. He met me at breakfast, his eyes dark through lack of sleep. "We're going." That's all he said.

'From West Orange a short train ride brought us to the little station of Raritan Township, where we were the only passengers to alight. The night was cold, an early snowfall dusting the land, but a brisk walk up the hill to the old Menlo Park facility warmed our bones.

' "I've not been back here since eighty-one," Edison smiled. "So many memories . . . "

'When we reached the crest of the hill his smile died.

'In its heyday Menlo had been called "the invention factory" and was the most sophisticated private laboratory in the US. It must have been a fine thing to see back then, the bustle of young men at their work, the grind and hammer from the machine shop, the bubble and smoke from the lab. Now all I could see was a sad ruin crowning the hillside.

'Silhouetted against the distant lights of New York and Brooklyn sat a collection of tumbledown buildings ringed about with a picket fence. The site was dominated by the huge two-storey laboratory. It looked to me like an oversized country church minus a steeple, and I suppose that in its own way it had been a place of worship. Miracles had taken place here.

' "You see that house yonder?"

'I followed Edison's finger to a large villa a short distance from the facility.

'"That was the house I bought for Mary, my first wife. She . . . " He drew on the last of his Havana and threw the stub to the ground. "She had no mind for invention . . . Come now, Ollie, light your torch, it'll be dark inside."

'I took out the flashlight while he unlatched the gate. The first thing the beam fell upon was the footmarks in the snow—a trail leading to the laboratory's porch steps and through the open door. So "R.W." had arrived ahead of us. I transferred the torch to my left hand, took a grip of the Colt revolver in my pocket, and led the way to the door. We entered a small office with a bare floor and empty bookcases thick with dust. Aside from some wet marks on the ground there was no sign of the letter writer.

'From the office we passed into a cavernous chamber that took up the rest of the building. Save for a few battered benches this space was also empty. The boards above our heads creaked. R.W. was waiting for us in the upstairs lab. I raised the revolver and headed for the stairs, Edison at my back. I'd faced many dangers in my short life—the Hun at the Second Battle of Marne, desperate hoodlums armed to the teeth—and my hand had never shaken. Now, as I mounted these groaning stairs, the revolver trembled in my fist.

'It was a little lighter in the lab. The rows of floor to ceiling windows threw slabs of silver moonlight onto the floor, the gaps between them black as trench mud. Brown, green, clear, and cobalt blue, thousands of empty bottles sat on shelves around the walls. I raked the room with my eyes. I could have sworn we were alone, but then the voice came out of the shadows—

'"Welcome, Thomas. You return to the scene of your greatest triumphs."

'A pair of violet eyes shone through the gloom.

'"But now, as you enter the final chapter of your life, it is time you learned humility. Good evening, gentlemen . . ."

'A face emerging from nowhere.

'A smile where there had been only darkness.

'"I am the necromancer Randall Wolfe."

15

Nick lifted the needle and turned the record over. He was about to crank the phonograph handle and start playing the reverse side when Emma called a halt.

'Hold on. The necromancer Edison met in 1920 was Randall Wolfe? The same man your grandfather studied with?'

Nick nodded.

'But Edison said he'd met Wolfe when he was a kid in—'

'1862.'

'And Wolfe died just last month. So how old was the guy?' She did a rough calculation. 'A hundred and seventy?'

'At least.'

'Well, that's that mystery cleared up, thanks,' Emma said sarcastically.

'Have patience,' he smiled, and set the needle on its bumping circuit.

Again, the crackle of the bygone barn:

'The man's flawless skin and narrow shoulders suggested a youth of no more than twenty, yet there was something in those violet eyes, deep and knowing . . .

' "You can put that toy away, Oliver," he said, waving dismissively at my gun.

' "Colt's been a good friend of mine." I tried to keep the tremor out of my voice. How did he know my name? "He may yet have cause to speak."

' "How very American," Wolfe smiled.

'I turned to Edison and found the inventor open-mouthed.

' "It *is* you," he said. "The Englishman who saved me from the baggage master."

' "Take a hold of yourself, sir," said I. "You told me that man must be eighty years old."

' "Eighty?" Wolfe whistled. "Dear me, it has been a long time."

'Edison cast haunted eyes around the room. "Why have you brought me here?"

' "This where it happened," Wolfe spun on the spot, "the cradle of the modern age. This is where the bright beacon of science flared and sent superstition scurrying away into shadow. And I foresaw it all."

' "You foretold the life of Thomas Edison?" Despite the fear, I laughed.

' "It was the summer of 1816," he said, "and I was visiting friends at the charming Villa Diodati on Lake Geneva. We were all up late one night telling ghost stories when I felt the pull of an unseen spirit. I made excuses to my lordly host and retired to my room. After some trouble I called forth an unmade who told me that, in thirty years' time, a boy would be born in the town of Milan, Ohio. A child that would change the world. I determined then to find and follow this child."

'"You say you've been with me all this time?"

'"Not just the baggage car. I was there when you established your first manufacturing shops in Newark, where you met poor, neglected Mary. There when you moved on from experiments with duplex telegraphs to the telephone, then the phonograph, then the electric light. I stood in the street of Menlo Park on New Year's Day 1879 when you lit up the town with your electric wonder. And I stood outside the house yonder when the blinds were drawn in 1884."

'"Mary," Edison murmured.

'"I was there again when you married Mina just two years later."

'"But why?"

'"For this moment. I had to wait until you'd reached the end of your road. There are no more great inventions ahead of you, but perhaps I can show you a final wonder."

'"A machine for talking with ghosts!" I snorted. "Even if it was possible, do you think people would pay for such a horrible thing?"

'"Of course they would," Edison said, a glint in his eye. "To hear the voice of a dead child, to speak again with a lost loved one, they'd sell their souls for such a chance." He stepped towards the necromancer. "I must see it."

'"You've brought what I asked for?"

'"Give him the telephone."

'"But, Mr Edison—"

'"Give him the damn phone," the Old Man growled, "or I'll make sure you're kicked out of Pinkerton's and ruined for life."

'Finally, I'd seen it: the ruthlessness that was as much a part of the Edison legend as his industry and genius. I took the phone from my overcoat pocket; as Wolfe had requested, it was a perfectly ordinary candlestick model.

'"You've ensured the lines are connected?" he asked. "Good. It's not strictly necessary but the ectoplasmic field generated through the wires should strengthen the signal. Now, Oliver, set the instrument on this table."

'I obeyed, placing the telephone in a band of snowy moonlight.

'"Thomas, if you would be so good as to undo the mouthpiece."

'While Edison fumbled unscrewing the cap, the violet-eyed man continued in his soft-spoken way. "I attended the US Centennial Exhibition in seventy-six where Alexander Graham Bell's telephone was first demonstrated. It was the sensation of the decade."

'"I'd been experimenting on my own device long before Bell," Edison grunted.

'Wolfe smiled. "You know as well as I that, in the beginning, you dismissed Bell's invention as a mere toy. It was only when you saw that money could be made from it that you applied your genius to the telephone. What you saw that Bell did not was that variations in the resistance of the circuit could be achieved by the raising and lowering of the voice, thereby strengthening the transmission of sound over a much greater distance. After much trial and error you achieved your best results using carbon transmitters, which produced voices of amazing clarity."

'"I know all this." Edison held up the uncovered mouthpiece. "I was there."

Wolfe ignored him. 'Now we need to adapt your invention. To communicate across dimensions a carbon transmitter will not do. We need a different kind of material.'

'From his inside pocket, Wolfe took out a fragment of cloth-like material not much larger than a postage stamp. It gave off a startling green light that flooded the laboratory.

'"What is it?" Edison blinked. "Silk dipped in some kind of phosphorous?"

'"It is ectoplasm."

'"Bull," I said. "There's no such thing."

'"It is very rare," Wolfe conceded, "especially in a stable condition. Ectoplasm tends to disintegrate after a few days in our reality. This is the only scrap in the world able to hold its form."

'"How?" Edison asked.

'"That is my secret. Suffice to say, I'm the only necromancer to have conjured an indestructible sample. Now, I want you to take out the transmitter and replace it with this . . . "

'He handed Edison the miraculous fabric.

'"It's ice cold," the inventor hissed.

'Using one of the screwdrivers he always carried with him, the Old Man removed the delicate diaphragm and began to unscrew the metal plate and its carbon transmitter. Wolfe stood behind him and watched the careful work.

'"There," Edison muttered, "it's in place."

'Wolfe took the telephone from the inventor and screwed on the cap. Spears of green light shone through the arrangement of tiny holes in the mouthpiece, hit the ceiling and hovered there like an eerie constellation. Wolfe then asked Edison to attach the telephone wire to the reconnected line.

'"What now?" the inventor puffed.

'"The clang of a bell in a ritual has always been a weak way to summon spirits. Now we have a more focused method." Wolfe ran his hands over the candlestick instrument. "With a human voice passed through an electro-ectoplasmic transmitter the summoning will become so powerful I'll be able to conjure any spirit of my choosing."

'"You could've done this yourself," I said. "Why did you need Mr Edison?"

'Wolfe smiled at the man whose long life he had followed so studiously.

'"I've chosen you, Thomas, because you embody the forces of science that are transforming this world. Well, now I will prove that there are mysteries that defy those forces." He took Edison's hand and guided it to the phone's rotary dial. "Think of those you have lost."

'He placed the Old Man's finger in the first hole and turned the dial.

'"This is the number key of the dead: 2 for duality, the link between our world and the gates; 3 for the triad of birth, life, and death; 7 for the pillars of wisdom to guide our summoning; 4 and 0 for the privations of the unmade; 1 and 2 to complete the cycle."

'Long minutes passed. Outside, the wind sang its mournful song among the telephone wires. I was slowly coming round to the belief that, for all his uncanny knowledge, Randall Wolfe was a crank after all when then the bell rang out.

'The Old Man jumped back from the phone, but the sound was not coming from that device. It was like listening to a telephone ringing in a nearby room.

'"We've made the connection," Wolfe said. "Now let's see who answers."

'The ringing stopped. Silence, but for the singing wires.

'My heart had just settled when the candlestick called. Such a small sound—the tiny *ting* of a brass bell—but it might as well have been a monstrous roar. All my army training deserted me and I dropped the revolver and staggered away from the workbench. Curiosity had clearly overcome any terror on Edison's part. With the light from the mouthpiece dying his flyaway hair a ghastly shade of green, he gestured towards the phone.

'"It's for you." Wolfe nodded.

'"But who?"

'"That depends how focused your thoughts were."

'Wolfe picked up the receiver. The bell stopped. He placed the candlestick in the inventor's left hand, the receiver in his right. The apple bobbed in his straggly throat as Edison forced out his greeting.

'"H-hullo?"

'When it came the voice seemed amplified, so that the word hissed in every corner.

'"*Thomasssss.*"

'Edison closed his eyes. "Mary? Is . . . is that you?"

'"*Husband. It has been such a* long *time.*"

'"Mary, w-where are you?"

'"*Behind the gates, of course. I did not take the light because I knew that my children*—our *children*—*still had need of me. And I was right. You remarried, built yourself a new family as easily as you might build a new machine in your precious laboratory. But what of your firstborns? The daughter sent away, the sons made to feel less than dirt under their father's boot. And me? I was soon forgotten . . .* "

'The Old Man could barely speak. "I'm sorry. I—"

'"*You have words for me now that I am dead, but where were your words then? You never cared for me.* NEVER!"

'The line went dead. Or so I thought.

'Shaken to his core, Edison was about to set the phone back on the bench when the bell rang again. He moved in a daze, lifting the receiver to his ear . . .

'"Mar—?"

'A green hand lurched out of the earpiece and locked fingers around the inventor's throat. Seized with terror, Edison seemed unable to relinquish his hold on the phone. My courage returned to me then. I snatched up the fallen Colt, tried to take aim.

'The Old Man had come to his senses and let go of the phone. The fingers slipped from his throat and the candlestick hit the ground with a soft crack. The bell inside *tringed* but the casing appeared to be undamaged. Reaching out of the earpiece, the green hand clawed against the wooden floor, fingernails digging into the boards. Suddenly, a complete arm emerged, then a shoulder, then strands of hair, dark and matted with dirt.

'Mary Edison's head was lying flat against her arm, like a sleeper in repose. I cannot properly tell how that face came to siphon its way out of the receiver—it seemed to appear at first in miniature, like a crushed doll's head. Then, feature by feature, the face inflated to its normal dimensions, Mary's eyes popping wetly into their sockets and her nose cracking as it straightened. Torso and legs followed as, piece by piece, the woman slithered out of the phone.

'Dressed in the remains of her shroud, she rose shakily to her feet. The brilliant greenness was gone; now she shimmered white in a block of hazy moonlight. Edison stood with his back pressed against a workbench, unable to move. Wolfe was by one of the tall windows, his face unreadable in the shadows.

'"No," the Old Man whimpered. "Please God, no . . . "

'"*Flesh.*" Her tongue luxuriated over the word. "*Give me your flesh and I'll forgive you.*" A hand went to his face, caressed the grey bristle of his cheek. "*You want forgiveness, don't you? For all the people you've wronged, for all the lies you've told.*"

'Her fingers seemed to melt into the Old Man's skin and he cried out. They were so close it was impossible for me to get a clear shot.

'"What are you searching for?" Edison gasped. "I h-have nothing to give you."

'"*Your soul is here, husband, and I* will *crush it. It is no more than you deser—*"

'I saw the movement out of the corner of my eye: the necromancer flickering into the moonlight. He held out his hand behind the dead woman's head and blew some fine dark dust from his palm. It scattered around her in a cloud.

'Mary Edison opened her mouth and screamed. Veteran of the battlefield that I was, I had never before heard such a hopeless shriek. Her head, her torso, her entire body appeared to collapse in on itself. Soon there was little more than a green pool lapping on the floor, a rough face at its centre. We three of us stood over the puddle, but the thing only had eyes for Edison.

'"*Enjoy your final years, husband, for you will know darkness and silence before the end . . .* "

'And with that, the pool vanished.

'"Where has it gone?" I heard my words but the voice seemed distant, not my own.

'"Back to the gates." Wolfe dusted off his hands. "Iron shavings."

'I nodded as if I understood his explanation.

'"Why did you show me this?" the Old Man trembled. "In God's name, *why*?"

'"I told you why. You wish enlightenment, Tom? You have been enlightened."

'The Old Man looked at Wolfe as if he were a demon.

'"Damn you." He touched the place where the fingers of his late wife had melted into his flesh. "Curse you!"

'The great man turned and fled. Fled from the laboratory in which he had achieved his greatest triumphs. Fled from Menlo Park and its ghosts. He would never return.

'"There is a hard time coming for you, Oliver." Wolfe laid a hand on my shoulder. For once, his violet eyes seemed kind. 'I'm sorry to have brought you into this . . . When he needs me, send him to London."

'"Who? Edison?"

'Wolfe shook his head. "When the time comes you'll know who I mean."

'Eleven years on, I still do not know. I pray I never will.

'It was a silent journey back to West Orange. I retired to my boarding house in the town, Edison to his beloved library. Next morning, I was stopped at the gate. My services had been terminated and I was recalled to Chicago. There Pinkerton's had a month's salary waiting for me and a train ticket back to Mearsville. The boss was apologetic but said that Mr Edison was an important client, and if he wanted a man gone then that man had better get gone.

'The reason for the Old Man's rough treatment of me is there in his deathbed letter. He just wanted to forget. Ah well, I hope the old coot rests easy now. Just as I hope you, Grady, never have cause to meet Randall Wolfe, the necromancer. He took his machine with him, telling me that it would remain one of a kind. In turn, I told him to guard it well. I do not care to think what might happen if such a device ever fell into evil or foolish hands . . . '

16

He lifted the needle and the record slowed to a stop.

'May I see that?'

Throughout the bizarre story of Nick's great-grandfather a more practical mystery had been troubling Emma. For over eighty years the record had been remarkably well preserved; only once had the needle skipped. She held the disc up to the firelight and examined the outermost grooves. There it was, a nick in the coating. How strange that the only scratch should be located at that precise point: *My name is Oliver* skip—*dway.*

Nick stored the gramophone and record away in their crate and returned to sit cross-legged on the rug.

'Randall Wolfe meant Grady, didn't he?' she said. 'Oliver's son, your grandfather.'

'Grandpa became interested in necromancy after hearing his dad's story,' Nick nodded. 'Just as Wolfe foretold, he travelled to London to seek him out.'

'How old was your father when Grady left?'

'I don't want to talk about my father.'

Emma sensed that all the pieces were there, jumbled up in front of her: Randall Wolfe and the creation of the ghost machine; Grandpa Grady and his necromancy studies; Nick's soldier father, who had died in some recent war. And what of Emma's vision of the farm? How did that fit in? Was the middle-aged man she'd seen on the porch Grady Redway? Had he returned from London for a visit? Or was it someone else?

'OK,' she breathed, 'so tell me more about Wolfe. How old was he? Did your grandad ever find out?'

Nick smiled. 'Wolfe liked to tease Grady with stories of adventures going back centuries. The necromancer had a wicked sense of humour, you'd have liked him.'

'I don't know. The way he treated Edison just to prove a point? Seems to me he was a cruel man.'

'Not cruel. He just had a different take on what it means to be kind. He was *very* kind to my pop . . . Exactly how kind we didn't find out until the end.'

Emma knew it was pointless to push that line of questioning.

'Tell me more about the machine.'

'With the powerful signal given off by the device, Wolfe could draw a spirit directly to him,' Nick said. 'But he was aware of the dangers posed by his invention. Necromancy is difficult for a reason. You have to study long and hard so that you know how to control the spirits when they come through. Wolfe's nightmare was that a group of unskilled people would get their hands on it.'

'So for all this time he kept it to himself. But there were rumours it existed?'

Nick nodded. 'Word started to spread—whoever possessed the machine would hold dominion over the dead.'

'But no one managed to steal it until last month?'

'They tried, and every rival necromancer fell at the gates of Wolfe's mansion. His magical protections were powerful.'

'So generations of necromancers failed, but the Milton Lake Circle kicked down Randall Wolfe's door and took it from his cold, dead hand?' Emma frowned.

'You're right, the Circle couldn't possibly have stolen the machine.'

'Then how come they're using it now?'

'Honestly? I've no idea. There was one man who was almost Randall Wolfe's equal. If the machine had been stolen by him then I'd be both comforted and concerned. Comforted because he'd know how to use it properly. Concerned because Wolfe thought him just about the darkest necromancer he'd ever known. What I can't understand is how the machine ended up in the Circle's hands, and why Edgar Dritch hasn't come to claim it.'

'Dritch?'

'Wolfe described him as "the Devil in human skin". '

'Didn't your grandfather see anything the night the machine was stolen?'

'It was chaos, so he said. The battle had barely started when a hex knocked him to the ground. When he came to the machine was gone and Wolfe lay dying.'

'Did he say anything?'

A strained look entered Nick's eyes. '"It's time. Let the boy take it from here."'

'Meaning you?'

'Wolfe saw . . . ' Nick swallowed hard. 'Saw that my grandfather was badly injured. Dying himself. I was the only one who could go after the machine.'

'So you came over from America.'

'Soon as I heard the news. I was with Grady when he passed.'

Emma squeezed his hand. Through a film of tears he smiled at her.

'He was a good man. He'd made some bad mistakes early on, but he sacrificed almost sixty years to put things right. Wolfe knew he was a good man, too. That's why he . . . ' Nick caught himself. 'Sometimes we do terrible things to atone.'

The last of the logs collapsed and a curtain of darkness fell across the room. In the sudden gloom, Nick's features stood out sharp and clear. He looked exhausted.

'It's late,' Emma murmured. 'We should probably—'

'Of course.'

He led her to the corridor where a draught had set the soul-catchers jangling. They said their goodnights, and before she knew it, Emma was at her own door, latchkey in hand. A rush of cinnamon-spiced air greeted her as she stepped inside.

'There you are,' Aunt Julia said, poking her flour-dusted face into the hall. 'Would you like a slice of coffee cake?'

'You're baking? It's almost eleven.'

'Oh, I often bake at night. Good for the nerves, you know. Come into the kitchen, it's been ages since we've had a good, long natter.'

We've never *had a good, long natter.* 'I'm tired, thanks anyway.'

'Very well. Your father's sleeping like the dead.'

Had she meant that as some kind of threat? Bob was her brother, surely Julia wouldn't allow the Circle to harm him. If it was a threat, maybe it was meant kindly—a plea for Emma and Nick not to interfere.

Once inside her room, Emma collapsed onto the bed and scrolled through her phone. For a long time she just lay there staring at the highlighted name: HENRY. She had promised to call him but Nick had forbidden it. Biting her lip, she scrolled on until she reached MILES. The call was answered after three rings.

'Ems?' He sounded sleepy. 'Whaddaya want?'

'Just checking to see if you're OK.'

'Why wouldn't I be?'

'No reason. You seemed a bit fried at school today.'

'Yeah. Skipped afternoon classes. Feeling a bit rough. 'S jus' a fever.'

It seemed that Nick's powers of hypnosis were just as potent as the Circle's.

'OK, well I'll catch you later.'

'Hold on.' She could hear the puzzlement in his voice. 'You sound . . . different.'

'Different?'

'Like you used to sound, back when we were . . . Is it that kid Chan and the girls are talking about? The Yank?' A steely edge slipped in. 'So you can go back to being the old Ems for some kid you hardly know but you couldn't do it for me? I lov—' He stopped himself. 'Who is he, anyway?'

'Night, Miles.'

He tried phoning back but she cancelled the call.

Who is he anyway? Fair question. If Nick's story of a life in Mearsville could be trusted—and that was the one part that seemed to come straight from the heart—she still knew very little about him.

He seemed to have picked up necromancy knowledge from his grandpa, enough to take on the task of tracing the machine and dealing with the unmade, but that in itself was strange. Nick had arrived just in time for Grady's dying hours; if his grandfather hadn't passed on necromancy skills to him before—and the Mearsville childhood suggested they'd had little real contact—how had Nick acquired such knowledge?

She had enough information now to make serious inroads into the conundrum. She could research Randall Wolfe, find out whether there was an online directory of Pinkerton agents from the 1920s, even cross-reference 'Oliver —dway' with 'Mearsville' and maybe track down that article from the *Cumberland Chronicle*.

But she had made a promise to her mysterious friend not to go snooping into his past.

It was a promise she intended to keep.

17

Despite a night of snow hurling itself at the door, the chalk circle remained undimmed. Emma ran her finger around its whirls while Bob called out from his temporary bedroom, complaining about the draught. From a steaming kitchen, Julia emerged with a tray of freshly baked biscuits.

'Off to see that friend of yours? Have you asked him about our Christmas Eve party? Seven sharp, remember.'

'We've other plans.'

The buttery smile melted. 'Oh. Very well.'

She was near the road when Julia called her back. Up close, her aunt's skin was splotchy from the heat of the oven and it looked as if she'd been crying.

'I just wanted to say . . . Well, I care very deeply for you, Emma. After Richie passed away and your mother left, I wanted to—'

'Don't say that,' Emma snapped. '"Passed away"?' Her eyes flickered to the kerb outside the Sparrow House. 'You know how he died.' All this twittering was too much. She mounted the step. 'I know why you're here, and I swear to God, if you hurt Bob—'

Julia's mouth made a big 'O'. 'Robert's my brother! I would never—'

Emma turned and marched away.

'I only want to help!' Julia called after her. 'It's all I've ever wanted.'

She cleared the porch steps in a single bound and was reaching for the Sparrow House door when her body twisted on the spot. It didn't feel like a conscious action. It was more like someone had taken hold of her wrist and yanked her round.

There they stood: Mrs Glock in a hideous pink coat, Farter Carter twirling keys around his fat finger, and a man with a beard so unkempt it looked as if a careless bird had woven a nest around his chin. This, she assumed, was Mr Merriglass the vicar. Four Circle members gathered together on the Glocks' driveway.

The door behind her opened and Nick drew her into comforting shadows.

'So much for us watching *them*,' he said. 'Come on, I've got something to show you.'

He led her into the parlour and took the spirit detector from the mantelpiece. Behind its little window, the arrow hovered just above zero.

'You mean they've stopped using the machine?'

'Looks like. Nothing's registered since the soldier came through yesterday.'

'Maybe they decided to give it a rest for a bit.'

'But why?' He slumped onto one of the packing crates. 'Knowledge and power is within their grasp, and yet they hesitate.'

'You almost sound like you want the unmade to come through.'

'Not that. I just want . . . ' He lowered his eyes. 'I want to have this over and done with. I can't stand it, Emma. Sending the unmade back—the fear in their eyes, their screams. It's so familiar to me now it's almost like my own fear, my own scream.'

Suddenly he was shaking. Trembling like a haunted child abandoned in some nightmare place. Emma pulled him into her arms. She could feel the frantic thud of his heart, like an engine tearing itself to pieces. And then . . .

'Emma? Emma, can you hear me . . . ?'

. . . he was gone, and with him, the world she knew.

Again, the farmhouse, the roadside stall, the patrol car with its drooping, fizzing radio. The screech of metal was echoed by the black bird circling the chimney. The sheriff barked his curse. Then the middle-aged man (Grandpa Grady?) appeared on the porch and called out: '*Both?*' She heard the slosh of the sheriff returning to the road.

All at once, the man himself hove into view. From her fixed position, Emma could only make out his bottom half—the sodden trousers, the gleaming boots, a big callused hand swinging down and snatching up the radio. Beyond the sheriff, the middle-aged man had crossed the yard and was hurrying down the road.

'Accident out at Slumberneck Creek,' the sheriff reported. 'Ambulance needed quick as . . . '

The man had reached a point outside Emma's line of sight. She heard the splash as his body entered the water.

'Goddamn it!' the sheriff hollered. 'Get the hell out of there . . . OLIVER!'

The vision faded and fractured again. As Nick and the parlour materialized before her, all she could think of was the name spoken by the sheriff. Because she'd assumed the visions had a close connection with Nick, Emma had guessed that the middle-aged man had to be Grady Redway. But if it was *Oliver* she was seeing then that meant the scene couldn't have happened recently. Oliver was thirty-six in 1931. The man on the porch had looked to be in his late fifties. So whatever the relevance of the vision, it couldn't have any direct connection with Nick, who wouldn't have been born for at least another forty years. She wondered if one of the people in the water had been Oliver's son Grady, and if the other might have been Nick's father. If so then the drama had to have had a happy ending: both must have survived or else Nick wouldn't be here now.

But then what to make of the newspaper article? ***Mearsville Tragedy Latest*** . . .

Nick seemed to see the ghost of the vision in her eyes.

'Please, don't ask.'

She nodded, her promise kept, and moved slowly to the window. Through a gap in the boards she could see the whole street. It had started snowing again, flakes as big as her hand.

'Any sign of them?'

She shook her head. The Circle had vanished. He came to stand beside her, his sharp, pale face reflected in the darkened glass.

'Where will you go . . . ?' she hesitated. 'When it's over?'

'Home.' He smiled. 'There are roads there that never end. Black ribbon roads that scratch their way over snowy mountains and yellow deserts. It's a country you can lose yourself in.'

'Do you want to be lost? Alone?'

He turned her round so that she faced him.

'Emma, don't you see? Lost isn't always—' His expression darkened. 'Someone's here.'

She heard it: the sorrowful creak of old hinges, a whistle of wind and the song of the soul-catchers. Nick motioned for her to stay where she was while he took up position behind the door. Floorboards thumped thickly under the tread of heavy boots. She gave Nick a nod and saw white teeth clench behind snarled lips. A shadow leapt against the firelight as the stranger came lumbering into the parlour.

'Stop!' The words were out of her mouth but it was too late.

They hit the floor together and a spray of snow flashed from the intruder's coat. The rug rumpled beneath them as they tumbled body over body towards the window. Hitting one of the crates with a bone-juddering smack, Nick scrambled onto his opponent's back and locked an arm around his throat. His bicep strained as he lifted his head and tried to shake his senses into focus. The strength of the intruder had unbalanced him. Emma was about to call out again when Nick's vision seemed to clear.

'*Sas?*' He released the chokehold and staggered to his feet.

'You b-bloody maniac!'

'Are you OK?' Emma asked, helping Sas to a seat on one of the crates.

'C-course not. How could anyone be OK after being attacked by that ass-assh—'

'No need for profanity, there's a lady present,' Nick cut in. He held out his hand. 'Truce?'

Sas considered before shaking it. 'So, any reason for the warm welcome?'

Nick puffed. 'Oh, I don't know, might have something to do with a complete stranger breaking into my house.'

'I'm not a stranger! I'm your girlfriend's cousin's best mate.'

'I'm not his girlfriend,' Emma insisted.

'Well that's what Madeleine Chow and Lola Flick's been telling everyone.'

'Great.' Emma groaned inwardly. 'Anything else they've been saying?'

'That whoever this guy is, he hasn't made you any less crazy. Not that anyone's paying them much attention.'

'They're not? Why?'

'Because all the cool kids can talk about is "the cute American guy" and how he's really into you. Miles and Chantelle are steaming mad about the whole thing.'

'Because?'

'They were *the* Tennyson couple, and now you are.' Sas shrugged. 'Chan's tearing her curly blonde hair out and Miles has gone into full-on brooding mode. They're such ass—' He caught Nick's eye. 'Idiots.'

Emma thought back to last night's phone call. Bitterness had rippled through her ex-boyfriend's voice as he spat out the words—*So you can go back to being the old Ems for some kid you hardly know but you couldn't do it for me?* Miles's anger ran deeper than being bested in some stupid popularity contest.

'So to what do we owe the pleasure?' Nick rolled his shoulders. 'And haven't you ever heard of a doorbell?'

'Tried it, didn't work. I'm here because *you*—' he threw Emma an accusing glance, 'won't answer Henry's calls. We sat up all night talking about what's been going on. I told him that you'd broken into the house and that his folks had him handcuffed to the bed. I still don't think he believes that part. He wants to know the truth, and so do I.'

Nick sighed. 'You've no cause to trust me, Brandon, but do you trust her?' He turned to Emma. Without the slightest hesitation, Sas nodded. 'You're a wise judge of character. Now, I can't tell you the truth about what's happening in this town. Why? Because *I* can't trust you. Not because I doubt your integrity, but because there are forces out there that have the power to make you speak against your will. Do you understand?'

'Course I don't!' Sas cried. 'But I guess if Emma trusts you then that's good enough for me. You trust him, right?'

'With my life.'

The words were out before she had time to think about them. Immediately they struck her as both strange and true.

'Ah, that's lovely,' Sas pouted. 'Really, I'm all warm and squishy inside, but it still feels like Henry and me are being treated like little kids. Henry can't do much, his dad's got him on lockdown, but I could help.'

Nick looked as if he was about to argue before a smile broke out. 'Maybe there is something you can do. There's a party tomorrow night at the Torves' and Emma and I need to be there. At the same time we have to be at the visitor centre by the lake.'

'Two places at once,' Sas said. 'You're either smarter or dumber than you look.'

'We also need a plausible explanation as to why the centre's been broken into. One that won't cause certain people to look into the situation more closely. Understand?'

Sas sucked his teeth. 'Again, gonna say "no". So what do you want me to do?'

Nick sketched out a plan in the vaguest terms he could. If Sas was under hypnotic suggestion then the Circle would get only the scantest of information.

'Do you think you can persuade the Chainers to go along with it?' Emma asked.

Sas considered. 'They're not the bravest kids in the world—running the Funland gauntlet's about as daring as they get—but I think I can convince them.'

Emma teetered onto tiptoes and planted a kiss on his hot cheek.

At the door of the Sparrow House, she watched the boy-giant lumber out into the snowstorm until he vanished amid white-flecked shadows. Then she turned to Nick.

'What say we give the ghost-hunting a rest for a few hours? There's something I've been meaning to show you.'

18

Capped with snow, Spring Fell, Summer Rise, and Winter Heights rose above the valley like the heads of three frost giants gathered around their supper. Emma didn't think she had ever seen the hills look quite so beautiful. In fact the whole town had kind of a pristine splendour to it, the grime and dirt swept under a white carpet. In the packed market square people traipsed from shop to shop, their arms laden down with last minute Christmas gifts.

'Look at them,' she murmured. 'So many . . . '

Her gaze raked the crowd: mothers and fathers pushing pink-nosed bundles; elderly couples clinging to each other on icy pavements; teenagers trading snowballs.

'This town was founded over five hundred years ago, Nick. How many ghosts are we talking about? Hundreds of thousands? Maybe even millions. All of them hungry.'

'You're shivering.'

'Of course I'm shivering! Why aren't you?'

'Because there's hope. Come on, let's get you into the warm.'

The steam of wet coats combined to form a sweating fog in the air of the Copper Kettle Café. Nick found a table towards the back and tried to catch the eye of a passing waitress. A girl of about seventeen came bounding over and took their order. When she returned to the kitchen, Nick slid the detector from his pocket and checked the dial.

'See the distance between these points?' He indicated the gap between the 0 and the 1. 'That's where hope rests. Until we find the ghost machine, we focus our prayers on this space.'

She leant forward. 'Do you pray?'

'I used to. I don't have to believe in an afterlife, Emma, I've known the company of ghosts. But if you pray you have to believe that someone's listening, right?'

'After Richie's accident I prayed that Bob and Rowan wouldn't agree to switch off his life support,' she said slowly. 'But they did. That was *their* decision, and it meant that I couldn't ever tell him . . . ' She shook her head.

Their order arrived with a cold smile for Emma and a warm wink for Nick. The waitress had attached a sprig of mistletoe to the handle of his mug and suggested, if he needed a refill, he should wave the cup over his head and she'd come running. Emma rolled her eyes.

'When I was little I'd gather up mistletoe from the woods around our farm and go sell it door to door,' he said, disentangling the sprig. 'I'd use the money to buy Christmas gifts for Pop and Grandpa.'

So it had been just the three of them: Nick, his father, and Grandpa Grady. Grady Redway, who must have left soon after to begin his studies under Randall Wolfe.

'Before he shipped out to war, my pop loved Christmas.' Nick twirled the mistletoe between his fingers. 'When he came back, I'm not sure he loved anything much. He just stared at the walls until it was time for the bars to open. Then he'd get into his truck, sink a gutful, and stare at some different walls.'

'Was that what killed him?' Emma asked gently. 'You said he died in battle—'

'It was a battle. Between him and the demons he brought home. Not all wars are fought with guns, Emma. You know how the US ended World War Two?'

'The atom bomb,' she nodded. 'Hiroshima. Nagasaki.'

'Sometimes it takes a colossal event to shock the world out of its madness. No one could talk to my father, no one could make him see. Not until a bomb was dropped on his head.' He took a savage bite out of his sandwich. 'We're a festive pair, aren't we?'

'My mum used to say Christmas was all nonsense anyway. "A pagan celebration of mid-winter hijacked by Christians and dressed up by capitalists." Bob would screw up his face and say, "Bah, humbug," and Richie'd laugh. Then she'd start laughing too.' Emma pushed her sandwich away. 'There wasn't much laughter after she quit her job at the university.'

'Dr Rowan Rhodes.' Nick nodded. 'Your mother was a respected expert in her field.'

Emma shrugged. 'Her students seemed to like her.'

'I'm not talking about her work at the university. I meant her studies as a member of the Lysanna faith.'

Emma's heart leapt into her throat. All this time they had spent together and Nick hadn't once mentioned her mother.

'What do you know about Rowan?' she demanded.

He held up his hands. 'If what little I know was important, I would've told you straight away. I promise.'

She sat back, arms folded, eyes like daggers. 'So?'

'You first. Tell me how it started.'

She took a deep breath. 'A few years ago Rowan began a project investigating modern day witches and their roots in pagan worship. She started out as she always did, treating her work like a proper academic. She spent three months living with the Lysanna followers at their camp in Devon. At first we heard from her once a week, then it was every other week, in the last month she didn't call at all. By the time she came home she was a true believer in white magic. Bob thought she'd been brainwashed.'

'What did you think?'

Emma sighed. 'I thought it was all pretty harmless, but Bob couldn't accept it. You've got to understand, his world is defined by science, everything else is . . . ' She struggled for the right word. 'A kind of superstitious abomination. That was why the rows got so bad. And after Richie died, there was nothing to keep Rowan at home. I guess she went back to the Lysa—'

'She isn't there, Emma.'

'What?'

'Like I told you, I did a little digging on the people from

Milton Lake. Your mother never returned to the Lysanna faithful.'

'Then where is she?'

'I don't know. No one does. That's why I didn't tell you, there was no point.'

She grabbed her coat. 'Come on, I need some air.'

As they walked, Emma's mind roiled with questions. The story of Nick's war-damaged father had made her heart ache. Had Grady really abandoned his grandson to the care of a man who spent his days drinking and staring at walls? And what had Nick meant by a bomb being dropped on his father's head? Then there were the questions that really stung. Those about her mother. Rowan had never returned to the Lysanna camp, so where was she?

At the outskirts of town, they passed into the sullen shadows of Black Acre. Away to their right, the lake glinted in the spaces between the trees. They moved deeper, the snow falling around them, soft and silent, a cemetery of leaves shushing underfoot. After a short hike, they came suddenly into the clearing and Nick stopped in his tracks.

'My God . . . It's beautiful.'

Emma smiled. It *was* beautiful.

The Kinema by the Lake had first opened its barn-size doors in 1919 and had been showing movies ever since. A string of multi-coloured lights ran across its peaked roof and tumbled down its Egyptian-pillared entrance. Two moss-maned sphinxes stood by the doors like stony-faced ticket collectors. Housed behind glass frames, film posters decorated the outside walls—works of art from old movies like *Ben*

Hur, *Sunset Boulevard*, *Carousel*, *The Old Dark House*, and *The Creature from the Black Lagoon*.

The doors stood firmly shut, the lights were dimmed. Nick crossed the car park and placed his palm against one of the poster cases. The film was *Singing in the Rain*, a musical Emma and Bob had caught during the Kinema's season of 'Hollywood Classics' a few years back.

'My pop loved this movie,' Nick said. 'When he came home I tried to take him to see it at one of the nabes. He wouldn't go. No matter how much I begged, he just sat in his chair staring at that same damned spot on the wall. The things he'd seen out there, Grandpa said they'd broken something deep inside . . . '

He ran his fingers through the mop of hair that curtained his forehead. For a moment, the white scar was unveiled, bright as a brand. 'I still don't know what he saw in that wall. Even now, when so much of what he thought and felt is clear to me, I still . . . '

The crunch of snow cut him dead.

Emma turned in time to see four familiar figures emerging from the forest.

19

Throwing the baseball bat from hand to hand, Miles led the way into the car park. Behind him, Chan, Madeleine, and Lola had to scurry to keep up.

'Let's go,' Emma said, catching at Nick's sleeve.

His mouth was set in a thin line, but he nodded agreement. As they started towards the forest, Miles moved quickly to intercept them. The bat swooped over their heads and came to rest with a tender tap against Nick's chest.

'What's the hurry?'

Nick's eyes fixed on the barrel of the bat. The terrible focus of that stare made Emma tremble.

'There's no need for this,' she said. 'You can keep your stupid "it couple" crown, we don't want it.'

She saw straight away that she'd made a terrible mistake. Miles's lips twitched and Chan's face turned an ugly shade of crimson.

'I'm sorry.' The words were like poison in her throat. 'Just please let us go.'

Miles dug the end of the bat into Nick's sternum. 'First this guy needs to be taught a lesson.'

'You won't hurt her,' Nick said.

'Hurt her?' Miles seethed. 'I'd never hurt her. I love—*loved* her.'

The slip had been made, and now Chan's manicured nails dug into Emma's arm and she was hauled backwards. Madeleine and Lola grabbed her shoulders while their wild-eyed leader fastened fingers around Emma's throat.

'We so didn't mean any of the stuff we said to this freak,' Madeleine squawked.

'We were just messing with her,' Lola agreed. 'Pretending we wanted to be friends.'

'Play nicely, girls,' Miles ordered. The king's command was law, at least as far as his queen and her empty-headed handmaidens were concerned. The chattering voices fell silent. 'Now, Ems, like I was saying to your boyfriend here, I'd never hurt you. I really did care about you and I wanted to be there for you. But you shut me out.'

The bat jabbed against Nick's chest.

'What happened to Richie was tragic.'

Jab.

'I even felt a bit responsible.'

Jab.

'After all, you *were* on the phone to me when it happened.'

Jab.

'And I was sorry about it. Really. I liked the little dude.'

'Stop talking about my brother,' Emma spat.

'Ah, but that was always your problem, wasn't it? Not talking. I would've listened.' *Jab*, *jab*, *jab*. 'But you wouldn't let me. And then this guy turns up and suddenly the old Ems is back. What is it about *you* that's so bloody special, eh?'

The bat travelled up from Nick's sternum and dropped into the little well above his collarbone. Miles dug the blunt end into his throat while Nick stood his ground.

'Gonna answer my question or just stand there glaring?' Miles cocked his head to one side. 'Come on, Yank, how did you bring her back?'

As the baseball bat moved on, grazing a path along the side of Nick's face, bumping over the sharp contours of his jaw and cheekbone, the question remained unanswered. Emma herself had no clear explanation. Had the danger posed to Milton Lake by the ghost machine wrenched her free from guilt and grief? Or was it something deeper? One haunted soul reaching out to another . . .

'If you don't tell me I might just have to go looking for the answer. If I crack your skull open then maybe, just maybe . . . ' he knocked the bat against Nick's temple—an insistent rap made all the more terrible by its tenderness, 'the secret will come tumbling out.'

Lola and Madeleine exchanged worried glances. Cruel jokes and dirty looks were the limit of their sadism. Emma, who had dated the star midfielder for almost eight months, was just as surprised. Miles might be a bit self-absorbed but she would never have thought him capable of this kind of violence. For all his dark words, she wondered if even he knew what he was going to do next.

The hold around Emma's throat loosened a little.

'Come on, M-Tag, we've already scared these freaks silly!' Chan's laugh was horribly shrill. 'Let's go home and raid my dad's booze cabinet.'

'Shut up!'

Miles twisted sideways and the muscles in his neck and shoulders tensed. The bat hovered a hair's breadth from Nick's face.

'So what about it, Yank? You're gonna spill one way or another . . . ' He pulled the bat over his right shoulder. 'Brains or secrets, 's your choi—'

A powerful uppercut landed on the underside of Miles's jaw, snapping his teeth together with a loud *cluck*. The baseball bat fell from his fingers and he staggered backwards, one hand cradling his chin, the other held out to ward off his attacker. Gone was the menace of a moment ago, replaced by a kind of bewildered terror.

Nick pressed his advantage. Two quicksilver jabs opened up cuts on either side of Miles's face, and now Nick was ducking under his opponent's hands, executing blow after blow to the boy's ribs and abdomen. When Miles crouched low to protect those parts of his body, fresh punches were landed to his unguarded head.

Hands dropping to his sides, a dazed and bloodied Miles straightened up. Nick's grin turned wolfish. Putting all his weight behind his fist, he landed a killer punch in the sweet spot at the centre of Miles's face. The midfielder's nose cracked and a festive red ribbon laced through the air. Miles hit the snow and stayed there.

All this had happened within the space of a few short seconds. The girls were still clustered around Emma, although now it felt as if they were clinging on to her for support rather than holding her hostage. Lola and Madeleine gawped like a pair of stunned halibuts while Chan made mewling noises at the back of her throat. Meanwhile, Nick sat astride Miles's chest and delivered a brain-rattling blow to the right side of his face.

'Apologize.'

Crunch.

'Say you're sorry for all the pain you caused her.'

Crunch.

'Tell her what a miserable little worm you are or I swear to God—'

Miles held up a shivering hand. 'Pw-pwease.'

Nick grabbed him by the collar and turned his head in Emma's direction.

'Say it.'

She felt the restraining hands release her.

'E-Ems, I'm s-sorry. I'm a w-w-worm, a sn-snake, w-whatever he s-said. Please f-forgive me.' Through swelling slits he looked up at Nick. 'D-uh did I d-do it r-right?'

A bloodstain sinking into the snow hooked Nick's attention. He watched the crimson star spread and lose its vibrancy until only a pale pink blot remained. Then, very gently, he laid Miles back down upon the ground.

'I'm sorry.' He turned to Emma. 'I'm so sorry.'

She shook her head. It was only as tears flew from the corners of her eyes that she realized she'd been crying. Nick took Miles's hand and bent down to whisper in his ear. When he'd finished, he moved on to Lola, Madeleine, and Chan, each too shell-shocked to resist his hypnosis. They would call an ambulance and accompany Miles back to town where a story about a fight with a motorcycle gang would be reported to the police.

Emma fled from the clearing. Her heart felt strangely loose in her chest, as if it had slipped free from the veins and arteries that anchored it to her body. The sleeping trees whipped by and she did not look back until she reached the lake. She stood at the very edge where the grey-green waters nibbled the shingle shore. Below the surface, reeds reached up like silken fingers and caressed the reflection of the three hills.

'Please come away from there.'

Nick stood in the forest, knuckles bloodied, hair plastered to his brow.

'Come away,' he repeated. 'Emma, *please* . . . '

She mounted the bank, took his bruised hand and guided him into the trees. The afternoon had worn thin and the light was failing. Although she wanted desperately to keep hold of his hand, the memory of Miles, beaten and uncrowned, wouldn't allow her to do so. She moved away and went to stand with her back against a towering oak.

He asked, 'Do you hate me?'

'No.'

'Why not?'

'He was going to hurt you. It was self-defence.'

'Don't lie for me. He was never going to use the bat, we both know it.'

'Then why?'

'Because he was cruel. Cruel to a girl who feels pain so deeply she's been blinded to the truth all around her.'

They stood quietly while twilight bruised the air of the forest.

'Something happened to me when I was young,' Nick said. 'A terrible thing.'

The farmhouse, the sheriff, the man on the porch. Emma blinked the vision away.

'It had something to do with your father, didn't it?'

'My pop . . . yes.' It was too dark to see, but she could hear the tears in his voice. 'Afterwards I wasn't myself for a long, long time. My grandpa helped set me straight. I owe him everything.'

Wind whistled through Black Acre, a desolate chant like a hymn sung at a funeral.

'The anger you saw is a relic from that time, I hardly ever feel it now . . . ' He took a step forward. 'Please say something.'

Her voice shook. 'I took you to one of the few good places in my life and you made it ugly.'

'I know.'

'You don't *know*.' Her own anger flickered out and surprised her. 'I was so scared, Nick. I haven't been that scared since . . . '

It was time. She felt it as clearly as a diver might feel the tipping point before plunging into the ocean. Slowly, slowly she worked her way up from the roots of the story: Richie had wanted to prove himself the equal of his daredevil sister, and so she'd devised a challenge—go and ring the bell of the Sparrow House. On that first attempt, he'd failed, but the house had cast its spell and Richie bided his time . . .

'It was a Saturday. Dad had to go into work to collect some exam papers and Mum was shopping in town. I'd arranged to meet Miles, but Bob said I had to stay home and watch Richie. I started moaning about always having to look after my annoying little brother. Do you know what I said as Bob left the house? "Go then, but if you're longer than an hour don't expect to find Richie still breathing when you get back." '

'I stormed into the kitchen. My brother was at the table with his colouring books and crayons. He'd screwed up the drawings he wasn't happy with and had scattered them all over the floor. I collected up all the paper and stuffed it into the recycling, but the bin was full. The bloody thing tipped over. That was when I swore.

'Richie had never heard that word before. He started repeating it over and over. I just knew he'd say it to Bob or Rowan when they got home. I told him to stop but he kept saying it, singing it, shouting it as loud as he could. I promised I'd take him to the park, buy him sweets. Nothing worked, so I grabbed him and shook him. Not hard, but he started crying. I couldn't stand it. I took his hand and dragged him down from the table.

' "Stop it!" he shouted. "You're pulling my arm out!" I kept telling him to shut up. I didn't know what I was doing . . . I pulled open the front door and threw him outside.

He was so small, so fragile, and I slammed the door in his face. I only meant to leave him for a few seconds—just a minute to calm down and think. Maybe if I spent a fortune on sweets I could convince him not to repeat *that* word ever again. My hand was reaching for the door when the phone rang in the hall.'

As twilight deepened, the boy opposite had transformed from a silhouette to an indistinct smudge. He stood perfectly still, listening.

'It was Miles wondering where I'd got to. That was when the letterbox flapped open—"Sorry for whatever I did wrong, Ems," Richie called through the door. "Can I come back inside?" I told him to be quiet, but he was going on and on. Then he started crying again. The phone's attached to the wall and the cord wouldn't stretch to the door. I guess I just snapped. "Stop being a whiney little baby!" I shouted. "Jesus, Richie, why can't you just grow up?" "I'm not a baby," he called back. "I'm just as brave as you!"'

Darkness had fallen across the wood. Emma addressed her confession to the pattering snow and the sighing trees.

'Miles was still talking. A minute had passed, maybe two. I wasn't thinking about Richie . . . First.' She closed her eyes. 'First came the scream. Then the squeal of brakes. Then more screams from the people in the street. Someone swore. The same word I'd used in the kitchen. I dropped the phone. Moved down the corridor. The air felt thick, like walking through treacle. I reached the door, turned the handle.

'The sun was bright, blinding. I saw the lorry tilted up on the kerb, people gathered round. The driver was sitting in the road, head in his hands. People were on their phones talking about a little boy, dead or dying . . .

'They tried to stop me, said it was better not to see. I pushed them all out of the way. Richie lay with his head on the kerb, like a pillow. His arms and legs were . . . all wrong. He stared up at the sky, and when I tried to put myself in front of him his pupils didn't focus. I told him I was there. Promised he'd be OK. He coughed. That was all. At the hospital, they said he was blind and deaf, but he heard me. I know he did. He heard, and later, when I broke my promise, he *knew*.'

Silence from the darkness.

'I blamed Bob and Rowan for pulling the plug, but they aren't responsible. It was me. You see that, don't you? Don't you, Nick? Don't you?'

They'd all insisted it wasn't her fault, but how to make *him* see that they were wrong. She had laid down the challenge and then abandoned her brother to the spell of the Sparrow House. He must understand that she was to blame.

He *must*.

20

Shadows shifted through shadows as he came forward. Emma pressed her back against the oak. Pressed hard, as if by sheer force she could sink into the bark and never be seen again. Eyes closed, she could sense him standing before her.

Nick lifted her head, brushed a strand of hair behind her ear, and in the darkness, kissed her. His lips were warm and tasted slightly salty. She realized that it was her own tears that flavoured them. Tears that spilled down her cheeks and ran into the valley between their lips. Taking her hand, he led her out of the darkness.

He was the only one who hadn't tried to tell her it wasn't her fault. Why? Because although he could not offer true forgiveness, he understood her need for it, just as he understood her need to feel some responsibility. That was what the kiss had meant: *I understand and I forgive.* Now they moved in silence as the trees thinned and the lights of Milton Lake burned bright.

'You'll come with me, won't you?' he said. 'When this is over, when I leave, I want—I *need* you to come with me.'

She could hardly believe what she was hearing. She had thought of him as a friend only, the boy who opened doors, and yet all this time he had been more than that. Wrapped in grief, she hadn't noticed how her feelings for him had been changing, becoming deeper and richer.

'But you said you wanted to go home, lose yourself on those long roads.'

'Emma, don't you see?' he smiled. 'Lost isn't always *alone*. I could lose myself with you.' He kissed her again. 'Will you come?'

'Of course I will!'

His laughter was warm and dusty, like a cornfield in summer. He lifted her by the waist, hugged her to his chest, spun on the spot until the town lights whirled.

Hand in hand, they drifted through the crisp streets, Nick chatting excitedly about plans for a long road trip once they reached the States, Emma's mind reeling. All her life she had dreamed of wandering this world, of breathing exotic air and walking under different stars. Now they would wander together. The town passed in a blur; she hardly noticed the gaunt spectacle of St Jerome's churchyard and the cosy huddle of the little cottage Sas shared with his mother. Before she knew it, they'd reached Connolly Avenue and her own front door.

'I want to come with you . . . ' she said, 'back to the Sparrow House.'

He took her hands in his. 'I'll see you tomorrow.'

'But I want to be with you.'

'I'm not going anywhere,' he promised. 'Now get inside before you catch your death.'

He let go of her hand and walked to the kerb. Frail gusts of snow blew listlessly down the avenue and tumbled in the spaces between the houses. The worst of the weather seemed to have passed.

'Why did you let me stay and watch the face in the pool?'

He looked back. 'Sorry?'

'That first night in the attic, you didn't need to hear what Percival Sparrow said, you could've got me out of there. Why didn't you?'

'Guess.'

'You were lonely. You wanted someone to share the—'

'Share the horror with. That would be very selfish of me, wouldn't it?'

'Not selfish. Just very human.'

He looked as if he was about to say something, then the wind picked up and blew the hair back from his scar. 'Goodnight, Emma.'

She watched him cross the road and vanish into the Sparrow House.

Stepping into the warmth of the hall, Emma looked in on Bob's temporary bedroom. She found him asleep on the sofa, his plastered arm propped up on pillows, his broken hand resting on his stomach. He made a weary snuffle but didn't wake. Returning to the corridor she was about to mount the stairs when Julia bustled out of the kitchen. They stared at each other for a moment, frozen by the memory of the strange and heated conversation they'd had that morning.

'How's he been today?' Emma asked.

'Quite well. Ate most of his supper.'

'I-I'm sorry,' she forced out the words, 'about earlier. I haven't been feeling well and I've had loads of stress at school. I didn't know what I was saying.'

'Think nothing of it. I'm always being snapped at by Arthur, I'm quite used to it.'

'Maybe you ought to snap back once in a while.'

Julia looked at her thoughtfully. 'Perhaps I should.'

'I'm not sure if this is going to make up for being rude, but Johnny—' she caught herself just before saying 'Nick', '—and I have decided to come to your Christmas Eve party.'

'Oh,' Julia said coolly. 'Yes, well, it'll be very nice to see you both.'

She hadn't expected her aunt to perform a dance of victory but a sly smile wouldn't have been out of place. Very strange.

Although it wasn't late, Emma felt physically and emotionally exhausted. After showering, she pulled on her pyjamas and slipped into bed. She had forgotten to draw the curtains. Through the snow-spotted pane, she could just make out the attic window across the street. That was where they had met four nights ago. Just *four nights* and so much had changed. Now there was talk of them leaving Milton Lake together, of waving goodbye to ghosts and losing themselves on black ribbon roads . . .

Emma drifted. Drifted back through time to the now familiar scene of the old farm under its frosty-blue New England sky. Soaked to the bone, the sheriff was speaking into his radio.

'Accident out at Slumberneck Creek. Ambulance needed quick as . . . '

The middle-aged man from the porch entered the water with a splash.

'Goddamn it! Get the hell out of there. OLIVER!'

Emma saw the sodden brown trousers race across her field of view—she still could not turn her head—and heard a second splash. The bird had returned to the rooftop, its pebble black eyes rooted on what Emma took to be the men in the water. A carrion bird waiting its chance. Again, that screech of metal.

'Keep away from there,' the sheriff warned. 'You can't do them any good.'

'Grady . . . ' Oliver's words carried on the breeze. 'Goddamn you, son! Goddamn your soul to hell!'

'I said stay back—'

'Take your hands off me.' Oliver did not shout but the menace in his voice was clear. 'This is my son and grandson. Now, you've done your duty, leave us be.'

'Ambulances are on their way.'

'Only one ambulance needed here, Sheriff.' A moment of stillness textured by the lap of water and the croak of the bird. 'Damn you to hell, Grady,' Oliver repeated. 'My poor Nathan. My poor boy . . . '

The scavenger squawked and launched itself from the roof. Emma knew that this was a vision of past times, the bird could not hurt her. Still, she cried out as wings battered the air and wicked talons reached for her face . . .

She woke, tangled in her bed sheets.

At first, she could not tell whether it was morning or night, so dark were the clouds boiling at the window. A glance at the clock radio informed her it was 10:35 a.m. She felt rested, although a new snippet of information from the vision immediately began to trouble her. *Nathan Redway*. It had to be the name of Nick's soldier father, the man who'd returned from war to stare at walls and drink himself into an early grave . . . Except that didn't make any sense. There had obviously been some kind of calamity forty or so years before Nick's birth. Two Redways had met with an accident in the wetlands surrounding the Mearsville farm. The implication from Oliver's words was that Nathan had died, but how could that be if his son was alive and well and living over the road?

There was only one explanation: despite Oliver's fears, Nathan had *not* died in the accident. As for that headline in the *Cumberland Chronicle*—'Mearsville Tragedy Latest'—the newspaper must have misreported the story. And yet why was she having these visions if it had all ended so happily?

She stared at the ceiling, turning the mystery over in her mind. Finally admitting defeat, she headed for the bathroom and a hot shower. She brushed her teeth, combed the tangles from her hair, and rushed back to her room to pull on some clothes. Slipping her laptop into its bag, she tiptoed downstairs.

At the sitting room door, she paused. She hadn't spoken to Bob since the night before; she really ought to see if he needed anything. Opening the door a crack, she found a Bob-shaped mound bundled up in blankets on the sofa . . .

'I told you I'd think about it and I have. I'm sorry, but the answer's no.'

Aunt Julia's voice carried from the kitchen, high and shrill. Unless someone was in there with her, she must be talking on the phone.

'You say you're acting from the best of intentions, but you don't know what you're dealing with. Some things are best left alone, believe me. Not only that, you're asking me to betray the people I love. And Emma is just a child, I won't do it.'

Emma remembered the conversation last night in which she'd suggested that Julia stand up to her bullying husband. Had the little mouse decided to stop taking orders from the Circle? Was she now trying to protect Emma and Bob?

'That's my final word on the matter,' Julia said firmly. 'You'll just have to play this devil's game without me.'

21

Before she could blink the snow from her eyes, he was kissing her. Emma reached around his thick neck and crushed her lips against his.

'Wow,' he murmured.

'Wow,' she echoed.

He was dressed in what she had come to think of as the Nicholas Redway uniform of white T-shirt, blue jeans, and black biker boots. His breath steamed the air of the corridor and bobbles of gooseflesh puckered his arms. She took his hand and they started towards the parlour.

'Let's make our morning reports,' he said. 'Anything been happening over the tracks?'

Emma thought about confronting him with the revelations from her dream: that whatever drama had played out in the wetlands surrounding the Mearsville farm, it had all happened long ago, and that Nick himself had played no part. Only the promise made her hesitate. She decided then that she would not ask him about Mearsville unless honouring her promise became practically impossible. If, for example, through her visions more information came to light and the truth was virtually staring her in the face. In the meantime, she reported the conversation between Julia and Arthur Torve.

'It sounded like she'd had enough and was telling the Circle they could forget about her spying for them.'

'Perhaps.'

'So why don't we talk to her? Maybe we could convince her to help us instead. She might even know where they're keeping the ghost machine.'

'It's too dangerous,' Nick said. 'You told me your aunt was weak-willed, she could change her mind and go back to them. And there's something very odd about that conversation.'

'Right. I've never heard her stand up to Uncle Arthur before.'

'I didn't mean that exactly. I just wonder why she's having second thoughts *now*.'

'Maybe they asked her to do something she wasn't comfortable with. She talked about betraying the people she loved.'

Nick shrugged. 'I guess we might find out at their meeting tonight.'

'Speaking of which.' Emma pulled the laptop from her bag. 'Are you ready to rehearse our little play?'

While she set up the computer on one of the crates, Nick prowled the parlour like a caged beast, checking the windows and tapping out his frustration on the mantelpiece.

'Still no ghost activity,' he muttered, speaking as much to himself as to her. 'That's almost forty-eight hours without an unmade coming through. What are the Circle playing at?'

'Are you sure the detector isn't faulty?' Emma asked, looking up from the laptop.

'I recalibrated it last night, the detector's fine.'

'Then I don't understand, why have they stopped using the machine?'

'There's a lot in Milton Lake that doesn't add up,' Nick sighed. 'The Circle, your aunt and uncle. And then there's you, Miss Rhodes.'

'Me?'

'The fact that you still don't see.'

'See what?'

'How remarkable you are.'

I'll tell you what doesn't add up, Mr Redway: YOU. I'm just about the least mysterious person anyone could imagine. You, on the other hand, make advanced quadratic equations look straightforward.

With the voice recorder program loaded, she called him over to the laptop.

'Do you think this is going to work?'

'It will or it won't,' he shrugged.

Emma's cursor hovered over the record icon. 'What'll we talk about?'

'Anything. We just need half an hour or so of aimless chatter. Remember to leave gaps for Sas and Henry to add the odd comment.'

She hit record. Trying to keep a straight face was difficult as they flipped back and forth, discussing subjects at random: the weather, schoolwork, old pop songs, plans for the Christmas holidays, books they'd read, and movies they'd seen. After thirty minutes, Nick signalled to stop and Emma fell back onto the rug, giving full vent to her laughter.

'Weirdest conversation ever! Not that I'm surprised, I *was* talking to you.'

Nick shook his head. 'You should know something, Emma: mocking me is a grave offence for which there is only one punishment.'

He loomed over her, fingers wiggling.

'Don't you da—*aarrggghhh*!'

He managed to get in a full minute of tickling before Emma wriggled free and bolted for the corridor. Stairs thundered, doors squealed and slammed, and from worm-wet cellar to web-weaved attic the once desolate Sparrow House rang with hysterical laughter. It was at that small attic door that they paused, hearts racing and lungs striving. There that the air seemed at once colder and sweeter and where Emma felt the strangest sensation. It was as if someone had taken her hand and placed it into Nick's, gently folding her fingers around his. She turned to find him smiling.

'You're beginning to see.'

22

Emma stowed her boots in a saddlebag slung across the rear of the bike and slipped into a pair of high heels. Although the worst of the snow had been cleared from the Torves' drive, her choice of footwear made the going hard. She threw dagger glances at Nick, who did his best to stifle a fit of giggles as she tottered towards the house.

At their approach, the big double doors swung open and a blast of light flooded into the chill darkness. Henry stood on the threshold, treating Emma to the kind of look that Julius Caesar might have thrown Brutus's way. He had opened his mouth to speak when his mother appeared in the hall behind him.

'Emma dear, welcome.' She smiled at Nick. 'I was just saying to your uncle that I haven't seen much of you, and here's the reason why. What a handsome young man.'

He did look handsome, Emma thought, in his charcoal blazer, burgundy tie, and crisp white shirt. Julia ushered them into the grand sitting room, twittering all the while.

'You mustn't fret about your father, I'm only staying for an hour or so . . . Ah, darling! Here's Emma and her young man.'

Arthur Torve cut short his conversation with the mayor and came slithering through the crowd. Before extending a skeletal hand, he studied Nick with the kind of cautious intensity with which a snake might examine a mongoose.

'Mr Bleeker, isn't it?' He tapped his forehead. 'Of course, your family's bought the old Sparrow House. How are you settling in?'

'Just fine.'

'Excellent . . . You're from New England, I hear.'

'Thereabouts.'

'Is "Bleeker" a deep-rooted name there? You'll forgive a small town solicitor's inquisitiveness, but I happened to look you up. Couldn't find a trace of anyone called Bleeker in the Maine area.'

'That so?'

'I also looked for "Harvey Dowd". Apparently the name was printed on some boxes delivered to Connolly Avenue. Drew a blank there, too.'

'How frustrating.'

Arthur frowned. 'Dear me, my boy, anyone might think you were being deliberately evasive.'

'My father and his father before him were military men, Mr Torve. Guess I inherited their dislike for aimless chatter.'

At that moment, Julia stepped forward and whispered in her husband's ear.

'Ah yes. I fear my interrogation must be cut short, Mr Bleeker.' A tight-lipped smile. 'I have an important call I must make to a client, I'll rejoin the party later.'

Emma glanced at her watch: 7:17. The game was on. Arthur had just disappeared into the hall when Sas loomed over Henry's shoulder, right on cue. Everyone was used to the boy's booming tones, so didn't take much notice when his voice rang out.

'Hey, Henry, let's show Emma your new sound system. Come on, guys, you gotta see this baby.'

Emma waited with baited breath. What if her cousin was so incensed by her ignoring his calls that he refused to play along? After a brief pause, Henry nodded and jerked his head in the direction of the stairs. Leaving the great and good of Milton Lake to their champagne and canapés, they had almost reached the landing when Julia called up to them.

'Henry, where are you taking our guests?'

'Just showing them my new speakers. C'mon, Mum, we don't want to hang out with all those old farts.'

'Henry Torve, keep a civil tongue in your head or I'll tell your fath—'

She stopped mid-sentence and cast a curious gaze over the quartet on the stairs. Emma was having trouble understanding her aunt's behaviour. Earlier today she'd overheard a conversation in which Julia seemed to have cast off her allegiance to the Circle, yet just now there had been no sign of hostility between husband and wife.

'Very well,' she murmured, 'off you go.'

Henry led the way to his bedroom, closed the door, and turned to Emma.

'Now what the hell's going on?' he demanded. 'Sas gives me a whole bunch of instructions and expects me to just—'

'We don't have time for this,' said Nick. 'Emma?' She took the memory stick from her pocket and handed it to him. 'We need you to play this. We've left spaces for you to speak so that the conversation seems natural. Now, we have to go.'

He crossed to the window and lifted the sash. A blade of arctic air cut into the room bringing with it a spill of fresh snow. Nick was about to climb onto the sill when Henry grabbed his blazer and tugged him back.

'You're not going anywhere until I get some answers.' For all his tiny stature, he seemed undaunted by the towering bulk of Nicholas Redway. 'Sas and me, we've been going over all the things that have happened since my . . . ' he struggled for the right word, 'experience in the ghost train. I still don't buy the bit about my parents handcuffing me, but weird things *have* been happening—like the chanting.'

'What chanting?' Emma asked.

'Those people—Sas says you call them "the Circle"—sometimes I hear them in my dad's study. They call out these strange words and numbers.'

'When was the last time you heard them?'

'This afternoon.'

Nick glanced at Emma. If the Circle was still using the ghost machine then why hadn't the detector activated? He turned to Henry.

'Your cousin and I are trying to stop something very bad from happening to this town. If we fail then everyone you care about, including your parents, will be in terrible danger. I can't tell you more than that, but I beg you to have faith, if not in me then in Emma.'

Henry didn't hesitate. 'Of course I have faith in Emma, I always have . . . ' He sighed. 'All right, but when this is over I *want* the truth.'

He took the memory stick from Nick and slotted it into a port on his laptop. The file popped up on screen and Sas jacked in the speakers of the new sound system. Emma gave her cousin's arm a reassuring squeeze as she headed for the window.

'We don't know if anyone will be listening outside the door,' she said. 'If they ask to come in you'll just have to stall as long as you can.'

Nick was reaching for the sill again when Henry spoke up.

'Sas says you've talked about stuff like necromancy and exorcism. Sounds pretty dark, and I guess my dad must be right in the middle of it.' He clenched his fists. 'I don't want him hurt. Whatever he's done, he's still my dad.'

'I'll do my best to keep that in mind,' Nick said, and jumped from the window.

The Thunderbird was where they had left it, propped beside the pavement. Emma exchanged high heels for boots and Nick fired up the engine. A little way past the Torves', the road turned with the forest and joined that crumbling arc of blacktop known locally as the lake road. Instead of following this route, Nick bumped the bike onto the pavement and headed straight into a curtain of trees.

The footpath ran in an almost arrow-straight direction to the visitor centre on the southern shore. Travelling by car, Arthur would have to take a more meandering route, which might give Emma and Nick a ten minute advantage. Not only that, but if Sas had worked his magic with the Chainers then the Circle might face a few unexpected delays.

Picked out by the headlight, the forest flew by in a rollercoaster haze of twisted trunks and thorny thickets. Although the nimble Thunderbird obeyed every command of her dexterous pilot, Emma couldn't help feeling a little queasy as they screeched along the frozen path. Away to her right, the black body of the lake flashed between the trees. She tapped Nick's shoulder and pointed to the clearing a few hundred metres ahead. He brought the bike to a grumbling halt and they stowed it behind a patch of overgrown bramble, covering any exposed parts with fallen branches.

They were making for the clearing when a figure burst from the undergrowth. Nick grabbed the stranger by his hoodie and the boy yelped like a startled pig.

'It's all right,' Emma said. 'It's Freakazoid.'

'Emma.' The leader of the Chainsaw Gang blinked at Nick. 'And you must be the mystery man from the Sparrow House. Seen any ghosts?'

'More'n a few. Sas gave you my instructions?'

Freakazoid Fred was so excited he almost snapped out a salute. 'Mike borrowed his dad's chainsaw and we cut down the tree this afternoon. Hey, I guess we really are the Chainsaw Gang now!'

'Did you fray the stump like I said? If it looks like it was deliberately felled—'

'It's done, so chill,' Fred soothed. 'But whatever you guys are up to, you better hurry. I've got a few of my people hiding out in a ditch by the road. Torve's car has just pulled up and him and Carter are getting a towrope around the tree.'

Nick nodded. 'Then let's move.'

A short jog brought them to their destination. Set to the rear of a snow-clogged car park, the Milton Lake Visitor Centre was a neat timber-frame building with a sloping slate roof and a long glass front. Built just over a decade ago, it housed a coffee shop, the town's museum, and a modest library. As they approached, Emma saw that the glass door had been smashed through. One of the wheeled skips from the back of the building had been used as a battering ram and now lay upturned on the floor of the coffee shop, green bin juice dribbling from its jaws.

'No alarm?'

'Nope,' Fred grinned. 'It's a looters' paradise.'

Nick turned baleful eyes on him. 'Did I say anything about stealing?'

'We'll put it back later,' Fred mumbled.

'See you do.'

They stepped through the shattered door and into the moonlit interior. To their left was the coffee shop, to their right, a library of groaning bookshelves and tidy notice boards. Beyond was the town museum, an airy space full of glass cabinets exhibiting all kinds of historical curios from Milton Lake's past. Nick turned on the torch he had brought from the

Thunderbird's saddlebag and played its beam over the walls. As per his instructions, the Chainers had been busy decorating. Every wall sported a fresh piece of graffiti—DayGlo smileys, neon-green stencils, luminous throw-ups, and fluorescent tags.

'OK, Fred, your work is done. You better scoot before they get here.'

Freakazoid glanced around the open spaces of the centre.

'Sure, but what are you guys gonna do? Even if they don't call the cops they'll search every inch of this place. There ain't nowhere to hide.'

'Not your concern. Just hand me one of your spray cans and be on your way.'

'Your funeral, dude.'

Fred tossed him a can from his backpack and darted for the door.

'OK,' Emma breathed, 'so far I'm following the plan. The Chainers make all this look like a random act of vandalism to cover for our break in, but what now?'

She turned to find Nick in a far corner of the museum, spray can in hand. She watched as he daubed a pair of symbols on adjoining walls, each about a metre out from the corner. Painted in blazing scarlet they didn't seem out of place among the other weird tags and designs:

'Mystic devices,' he said, answering her unasked question.

'It's why I got the Chainers to go to town. The Circle might recognize this symbol, it's a well known talisman, but I'm banking on it going unnoticed among all the other graffiti.'

'Clever,' Emma approved, 'but what does it do?'

'They're the signs of the eclipse. Their power is in conceal—'

A pair of headlights shone through the broken door. Nick took Emma's hand and pulled her into the triangular space between the walls and the two dripping symbols. Stretching his arms full width, he touched his fingertips to each painted eclipse and murmured a few words under his breath. Was it her imagination or had the symbols grown a little brighter during his incantation? If so, they had immediately dimmed again.

From outside came the sound of an engine cut dead and the slam of car doors. During the short time they'd been inside, the storm had gathered once more over Milton Lake. Now the wind could be heard screeching through the trees while hard pellets, more hail than snow, chattered against the windows.

'What the hell's happened here?'

Emma would know that voice anywhere. Sidney 'Farter' Carter. Stepping in behind the headmaster, the leader of the Circle cast a narrow-eyed glance around the visitor centre. Emma squeezed Nick's hand. They were both standing in plain sight.

'What do you think?' asked Arthur Torve.

'Kids by the look of it,' Carter sniffed. 'God, I hate children.'

Arthur shook his head. 'First the tree and now this.'

'Coincidence. Come on, man, hold your nerve.'

A dozen headlights cut through the veil of snow.

'Here we go,' Nick said, as boldly as if they had been the only people within earshot. He smiled at Emma's wondering glance. 'The symbols keep us slightly out of sync with the rest of reality. As long as they don't spot and recognize the eclipse then we can't be seen or heard.'

It took a few minutes for the Circle to assemble. Seven in all, they gathered together in the museum area not five metres from Nick and Emma's hiding place. Torve, Carter, Glock, Merriglass, Worple and Roper, and there, standing between her uncle and the doctor's wife, the seventh member. Mrs Christina Nugent fitted the Circle profile exactly—an ordinary, middle-aged woman who wouldn't have looked out of place at the Torve Christmas party. In fact, the only odd thing was the expression on her face, almost as if she didn't quite know where she was.

The Circle's chatter was cut short by their leader.

'Ladies and gentlemen, all this is something of a surprise.' Arthur gestured at the walls. 'But I'm in agreement with Sidney that it is merely the work of vandals. I believe our meeting should go ahead as planned.'

There was a murmur of consent.

'I've just telephoned home. As you know, my wife had to return to look after her brother, but I'm happy to report that Dr Glock has kept an eye on my niece and her mysterious new beau. They are being entertained by my son Henry. I do not believe, therefore, that this desecration has anything to do with them. Now, let us begin . . . '

Arthur bowed his head and his followers arranged themselves in a circle, hands joined. Taking his place at their head, he looked at each in turn.

'Before we subject our sister to this *unpleasantness*, I would ask you to make your report. Do any of you have an answer? Mr Merriglass, what word among the exorcists?'

The vicar shook his head. 'None.'

'Miss Roper? Miss Worple? What of the witches?'

'A good deal of chatter,' said Miss Roper.

'Nothing definite,' said Miss Worple.

'And the mediums, Mrs Glock? Mr Carter?'

'The spiritual ether is abuzz with talk of the device,' Margery Glock said.

'But that's all it is,' Carter snorted. 'Talk.'

'I myself have gleaned nothing from my necromancy colleagues.' Arthur turned to Christina Nugent. 'And what of you, sister?'

The confused woman did not speak.

'Then I'm sorry, but we have no choice.'

Mrs Glock looked up, tears shimmering. 'It's perfectly all right, really . . . '

Arthur raised his hands like a priest giving a benediction. 'Then let the question be asked.'

Each member of the Circle opened their mouths wide. From the back of gaping throats came a deep and unwavering hum. It was a strangely sad sound, like the drone of a late summer wasp dying on the windowsill. With eyes shut and hands firmly linked, the Circle did not stop for air but continued to project that haunting, melancholy note.

'They're summoning the *terrenus*,' Nick whispered. 'Using an old Babylonian ritual by the look of it. This is basic stuff.'

Arthur lowered his hands and came to stand at the centre of the Circle. His face was grey, his eyes like coals cooling in a mound of ash. As the wind screamed through the shattered door, he took a bone-handled dagger from his pocket. Without the slightest hesitation, he pressed the belly of the blade into his palm.

'*Terrenus phasmatis!* Latched spirit! Earthlocked soul, come to us! With thy knowledge of secret things and hidden mysteries, answer our question . . . '

Blood fell and a scarlet pool formed at Arthur's feet. A pool that began to spit and bubble like the contents of a cauldron.

'Where is the treasure?'

Emma felt a cold chill shiver along her spine. She glanced at Nick. His jaw was set rigid but he couldn't hide the shock in his eyes.

'Who in Milton Lake has possession of this most powerful device? Where can we lay our hands on the Edison machine? Tell us! TELL US!'

Emma felt her legs weaken. She almost stumbled outside the protective triangle.

The Circle did *not* possess the ghost machine.

They never had.

23

The Circle's uncanny humming came to a halt. Every eye was fixed on the smoking puddle of Arthur Torve's blood while the leader himself pocketed the dagger and stepped back to join hands with his followers. Emma's gaze roved around the circuit of strained faces. Reaching the white-haired Roper and Worple, she paused.

Suddenly that conversation between Mr Carter and the two old ladies came back to her. They had been talking about Henry's experience at Funland—

'*I suppose seeing Hiram Sparrow raised from the dead would be enough to scare anyone. Unfortunate, the boy being there.*'

'*Only if he forgets what he saw.*'

That jarring word: *forgets.* Believing that the Circle were the ones operating the machine, Emma and Nick had naturally concluded that Henry had been kept prisoner to prevent him telling anyone what he saw. Namely, that his father had been present when the first spirit came through. But if that was the case, then surely Miss Roper would have thought it unfortunate if Henry *remembered* what he saw. Now the odd phrasing made sense. The Circle hadn't been trying to wipe Henry's memories, they'd been attempting to extract them in order to find a clue as to the identity of the necromancer.

'We've all been chasing ghosts,' Nick laughed bitterly, 'while the real necromancer remains in the shadows.'

'Except the spirits aren't coming through any more,' Emma reminded him. 'Whoever's doing this, they've stopped.'

'For now. But the Circle won't allow the machine to sit idle. That's why they're summoning the *terrenus*—not for instructions on how to use it but to tell them where it is.'

Arthur's voice rose to a pitch that almost matched the screech of the wind.

'By the blood and the song, I call you. By the auras of the seven here assembled I bind you. Latched spirit, come forth!'

Emma narrowed her eyes against the gale howling through the shattered door. For a moment, it felt as if a breath of air had taken hold of her hand and was tugging her forward, out of the protective triangle and towards the Circle. In the next instant, the wind dropped to a whisper. The museum now looked like a winter wonderland, every surface glazed with snow. The Circle had not lifted their eyes from the frothing pool of blood.

All at once, the surface gave a violent shudder and a small hand broke through.

A child—a little girl—rose up out of the floor. First came the hand with its nails chewed to the quick; then the plump face framed with red curls and splashed with freckles; then the body clothed in a dress decades out of date. Barefoot, she stepped from the pool and padded over to where Margery Glock stood shivering and weeping.

'Hello, Mummy.'

Emma turned to Nick. 'I remember. Something Rowan told me ages ago: I'd been complaining about Mrs Glock, saying she was a nosy old busybody, and Mum said I shouldn't be too hard on her. That Dr and Mrs Glock had once suffered a terrible tragedy. They'd had a daughter called Alice who drowned in the lake. Mrs Glock had been sunbathing on the shore, she'd only closed her eyes for a couple of minutes. Next thing, people were screaming and rushing into the water. That was over thirty years ago . . .'

Now that she came to look closer, Emma could see that Alice Glock's dress was weighed down with lake water and that her curls were braided with reeds.

'Mrs Glock was there when she drowned,' Nick said. 'Alice latched on to her mother's aura. She's been with her ever since.'

'And Mrs Glock's known all this time?'

'She's a medium, a special case. Most people with latched spirits have no idea a ghost is sheltering in their aura. And even if they are aware, they can't directly communicate. Not unless the ghost wants to talk or it's summoned by ritual and bound to answer.'

Margery was on her knees before the spirit of her daughter.

'I'm sorry, darling, but we need your help.'

'I don't want to help you, Mother.' The little girl shook her head sadly. 'What you're doing is wrong. The unmade should never be summoned.'

Despite appearances, Alice spoke with maturity and confidence. Emma realized that, although she looked like a five-year-old child, she had in fact been at her mother's side for thirty years, watching and listening. The spirit had grown up while the body remained frozen at the point of death.

Arthur stared down at the dead girl with a coldness Emma had never seen before.

'You *will* answer our questions. You are bound by the blood and the song to do so. You must tell us the location of the Edison machine.'

Alice closed her eyes. Tracks of lake water coursed down her face like tears.

'The device was stolen from its creator, Randall Wolfe. It now resides in Milton Lake but its exact location is hidden.'

'You cannot tell us who has possession of it?' Mr Merriglass asked.

'No. It is masked.'

'There's a stranger in town,' Arthur said. 'An American. We've tried identity spells, but so far his real name has proven elusive. The indications from our spirit readers suggest that he is not in possession of the machine, for there appears to be no signal emanating from the Sparrow House. Still, his presence is strange. He has developed a relationship with my niece, Emma Rhodes, and she has shown knowledge of necromancy. Tell us, Alice, what is their role in this business?'

Watery eyes flashed to the corner of the room. 'They are hunters.'

'You mean they're looking for the machine, too?'

'They seek it to keep it safe from unskilled meddlers.'

'You are not here to judge us!'

Arthur came forward in a rush and took the ghost child by the throat. A cry of horror went up from the Circle and Mr Merriglass had to move quickly in order to catch Margery Glock. The mother of the latched spirit had fallen into a dead faint. Under Arthur's grasp, Alice writhed and choked, lake water gurgling from her lips.

'You must never touch a *terrenus*,' Nick growled. 'If you handle them too roughly their link to the host aura could be permanently severed.'

Standing over Alice, Arthur tightened his grip. The cries of neither the living nor the dead could move him.

'You will tell me the *exact* location of the machine.'

'I cannot!' Alice cried. 'The machine is masked. But I can tell you where it *was*, before it came here.'

'We know where it was. Randall Wolfe's mansion.'

'After that. It didn't come straight to the Lake. The machine was taken by the thief back to his lair. Taken to the Phantasmagorium.'

The Circle gave a collective gasp and Arthur stumbled away from the child. Out of the corner of her eye, Emma saw Nick's hands curl into fists.

'You—you may leave us,' Arthur murmured. 'The song is over, you are free.'

Alice padded over to where an unconscious Margery Glock had been laid on the snow-dusted floor. She squatted onto her haunches and took her mother's hand. Slowly, the pool of blood began to shrink until only a drop of crimson remained. When that too started to vanish, the little girl faded like a snowflake in the sun. As a shimmer, then a shadow, then a memory, she spoke her final warning.

'When the gates are broken and the dead fill the streets, the thief will come to reclaim his prize. Woe betide anyone who stands in the necromancer's path . . . '

Miss Roper was the first to break the silence.

'Well, there's an end to it.'

'Roper's right,' Miss Worple said. 'Whoever has possession of the machine, they are clearly an agent of the Phantasmagorium. If we act against them we'll be acting against *him*.'

Merriglass shivered. 'And that would be suicide.'

'Agreed,' Carter said solemnly.

Mrs Nugent opened her mouth as if to speak. Her lips did not form the words and the voice that projected from the back of her throat was not her own.

'Who is this man? I've not heard of him.'

Emma recognized the voice immediately.

'It's Mrs Lorne,' she said, dumbfounded. 'Sas's mother . . . Sas, he looks after his mum because she's pretty much housebound; she has problems with her legs and—'

'It's a temporary possession spell,' Nick nodded. 'Arthur found someone he knew for Mrs Lorne to possess. That way she could still attend the Circle's meetings without leaving home.'

'And Mrs Nugent? What about her?'

'The spell's harmless. She won't remember any of this, although her conscious mind is striving to take back control of her body.'

Emma was about to question him further when her attention was drawn back to the Circle. Mr Merriglass had mentioned a name that stirred a recent memory.

' . . . he is known by many aliases, but currently he is Edgar Lemuel Dritch. I suppose he likes the sound of it: E. L. Dritch, eldritch—an arcane word for a malevolent force. No one knows his real name nor how old he is. Some say he's lived in the shadows for centuries, one of the original Seven Necromancers.'

'Rubbish,' Carter cried. 'The Seven predate the Delphic Oracle, the Egyptian pantheon, the ancient Sumerian gods themselves!'

Merriglass shrugged. 'All I know is that Dritch was second only to Randall Wolfe in his knowledge and skill. For some reason, he's sent Wolfe's machine to Milton Lake. Up to this point, we can plead that everything we've done to steal it was carried out in ignorance of his plans. He may be merciful, but only if we withdraw from the field.'

'But what are his plans?' Worple wondered.

'Ours is not to reason why,' Merriglass said. 'Ours is but to stand aside, unless we have a hankering to see the colour of our entrails.'

'Is he really that dangerous?' asked the absent Mrs Lorne.

'If you believe the stories, and I *do*,' Merriglass emphasized, 'then the owner of the Phantasmagorium may well be the old enemy himself.'

Arthur cast a sullen glance at the vicar of St Jerome's.

'Merriglass is right. I've heard stories of Edgar Dritch . . . ' A flicker of fear entered those coal black eyes. 'This conclave is at an end.'

The lawyer's long coat snapped behind him as he stalked out of the museum and into the tempest. A nervous and defeated Circle exchanged a few unhappy words before following their leader's example, Merriglass and Carter carrying the still unconscious Margery Glock between them. When the last of the cars had pulled away, Nick stepped out of the protective triangle and towards the shattered door. Emma had to jog to keep up.

'What now?' she asked, breathless.

'Now? Nothing.'

'But there's still someone out there trying to summon the unmade.'

Nick passed through the door and into the car park.

'You're right,' he called over the gale. 'The Milton Lake necromancer has to be stopped, but here's the thing . . . '

They reached the forest. Through naked branches, snow was falling thick and fast.

'There's only one way to unmask our mystery necromancer: I have to go to the Phantasmagorium and find out why Dritch gave the machine away.'

'Great. So let's go.'

Long strides brought them to the thicket where the Thunderbird nested.

'*I* have to do this, Emma. Alone.'

'Don't be ridiculous,' she laughed. 'Of course I'm coming with you.'

'No, you're not. Didn't you hear a word of what was said back there? I told you the Circle was ruthless and desperate, yet all their schemes fell apart at the mention of one name. So no, I'm not going to take you to his lair, Emma. Do you think I don't care about you at all?'

He grabbed the handles of the bike and dragged it from the brambles.

'It's because I care about *you* that I'm going.'

'Emma, no.'

'I'm going with you, Nick.'

'I said, no.'

'I'm going with you or I'll slash your tyres.'

Quick as a flash, she whipped out her Swiss Army knife and grazed it along the back wheel. Furious hazel eyes snapped from the exposed blade to Emma's lopsided smile. Nick shook his head . . . and burst out laughing.

'You're completely insane!'

'Say something original.'

'All right. I love you.'

She opened her mouth to speak, then promptly closed it again.

Sitting astride the Thunderbird, Nick held out her helmet.

'Just gonna stand there gawping, Miss Rhodes? It's time we kicked up some dust.'

24

Nick killed the engine and Emma eased her aching body from the saddle. The city in which Edgar Dritch had his base was only a fifty-minute journey from Milton Lake; even so, the storm had made the drive hard going. Now, with wind and snow blasting against them, they pushed their way across the street.

PHANTASMAGORIUM

Painted in scrolling letters on a scarlet background, the faded sign arced over the little door. The Phantasmagorium, drab, hunched, and inconspicuous, stood amid a row of perfectly ordinary shops on a perfectly ordinary city street. Next door was a newsagent, on the other side, a pharmacy with a neon cross buzzing in the window. Passers-by might cast the odd baffled glance at the name, but the shop sported such a dull exterior it would hardly excite much curiosity. Stencilled onto the tinted windows were the words:

SPECIALIST TRADERS IN RARE ARTEFACTS

VIEWING BY APPOINTMENT ONLY

'Sure I can't talk you out of this?' Nick said.

She tried her best to sound brave. 'Pretty sure.'

'I'm serious. I don't want you going in there, Emma . . . but I won't stop you. My grandpa taught me a thing or two, protection spells and the like, but all they'll do is buy us some time. We don't even know what to look for,' Nick sighed. 'What if—?'

'Let's tackle one problem at a time. First we have to figure out *how* to get inside.'

It was as if she had spoken a magical command. The lock clicked and the door of the Phantasmagorium swung smoothly inwards. Beyond, a half-lit corridor stretched away like a yawning yellow throat.

'I guess this means we were expected.'

Nick turned away from the door and pressed his back against the window of the newsagent's. The revolver he pulled from his pocket gleamed under the orange streetlight. He snapped his wrist and the chamber was released. From another pocket, he took out six bullets, loaded the weapon and clicked the chamber back into position.

'My grandfather Oliver's Colt,' he whispered. 'Lead bullets.'

A high, cheerful voice with an edge of razor-sharp mockery called out from the gaping mouth of the Phantasmagorium:

'Come in and close the door behind you. It's colder than purgatory tonight.'

Nick took Emma's hand and together they crossed the threshold. No sooner were they inside than the door slammed shut. The crack reverberated down the dingy passage and echoed like a gunshot in some cavernous space beyond. The darkness was now almost complete; all that Emma could see of Nick was the pale print of his face floating beside her. Her palm was greased with sweat, yet his felt dry as a bone.

Nick pressed a small torch into her hand. Emma found the switch and was about to cast the beam around when he uttered a gargled oath.

'Don't . . . ' He swallowed. 'Whatever you do, don't look at the walls.'

Although she trusted him completely, Emma had never been able to resist a mystery. She moved the torchlight and, for the first time, saw the walls of the corridor clearly. A dull yellow, she had thought them, but close up those ratty strips of wallpaper looked more like the feverish yellow of jaundiced skin. Yes, very like human ski—

Her hand flew to her mouth and she looked back towards the door.

'Now, now, young lady,' called the mocking voice, 'there is no going back. You have come seeking answers and, being a generous soul, I'm willing to provide them. Muster your courage and venture forth into my Aladdin's cave.'

Nick stroked his thumb against the back of her hand, a gesture of reassurance.

At the end of the corridor a patch of blue light flickered like a will-o'-the-wisp. They followed this glimmer into what appeared to be a kind of warehouse. Judging by the tiny shop front, Emma would never have believed the interior of the

Phantasmagorium could be so large. Plain brick walls ran away into the distance and reached up to a ceiling that could only just be glimpsed. Things half-seen stirred in those faraway rafters; a host of bright-eyed, long-clawed, leather-skinned shadows that Emma hoped would remain hidden. It was almost as cold here as it had been in the street, although the crisp smell of snow had been replaced by the mouldy, medieval scent of incense and old books.

'What is this place?'

Nick squeezed her hand. 'The darkest treasure house in the world.'

It was indeed a maze of wonders. From the point at which they entered, several pathways branched off, the walls of which were made up of stack upon stack of bizarre artefacts. The source of the blue light was not obvious, yet its unearthly glow shimmered over every weird surface.

'Which way?' Emma asked.

The voice returned. 'Take the third path and do not deviate from it. There are certain items in my collection which do not like to be disturbed, especially by human hands.'

Together, they started down the third path. As their torchlight flashed over impossible marvels, Emma's eyes grew wider and her heart beat faster. Arranged along the thirteen shelves of an immensely long bookcase was a vast collection of specimen jars, each filled with thick grey fluid. Floating inside were what appeared to be the skinned bodies of a thousand felines. Far larger than any cat Emma had ever seen, these drowned monsters clawed at their glass cages as if still alive.

They hurried on, past a luminous broadsword that hovered in midair and a passage of mirrors in which they glimpsed themselves as animated corpses. Another turn brought them to a towering tree planted directly into the concrete floor. Instead of branches, human hands sprouted from the gnarled trunk, snatching, reaching, clutching, and grasping. Opposite the tree stood a great table cluttered with chalices and goblets. Insects the like of which Emma had never seen crawled from cup to cup, dragging tiny effigies of men behind them. Looking closer, she saw that the men were moving and their miniature mouths, screaming.

On, on. Past iron maidens with eyeholes full of blood; past the mummified heads of things half-animal, half-human; past a huge water tank in which the tentacles of some leviathan horror swooped and swirled. On, on. Down passages lined with monoliths that looked older than Stonehenge, each carved with dread and ancient symbols; down pathways filled with cages in which shrieking and invisible prisoners were held; down avenues piled high with the bodies of . . . No. Emma turned away.

More twists. More turns. More shrieks and sobs, slithers and scratchings. She was beginning to wonder if this labyrinth went on for ever when Nick came to a halt. They appeared to have reached the heart of the maze, a roughly circular space the size of Milton Lake's market square. The blue light was stronger here, yet still its glow was no brighter than a misty moonbeam. It illuminated a tall curtained box which stood by itself at the midst of the circle. Beside the box was a table upon which lay a leather-bound book, thick as a telephone directory.

'Welcome, children.' The mocking voice tittered from behind the curtain.

'What is that thing?' Emma asked.

'A spirit cabinet,' Nick said. 'Mediums used to be placed inside curtained cabinets during their séances. They'd be bound with ropes and chains while they communicated with the dead.'

'Very good, young man.'

The curtain was wrenched back. Seated inside the cabinet was one of the oldest men Emma had ever seen—a shrunken figure dwarfed by the armchair on which he was perched. The little man was dressed in a smart pinstriped suit with a pink carnation in the buttonhole. The skin was pulled tight around his hairless head so that, although clearly ancient, he did not possess a single wrinkle. With sunken eyes rolled white and a toothless mouth hanging open, the fearsome necromancer appeared to be fast asleep.

Nick took a step forward. 'You're not Edgar Dritch.'

The man shuffled his shoulders and rolled his head, as if shrugging off a twinge.

'*I* am Edgar Dritch. This—' like a badly operated string puppet, the man tapped the side of his hand against his breast, 'is my employee, Mr Kitsune.'

The voice of Dritch came fully formed through Kitsune's open lips.

'Temporary possession,' Emma said. 'Like Sas's mother and Mrs Nugent.'

'You've taught the girl well, my friend,' Dritch said. 'Who is she?'

'I thought you knew everything,' Nick answered. 'So where are you, shopkeeper?'

'Christmas in New York.' Something like a smile lifted the corners of the old man's mouth. 'I haven't set foot in this city since it was called New Amsterdam and all the settlers were wearing beaver pelts on their heads.'

'What are you doing there?'

'Buying a mirror, if you must know.'

'I didn't think you'd leave the country, not with such a powerful prize on your doorstep.' Nick took another step towards the cabinet. 'What's going on? A *terrenus* told us that you were the one who stole the ghost machine from Randall Wolfe. Why go to all that effort just to sell it to some hopeless necromancer from Milton Lake?'

'All about the secrets, aren't you, boy?' Dritch chuckled. 'You wish me to tell you a tale? Why not? For when the telling is done I'll have a little job for you and your pretty associate.'

Now it was Nick's turn to chuckle. 'You think we'd work for you?'

'I think you will, yes. In fact, I'd wager my treasure trove upon it.'

'You'd lose your bet.' Emma joined Nick in front of the curtain. It felt strange, addressing the necromancer through the senses of his aged employee. A bit like a human telephone, she supposed. 'There's no way Nick would ever help you.'

'Spirited,' the old man nodded. 'And blind to the wonders all around her.'

'Just tell your story,' Nick snapped.

'Mind your tongue, boy, or I'll tear it out and feed it to the pretties overhead.'

Emma lifted her gaze to the shadows in the rafters. When she looked down again, she saw Nick's hand steal to his pocket and tighten around the Colt.

'Now, are you sitting comfortably? Then I'll begin . . . I had, of course, always coveted the machine created by my rival, Randall Wolfe. The story of its construction you know. It was, after all, your forebear Oliver who witnessed its first testing. Wolfe's real genius lay in his discovery of a stable fragment of ectoplasm through which a call to the gates could be made. Try as I might, I could not replicate that achievement, and so was unable to build my own spirit telephone. Only one option then: I must steal the device and examine it for myself.

'Over eighty years passed, during which not only I but a host of necromancers tried to wrest control of the machine from Wolfe. None could overpower him. But then, just over a month ago, I saw my chance. Through various connections, I learned that Wolfe was about to attempt a summoning. It wasn't the greatest of necromancy feats, but it did mean his attention would be focused elsewhere. Knowing the timing of the ritual, if I could stage a sudden strike at his stronghold then the element of surprise might be enough to overwhelm his defences. So it proved. I smashed his magically trained guards and was inside the mansion before Wolfe had a chance to react. What happened next . . . '

Again, that mocking laughter. 'Well, I won't spoil the last chapter of someone else's story. Suffice to say, I managed to find my way to Wolfe's inner sanctum and deal my rival a lethal blow. I snatched the ghost machine from his cold, dead hand. At least, I *thought* he was dead, but the king of necromancers had one last surprise up his sleeve.'

All the merriment vanished from Edgar Dritch's voice. 'With his last breath, Wolfe cast a most ingenious spell. A curse upon his killer. I could steal, purchase, beg or borrow any supernatural object in existence, but I could not use it until its power had been *fully* accessed by another. Of course, in most cases that would mean the object would then be in the possession of a gifted magician who would not willingly hand it back to me. Moreover, in the case of the ghost machine, fully realizing its power would lead to the mass summoning of the unmade and the smashing of the gates. No sensible necromancer would do such a thing. It was an impossible dilemma. Until . . . '

'Someone from Milton Lake came looking for the machine,' Emma said. 'Someone desperate to summon ghosts.'

'Exactly. I sold the machine to this individual for a pittance.'

'But they've stopped using it,' Nick said. 'There hasn't been any spirit activity in the Lake for days.'

'Check your instrument.'

Nick pulled the detector from his pocket and made adjustments to the antennae.

'I'll focus the signal back towards the Lake. It should . . . Oh God.'

He turned the little window to Emma. The needle behind the glass had flipped into the red.

'They've started using it again. Some time after we left town . . . Hundreds and hundreds of calls. Emma, if this continues—'

'They'll blow a hole in the gates large enough for all the dead of Milton Lake to come streaming through.' Dritch nodded his puppet's head. 'Time for you to get back on that bike of yours and put an end to this. Afterwards, *if* you survive, Kitsune will make contact with you and arrange to collect my property.'

Emma bristled. 'Nick would never give the machine to you.'

'What choice does he have? Every addle-brained necromancer and two-bit Circle in the world will come looking for it. His life and yours will be in constant danger.'

'But you're just like them. You'll use it to hurt people.'

'Of course I will, but I'll also use it prudently. I know the limits of the machine and have no wish to swamp the world with the lunatic dead. So go back to your little town and do your best to save it. Kitsune will see you on the other side.'

Nick turned away from the cabinet. 'Come on, Emma.'

'But—'

'Come on,' he repeated. 'We have work to do.'

The black curtains swished together, hiding the old man from view.

'One last thing,' Dritch's voice rang out. 'If you wish to know the identity of our hopeless necromancer you need only consult the ledger on the table. Flip back to the fourteenth of the month and you'll find the name.'

Emma went straight to the leather-bound book. She rifled the crackling pages and a blur of neatly inscribed entries flashed by. Somewhere near the end of this vast tome lay the secret for which they had been searching. The name of the Milton Lake necromancer. She reached the page and traced a shaking finger down the entries.

A date and description:

14th December—

Randall Wolfe's 'Ghost Machine' (also known as the Edison Spirit Telephone). Sold to

She had to read the name three times. To see it written there, bold and clear, felt like a punch to the gut. And yet hadn't she suspected something like this all along? If not the Circle, then who else connected to Milton Lake could possibly be involved with the ghost machine?

Tears swam and made the name blurry.

She felt Nick's arm around her shoulder.

'It's her . . .'

And now they were running back down the avenue of horrors.

Running as fast as their legs could carry them.

Dr R Rhodes

'My mother.'

25

Emma could hardly hear the roar of the bike over the gale. Layer by layer, fold upon fold, the snow pressed down, shrinking the world to a narrow envelope. There was neither sky nor road, just grainy white walls wavering on every side. They had left the city over an hour ago, but without landmarks it was impossible to tell how far they had travelled. Lost in the storm of her thoughts, she clung to Nick.

Her mother had bought the stolen ghost machine from Dritch. Of course it was her: the woman who had pursued her studies into the supernatural until they'd taken over her life. The only person from Milton Lake, other than the Circle, who might have knowledge of the machine's existence and the contacts who could put her in touch with Dritch. Why had she purchased it? That was easy. It had always been about Richie . . .

Blue lights sliced through the storm. Nick eased up on the throttle as the police Land Rover came slowly into view, like a ghost ship emerging out of the fog. A barricade had been placed over the road, although the fence was already half-buried in snow. Emma caught sight of the 'Milton Lake Welcomes Careful Drivers' sign: they had reached the crest of Winter Heights and were within a few hundred metres of the dip leading down into the valley.

Nick turned off the engine and together they trudged towards the Land Rover.

'What's going on?' he bellowed over the gale.

A young officer eased himself out of the jeep and Emma caught a blast of warm air from the radiator. It felt like heaven.

'Avalanche. Big deposits of snow have collected up in the hills over the past few days. With the extra fall tonight, the weight was too much. No one injured, thank God.'

'Any other way in?'

'Nah. Entire town's cut off. Should have a digger out first thing. Meantime, there's a motel back on the motorway. I can call a car to take you there. Not safe.' He nodded towards the Thunderbird. 'Riding that in the storm.'

'This is real important,' Nick hissed through cold-clenched teeth. 'Life or death. That jeep of yours looks sturdy enough to handle a bit of snow. Can't you drive us?'

'No can do. Got orders to stay here and make sure people see the barricade.'

'Listen to me!' Nick shouted. 'There are people in danger. We need to—'

The officer snapped into authoritarian mode. 'You don't *need* to do anything, sir. Now step away from the vehicle or I'll be forced to . . . ' His snow-flaked lashes blinked as he focused on Emma. 'Miss, could you move into the headlights?'

'What for?'

'I need to get a better look at you.'

She rounded the front of the Land Rover, the screaming winds pressing hard, almost as if they were trying to push her back. Filtered through the snow, the headlights fluttered like weak yellow flames. The officer ducked into the Land Rover and grabbed a bundle of paperwork from the dash.

'Are you Emma Rhodes of Connolly Avenue?'

'Yes.'

'You go to Tennyson Academy?'

She knew what he was going to say before the words steamed from his lips.

'Miss Rhodes, I'm arresting you on suspicion of arson. You do not need to say—'

'What's all this about?' Nick cut in.

The officer turned stiffly. 'This evening we recovered CCTV footage from the fire that destroyed the Smedley Memorial Library. It shows Miss Rhodes at the scene.'

Emma guessed that the spirit of Evelyn Smedley had not shown up on film. All the investigating officers would have seen was Emma retreating from a room soon to be engulfed in flames. Even if she now claimed that the fire had started accidentally, they'd ask why she hadn't spoken up before.

Nick was busy playing defence barrister, arguing that the footage was only circumstantial evidence, when a high-pitched squeal sounded from his pocket. Lawyer act forgotten, he wrenched out the detector and turned its antennae towards the valley. The device gave a banshee shriek and the glass of the indicator panel cracked.

'It's happened.' He turned bleak eyes on Emma. 'She's made too many calls. The machine's gone into overdrive and the gates have been breached. We have to—'

An ear-splitting, air-shivering boom exploded out of Milton Lake. Its vibrations sent a tidal wave of snow streaming up the valley and over the heads of the three people gathered on the hill. The acoustic tsunami folded back the smaller trees of Black Acre, shattered the Land Rover's wing mirrors, and knocked Emma, Nick, and the officer onto their backs. A moment of darkness followed, although Emma didn't think she had passed out. It felt more like her senses rewiring themselves after a power overload.

Nick was already on his feet. Before joining him at the barricade, she checked on the officer. He'd been knocked out by the fall but didn't seem seriously hurt.

'Guess I won't be needing this any more.' Nick threw the broken detector into the forest. 'Jesus, Emma, what are we—?'

From the storm clouds it came, a spear of ectoplasmic light stabbing at the heart of Milton Lake. The snow stopped and the wind fell to a murmur. It was difficult to be sure where exactly the luminous green lance had touched down, although its huge rippling reflection suggested a location close to the lake. From the base of the column, several writhing tentacles lashed out towards the town.

Streetlights flickered as, block by block, houses dipped into darkness. Now the only light source was the spear itself, throbbing and casting a spectral sheen over the valley. As the last of the boom faded from her ears, Emma could make out a chorus of frightened dogs and the odd isolated scream.

'Is there any way to stop this?' she whispered.

'I don't know. Maybe. But first we have to get down there.'

Over a mile of treacherous hill road lay between them and the town. The Thunderbird had no chance of making it through the drifts. Emma marched over to the Land Rover and pulled open the passenger door.

'Are you coming?'

'I'll ride shotgun.' Nick shrugged. 'I can't drive stick.'

'But I've only ever driven Bob's Mini around an empty car park.'

'Then this should be quite an adventure.' He looked down at the sleeping policeman. 'What about Elliott Ness here?'

'Guess we'll have to take him with us. Get him into the back.'

Nick picked up the officer as if he weighed no more than a toddler and deposited him in the jeep. The policeman had left the motor running, probably to keep himself from freezing to death. Emma flexed her fingers over the hot air spluttering from the radiator vents, depressed the clutch and shoved the gear stick into first.

The Land Rover leapt forward, crushing the plastic barrier under heavy wheels. With its edges marked out by trees, the buried road rolled on like a white river, the jeep rising and tumbling over its frozen waves. Judging by the level of snow against the old cedars, they were at least a metre and a half above the tarmac.

It wasn't until they reached the fork leading off towards Funland that they saw the first unmade. Slithering out from the spear, a green tentacle had reached up the hill all the way to the amusement park. There was no mystery as to why it had been drawn there. Eleven years ago this earth had been watered with the blood of souls taken before their time. How many of those killed by Hiram had chosen the light? How many had found a loved one to latch on to? Very few, judging by the numbers that now swarmed into the road.

'Keep going,' Nick barked. 'Don't stop.'

'But what if one of them melts its way into the car?'

He took out his great-grandfather's Colt and wound down the window.

'You drive, I'll clear the way.'

Emma stamped the accelerator and the four-by-four sped into the spectral throng. Some of the unmade scattered; those that weren't quick enough, or who had turned ravenous eyes on the occupants of the Land Rover, took a bullet in the head. Mercifully, Nick only had to fire off six rounds before the rest of the horde vanished into the trees.

They drove on. Occasionally she'd glimpse figures in the forest traipsing towards the town, some still bearing the injuries that had killed them. They walked with severed limbs cradled to their chests and gaping wounds spilling ectoplasm onto the forest floor. Whatever their condition, they all sang the same song:

'*Give us your lives . . . Your souls . . . Your flesh . . .*'

At the bottom of the hill, the avalanche had come to rest as a white mountain too formidable even for the jeep. Emma cut the engine and clambered out.

'What about him?' she called to Nick.

The officer was still unconscious on the back seat.

'We can't carry him,' Nick said. 'Best we can do is cover him with something and hope the unmade don't notice as they pass by.'

Emma found a blanket in the boot and draped it over the man who, minutes earlier, had wanted to arrest her for arson. Then she took Nick's hand and together they ascended the avalanche.

'You'll *have* to take me with you now,' she smiled. 'Not only am I a wanted arsonist, I've stolen a police car.' She noticed his expression and her smile faltered. 'You'll keep your promise, won't you? When this is over, we're going to leave together. You said—'

'Emma, look.'

From the top of the avalanche, they could see most of Milton Lake laid out below. The shouts and screams of the townspeople had been blocked by the snow mountain, but now the cacophony rang clearly through the freezing air. Dozens of abandoned cars had careered into the bottom of the avalanche, as if desperate drivers had thought they could smash their way through the snowdrift. Then there were the marks on the face of the mountain—long trails suggesting that, having left their cars, people had tried to escape on foot only to be overtaken and dragged back down the slope. Emma and Nick had passed no living soul on the hill. Unless they'd fled through the forest, it was unlikely that anyone had made it out of the town.

Everywhere Emma looked the dead were at their hungry work: peasants in medieval rags pulling people from cars; ladies in fine dresses snarling like dogs over the body of a little girl; an armour-clad knight pressing his gauntleted fist into the face of an elderly woman; soldiers in Second World War uniforms holding down a policeman while their comrade crushed his soul; a druid with a long white beard sinking slowly into the body of a terrified teenager.

Emma looked to the spear that breached the clouds.

'The bridge is still open. More are coming through.'

Nick nodded. 'We have to get to Connolly Avenue.'

She was desperate to get home, too. Incapacitated by his injuries, Bob would need help to protect himself from the phantoms. Unless, of course, Julia had taken him back to the Torves'. If that was the case then, for the first time, Emma was grateful for the Circle's interest in the supernatural. Unskilled as they were, they might know enough to ward off the unmade. That could mean Henry and Sas were safe, too.

'Why do you need to get to the Sparrow House?' she gasped as they raced down the white mountain. 'Shouldn't we be heading to the lake?'

'It's a pit stop. Something I need to pick up.'

'A weapon?'

'Maybe. We'll see.'

It wasn't far from the base of the avalanche to the turn for Connolly Avenue. Nevertheless, they still had to run a nightmare gauntlet. On one corner they saw a woman in Elizabethan gown and ruff, jewelled fingers melting into the face of a weeping girl. It was only when she looked closer that Emma recognized Lola Flick.

'We can't help her,' Nick said, drawing her on.

'But you've got the gun—'

'They're connected now. If I use the gun on the ghost I'll kill the girl.'

The same was true for every phantom and victim they passed. Many ghosts were still in search of vessels to possess, but the majority of the townspeople had already been claimed. Housed within living bodies, the unmade tottered towards car windows so that they might admire their new reflections.

Among the few still unclaimed, Emma and Nick were soon identified as choice meat. Reloading the Colt as they ran, Nick fired off a dozen shots to clear their path. Showers of ectoplasm splattered across pavements and well-tended lawns, the shrieking dead falling to left and right.

It appeared to grow gradually quieter as they approached their destination. Like the rest of the roads, Connolly Avenue was choked with deserted cars and strewn with clothes and possessions abandoned in the rush. In the whole street only two doors were firmly shut: Emma's and the Sparrow House. Did that mean Bob and Julia were still inside or had they received early warning from Arthur Torve? Emma found it difficult to imagine her rational father surrounded by a circle of necromancers. Tonight, all of his beliefs would be called into question as Bob was confronted with life after death, diabolical possession, and hungry spectres.

Nick handed her the Colt. 'I'll meet you back here in a couple of minutes.'

'I've never fired a gun before.'

'It's easy.' He placed her finger inside the trigger guard and her thumb on the hammer. 'Release the safety, aim, and shoot. OK?'

'Yeah.' The Colt sank to her side. 'Don't be long.'

Nick sped across the road, cleared the tumbledown fence and disappeared into the Sparrow House. Emma gave the avenue a final glance. It was difficult to believe that this forsaken nightmare could be the same street on which Bob had taught her to ride a bike. Bob and Rowan. They were like fictional characters to her now, the father who'd pulled the plug and the mother who summoned spirits.

Bob's coat was missing from its peg and his key had gone from the hook. She checked every room, upstairs and down, clicking useless switches as she went. Sometimes Bob would leave a note by the fruit bowl, but when she re-entered the kitchen there was no note to be found. Her stomach rumbled. She couldn't remember the last time she'd eaten. She plucked an orange from the bowl and pressed it to her nose, breathing in the zesty tang of the peel. The scent stirred a memory—

Vvwwp, Vvwwp—Vvwwp, Vvwwp

The message alert almost shocked her into dropping the gun. She placed the Colt on the table and slipped the mobile from her pocket. Maybe it was Bob . . .

His Name is Medway. EL Dritch

The phone fell from her fingers and clattered to the floor.

In her mind, she heard again the jump of the record. The *deliberately* made scratch in the wax groove: *My name is Oliver* skip—*dway*. The name of his great-grandfather obscured. There could be only one reason for such concealment—the truth behind the name must be out there somewhere.

She hardly stopped to consider how Dritch had got hold of her number or why he'd given her this final clue. Perhaps he had some dark motive or simply wanted to cause trouble for Nick. Whatever his reasons, Emma could not ignore the information. She had honoured her promise as long as she could, now she must know. The final straw had been reached at the summit of the avalanche when she'd asked if he still intended to take her with him when he left Milton Lake. He had been so positive before, yet there, on the white mountain, it was as if he had changed his mind. Well, she could no longer build her hopes on the shifting sands of Nicholas Redway . . . Medway.

She went to Bob's study and started pulling books from the shelves. Luckily, her phone had only been scuffed by the fall and so she could use its light to read by. The thick Edison biography was hiding between an old Tennyson yearbook and a copy of Newton's *Arithmetica Universalis*. Emma slammed the book onto the desk and turned to the index. She found what she was looking for as a tiny footnote:

MEDWAY, Oliver: Pinkerton agent and bodyguard to Edison from c. April–November 1920.

The entry confirmed that the name Dritch had given was genuine. She pulled up a search engine on her phone and typed 'Nicholas Medway, Mearsville'. No direct results, but a related link from the archives of the *Cumberland Chronicle* almost caused her to drop the phone again. Her heart sang and tears spiked the corners of her eyes. The truth at last. The truth at her fingertips.

She clicked.

Mearsville Tragedy Latest

The print became a blur. She couldn't focus on the story. Her gaze passed over the black and white picture of the rutted road and clapboard farmhouse that she had seen so often in her visions. The only thing that mattered was the *other* picture. She clicked and enlarged until the grainy photograph filled the screen. Her blood thundered. Her thoughts burned. There was a rational explanation—there *had* to be.

The caption under the picture: *Nathan Medway, the deceased.*

Much as she tried to deny it, Emma knew the truth. She *knew* that face, had lost herself in those eyes, had kissed those lips. And now that she knew, the fragments began to slot into place. Like a modern necromancer, she summoned search engines to build the story that had been hidden from her . . .

A shadow in the doorway. She looked at him as if from the end of a long, dark tunnel. A tunnel of decades stretching back over sixty years to the Medway farm and the little town of Mearsville, Maine. She held out the phone with the photograph, and the boy nodded, his smile full of sorrow.

'Nicholas Redway doesn't exist. My name is Nathan. Grady Medway was my father, Oliver my grandfather. I was born October 23rd 1936 and I died December 17th 1953. I was seventeen years old when my father killed me.'

26

As she looked at him now, standing desolate in the doorway, Emma remembered something her father had said: *Most kids today live at a hundred miles an hour, but he has a quieter way about him.* Quieter, yes, almost as if he had lived at a time when the world moved at a slower pace. An era when the human race had stood on the threshold of annihilation . . . She remembered the incident of the school bell and how he'd dived under the desk. The automatic response of a child from the 1950s who had been taught the 'duck and cover' drill in case of nuclear attack.

And then there was the slip he had made about his soldier father and the Eighth Army Rangers. An online search had told her that this particular unit had been formed at the outbreak of the Korean War in 1950 and deactivated in 1951. It was Grady who, shell-shocked from service, had returned to Mearsville to spend his days staring at walls. And it was his son Nick—or Nathan to give him his proper name—who had tried to interest him again in his favourite movies.

The movies—*Harvey*, *The Wild One*, *Singing in the Rain*—all of them made in the fifties. She thought of the slang terms that had crept in unnoticed: the 'nabes', the 'greasers', the 'car-hops' and his ignorance of modern jargon like 'newbies' and 'down with that'. Then there were his dated manners which had so impressed Miss Lucas.

These and a hundred other clues had been obvious from the start. The crate of belongings that he'd claimed was his grandfather's but which in fact contained his own toys, magazines, and records. The lyrics of that song she had heard him crooning in the shower. A quick search had identified it as 'Something's Wrong', a Fats Domino number from 1953. The year of his death . . .

'Tell me.'

'Emma,' he sighed, 'we have to go.'

'Tell me!'

He bowed his head. 'Most of what I told you is true.'

'All the best lies are based on truth,' she snapped.

He came into the room and dropped onto the sofa opposite her father's desk, his head in his hands.

'I wanted to tell you, but how could I? You felt something for me, and I . . . ' He brushed back the tousled hair from his scar. 'I'd been alone for such a long time. I was scared that if you knew what I was, what I am, you wouldn't come with me. When I left.'

Despite the horrific story that she knew must come, a bud of hope blossomed in Emma's heart. He still meant her to go with him. The only question was whether she would feel the same, once his tale was told.

'Like I said, I was born October 23rd 1936. Grady and my mom were only fifteen years old. Grandpa Oliver had lost his wife five years before and didn't have a clue what to do with an unmarried son with a baby on the way. Soon as they turned sixteen, Mom and Pop got hitched and she came to live on the farm. I never knew my mother. Cancer took her before I could crawl. Mom's family didn't want anything to do with me after that, so it was left to Pop and Grandpa to bring me up.

'Soon as I could toddle, I was helping out on the farm. It was a hard life but a good one. Every night Oliver would tell us stories by the stove. My pop was about twenty years old by then, but he wasn't too grown up for a tale, even though he must've heard them a hundred times over. The only story Grandpa never told was the one about Edison and the ghost machine. He'd made the recording in thirty-one, but didn't play it to Grady until he'd reached eighteen. At the time, I don't think Pop believed his dad's wild story . . . '

'Life went on. When America entered the Second World War, my pop followed in his father's soldier footsteps. I was six years old and didn't understand what was going on. Grandpa's war stories seemed like romantic adventures, but here was my pop in army uniform, going away to face Messerschmitts and machine guns. I was terrified. But he came home all in one piece, just the same old pop as he'd ever been.

'I grew up a lot in those years. I don't know if it was all the exercise I was getting on the farm, but I seemed to shoot up and broaden out. By the time I reached high school, I was a head taller than anyone in my class and first pick for captain of the football team. 1950. This was our time, Emma. The decade of the teenager had begun, and I loved every minute of it—the clothes, the movies, the blues! Even the TV dinners.'

His smile faltered and a rutted track glistening with ice rose up in Emma's mind.

'But there was a darkness to those years, too. America was in an arms race with the Russians and everyone thought nuclear war was inevitable. Then, in June 1950, the US intervened to defend the South Koreans from an invasion by the communist North. The Korean War had begun. My dad was twenty-nine and eager to join up. Due to his experience in Germany, he was drafted into a special operations unit called the Eighth Army Ranger Company. He came back a year later, changed for ever.' Nick's face crumpled. 'I know now what he saw in Korea. I remember the horror as he remembered it, and so it's clear to me why he came home and stared at walls . . .'

Nick closed his eyes. 'It was a cold night in December fifty-three when I got the call. It was Maisie Hannigan, a waitress at the Mearsville Roadhouse. She said Pop had gotten himself into a fight with a couple of pool sharks and had come off worse. Grandpa was asleep so I took out our old flatbed truck and headed into town.

'Seventeen,' Nick sighed, 'and not a clue as I pulled into the Roadhouse that my final minutes were ticking by. Pop was hunched like a gargoyle on the trunk of a rusted to hell

Chevy sedan. He looked up as I sounded the horn and came staggering over. The only time he was mean was when he was oiled, and tonight he could barely stand. He barked at me to get out, he wanted to drive. I told him no, he could either ride beside me or on the flatbed. Eventually, he came round to the passenger side, hollering and cursing.

'It wasn't until we turned onto the farm track that the devil really got inside him. He . . . ' Nick glanced up. 'Emma, are you OK? Stay with me . . . '

His voice drifted, and with it, her father's study and the little house she had grown up in. The entire spirit-haunted town of Milton Lake faded away as she was dragged back through the decades.

Back to that fateful December night in 1953.

Perhaps it had been the promise that had kept her vision frozen on the road. Now that the truth had been told, Emma found herself free to float through the unfolding tragedy. It was as if she were a third passenger in the truck's cab. Through the flyspecked windscreen she could make out the farmhouse in the distance, pale streamers of dawn fluttering over its peaked roof. The truck jounced along the track. Behind the wheel, a boy of seventeen, careworn, yet without the deep sadness that she had seen in Nick's eyes. Next to him, a red-faced wreck with the same tousled brown hair and strong features.

'No respec',' he slurred. 'Hear me, boy? I sh'aid you got no resh'pec.'

Nick's knuckles were white around the wheel. 'I heard you, Pop.'

'Not you nor that ol' coot neither. The things I've sh'een. I deserve resh-pec!'

'You do. You got it.'

A bloodshot eye gave a sidelong blink. 'Mocking me, Nate?'

'No, sir.'

'Don't take kindly to mockery. Over there I . . . ' He slammed his big farmer's fist against the dash. 'You mocking the things I done and sh'een?'

'Pop, no. Never.'

The hurt in Nick's voice made Emma want to shout: *Leave him alone!* But she could no more speak than she could intervene when Grady grabbed the wheel.

'Lemme drive. Think I can't? I've drove sh'upply trucks through minefields. Gimme the goddam wheel or I'll beat you to Portland an' back—'

'Stop it! Pop, please . . . '

And now she was out of the cab and standing on the track. To her right, the roadside stall from which Nick and Oliver sold the farm's fruits and vegetables. To her left, the great shimmering wetland reaching out to a distant fringe of trees. Behind her, the farmhouse; in front, the leaping dazzle of the truck's headlights. They bore down on her, but Emma was not afraid, at least not for herself.

Tyres screeched on the ice-dusted ground as the truck swung violently to the right. The road stood a metre or so proud of the wetland, and so for a second or two the flatbed sailed through the air before nose-diving into the water. It was surprising how little noise it made, just a flat smack followed by a couple of throaty gurgles.

Emma was inside the cab again. She didn't feel the water nor the blows of Grady Medway as he thrashed about like a harpooned eel. His leg was caught under his seat and he was trying to lift his head above the rising water. He pressed his face into the envelope of air under the cab's roof while his hand grasped at his side. It was only as the vision panned down that Emma saw what he was reaching for.

'For the love of Jesus, grab hold! I'm sorry, Nate, so sorry, but you can't be . . . ' He hissed through his teeth, unable to say the word. 'Hold on, son!'

But Nathan—Nick—was already . . . *that* word. He had struck his head against the steering wheel and bright flowers of blood were blooming all around. There was no movement, no struggle to breathe. All Emma could think was *at least he didn't drown*. It was that comfort, cold as the wetlands, which accompanied her out of the vision . . .

Nick came slowly into focus. He had carried her to the sofa and propped a pillow under her head. She lifted a shaking hand and brushed back the hair from his scar.

'I saw you die. How . . . ?'

His smile was the saddest she had ever known.

'Sheriff arrived early to speak to Pop about the brawl at the Roadhouse. I think you've seen most of what happened next. Pop was half-dead when they dragged him out of the truck. Me?' Another sad smile. 'I was full dead.'

'So you latched onto your father,' Emma said. 'You became a *terrenus*.'

'No, Emma. The Night Watchmen came for me. Those hooded bastards took me to the gates and that's where I stayed for sixty years. Unmade.'

Emma thought she was going to be sick. 'But how? Why?'

'Why didn't I latch? Imagine your soul being wrenched from your body and knowing that your own father was the cause. How could I shelter in his aura?'

'OK,' Emma breathed, 'what happened next?'

'Pop was arrested. He admitted everything, even requested that the judge give him the longest sentence possible. The court ruled he was to serve ten years. It was five before Grandpa answered his letters and went upstate for a prison visit. Way Pop remembers it, they didn't speak two words to each other. Grandpa just handed over the record and went on his way. He died the following year.'

'The story of Thomas Edison and Randall Wolfe,' Emma nodded. 'Wolfe talked about Oliver sending someone to find him in London. He meant your father . . . '

'They released Pop in sixty-four and, with a small inheritance from Grandpa, he took the first flight to London. He found the ever-youthful necromancer waiting for him at the airport. Wolfe took my father to his mansion, where Pop demanded that he summon me back from the gates.'

Nick looked up as a pulse of green light throbbed through the study window.

'Emma, we need to go.'

Rising from the sofa, he picked up an object that he must have thrown onto the desk when Emma's vision had claimed her. It was a small curved dagger, its ivory hilt inset with blood-red rubies.

'What's that?'

He slipped the blade into a sheath on his belt and turned to the door.

'Come on, I'll tell you the rest on the way.'

The street outside remained deserted and an uneasy stillness had settled over Milton Lake. Emma and Nick had almost reached the corner when a front door swung open and Dr and Mrs Glock came stumbling out. Except it wasn't the Glocks. One look at those shuffling figures was enough to tell Emma that the doctor and his wife were now hosts to the unmade.

Nick pulled her behind a row of bins. They watched the 'Glocks' zombie-walk around the bend and pass out of sight. Emma wondered if the entire Circle had now been claimed by the kind of spectres that, for so many years, they had strived to summon. A bitter irony if so, and a worrying development. She had trusted in their meagre skills to provide safety for Henry, Sas, Bob, and Aunt Julia.

'Coast's clear,' Nick said. They were up and running again. 'We'll track through the forest, come to the lake under the cover of the trees.'

The lake. She remembered how reluctant he had been to approach those waters.

'Will you finish your story?'

A short run had brought them to the edge of Black Acre. From here it could be no more than a ten-minute walk to the point where the spear touched down. The place where

Dr Rowan Rhodes was busy working her necromancy madness. She had sacrificed an entire town in a desperate attempt to locate one particular soul. Emma glanced at Nick. After all the horrors she'd witnessed, *this* was the most terrifying revelation of all: the lengths to which a parent would go for the love of their child.

Nick resumed his tale.

27

'For ten years, all that Pop had been able to think about was his father's story of Edison and the ghost machine. He would pay any price, meet any challenge, as long as Wolfe agreed to summon me back from the dead.

' "We could use the machine to draw Nathan through the gates," Wolfe told him. "But it is *you* who must summon your son. You have a blood connection and so your voice will be the strongest."

'Pop jumped to his feet, eager to get started, but the necromancer didn't stir from his chair. He told my father that the summoning would take some time.

' "How long?"

' "Years." Wolfe shrugged. "Decades."

' "But Edison's wife came straight through."

' "That was a different case entirely," Wolfe said. "Why, you ask? Because, Mr Medway, Thomas Edison didn't kill his wife. You must understand, I created the ghost machine in order to hone the summoning signal so that a necromancer might call forth any spirit of his choosing—"

' "And that's just what I want to do!"

' "But spirits can hide themselves. Even with the ghost machine, I cannot locate an unmade that doesn't want to be found. Why would your son answer the summons of the man who killed him?"

' "Then I've lost him for ever."

' "I did not say that."

'Wolfe rose from his desk and went to a safe at the back of the room. He spun the combination dial and heaved open the heavy, armour-plated door. He returned a moment later with the machine in his hands.

' "I can teach you the mystic numerals, that is the work of moments, but then you must focus clearly on the soul you wish to summon. The realm beyond the gates is vast and the numbers of the unmade swell daily. It could take you a lifetime to find your son. In the meantime, you'll be my honoured guest. Perhaps I'll even teach you a few tricks of my trade." The necromancer smiled. 'It's been a long time since I had an apprentice . . . " '

Nick and Emma ploughed through the snow-smothered forest. To the west, the column of ectoplasmic energy grew brighter as they closed in on its source.

'It was a lie, of course,' Nick said.

'A lie? Didn't Wolfe want Grady as his apprentice?'

'Oh, he wanted that all right. He was lying about how long it would take to find me. For fifty years, Wolfe kept Grady at his side, teaching him the mysteries of the unseen world. All the while he pretended to help my father, telling him that with each call they were getting closer to finding me. It wasn't until the end, when Pop was old and grey, that he revealed the greatest secret of all: on that first night, the necromancer could have used the machine to summon me straight from the gates.'

Emma turned a horrified gaze on Nick. 'You weren't hiding? But why would Wolfe do such an evil thing?'

'It wasn't evil, it was kind. Just how kind Pop didn't realize until the end.' Nick sighed. 'Wolfe understood, you see?'

'Understood what?'

'That Grady was a good man, and that he didn't deserve the fate he was rushing towards. From his point of view, he was protecting his friend; saving a life until that life was almost spent. A month ago, my pop reached his ninety-second birthday. The time had finally arrived for Wolfe to tell his apprentice the truth.'

'What was Grady's reaction?'

'He asked Wolfe to prepare the ghost machine for a midnight summoning. As far as he was concerned, their friendship was over.'

Despite his deceptions, Emma couldn't help feeling a little sorry for the ageless necromancer. After fifty years, his faithful pupil had rejected him.

'Someone in the house must have overheard the conversation and reported it to Dritch,' Nick continued. 'That was how he knew when to launch his attack—just as Wolfe's attention was diverted by the summoning.'

'Do you remember how it happened?' Emma asked. 'From your side, I mean.'

'I remember very little of my time behind the gates. Sometimes I get the odd flash, but I think the horror is too much for a mortal mind to cope with. All I remember clearly is a feeling of being wrenched from one place into another. A sense of passing from a state of un-being into being. For the first time in decades, I was seeing with human eyes, feeling with human hands. The world crowded in on me.'

Emma could hardly bring herself to say the words. 'Wolfe had summoned you with the ghost machine. And you . . . '

'My hands melted into his face, my fingers started crushing his soul. Yes—' He looked up into the starless reaches of the night. 'I possessed my father.'

Silence, but for the crunch of their boots in the snow.

'He was so happy. I heard his voice in the mind that we now shared: he said he'd stay with me, just until I'd found myself again. In those first moments, I didn't recognize him. I went on crushing and crushing, his soul breaking apart slowly in my hand. He fought against me, but only so that he might stay long enough to help me remember the person I'd been . . . The next thing I knew, there was a deafening roar as Randall Wolfe's study was blown apart.'

'Dritch.'

'I didn't know for sure it was him until tonight. The fact that the ghost machine turned up in Milton Lake seemed to suggest he wasn't involved.' Nick shook his head. 'When I came round, Wolfe was lying beside me in the rubble. Whoever the thief was, he had dealt the necromancer a mortal blow. His last words to me—to Grady—were these: "It's time. Let the boy take it from here." '

'He trusted you to hunt down the ghost machine? But he didn't know you.'

'He knew my father. Over the next three days, Pop eased me back into the living world. He whispered to me, told me stories of Grandpa and my childhood on the farm. Gradually, I reclaimed my soul from the darkness. I was Nathan Medway of Mearsville, Maine. I was me again, not just in spirit but in body.'

Emma remembered what Nick had told her about how an invading ghost could alter the form of its host body. How it might choose to keep the same appearance, as Peter Taggart had done when in control of his grandson, or opt to convert skin, organs, and bone structure until it resembled the body it had possessed in life. Nick had taken the second path, transforming a ninety-two-year-old man into a boy of seventeen. He had even chosen to keep the scar from where his head had struck the steering wheel—a memento of an old life cut short.

'My pop allowed the last fragment of his soul to crumble away. I tried to hold on to him, tried to tell him I was sorry. With his last whisper he said . . . ' Blinded by tears, Nick stumbled on, 'I hadn't crushed his spirit, I'd given it back to him.'

Emma squeezed his hand. 'You haven't lost him. Peter Taggart said he had access to all of Miles's memories. You know so much about necromancy—I'm guessing you can remember everything about those years Grady spent with Randall Wolfe.'

'All the things they saw, everything they learned.' He tapped his forehead.

'But there's something else you remember too,' Emma said. 'Hazy memories of your years behind the gates. That's why you feel sorry for them.'

Nick nodded. 'They have to be sent back, I know that, but in a way they're all my brothers and sisters. They aren't evil, they're just . . . '

'Hungry. One final question,' Emma said. 'Why did the visions come to *me*?'

'I can't tell you.'

'Nick—'

'I can't. You have to see it for yourself or not at all. It's so clear now, but you're afraid to look.' He reached out and folded a strand of hair behind her ear. 'You shouldn't be scared, it's a wonderful sight.'

Under the swamp-green glow of the spear, they kissed. There was a kind of desperation in the way he pressed his lips to hers, an almost fearful intensity.

'You won't ever forget me, will you?'

She pulled away, suddenly afraid. 'Nick, what's wrong?'

The trees rustled behind them and two figures came stumbling through the bracken. Nick moved like lightning, placing himself between Emma and the newcomers.

'Ems, is it really you?' Henry came forward. 'Jesus, what's happening?'

He was reaching for his cousin when Nick pulled out

Oliver Medway's service revolver and trained it on the boy. Emma had forgotten all about the weapon; he must have collected it from the kitchen table before they left the house. Already traumatized by whatever horrors he had witnessed, Henry fell back with a shivery yelp.

'What do you think you're doing?' Emma gasped. 'It's Henry, it's Sas.'

'Is it?'

He was right: how could they be sure the boys hadn't been possessed? Any invading spirit would have full access to their thoughts and memories.

'Someone *please* tell me what's going on,' Henry cried.

'First you tell *us* what happened,' Nick demanded.

Sas's face was a muddle of fear, confusion, and anger. He spat his words at Emma and Nick, almost as if he suspected *them* of having something to do with the supernatural forces that had overtaken the town.

'We were still up in Henry's room playing that stupid audio file. Next thing we know, his dad arrives home and starts throwing everyone out of the house.'

'I've never seen him like that. He looked . . .' Henry frowned. 'Lost.'

'The only people who stayed were that weird crew—"the Circle", you called 'em. All except Mrs Glock.'

Her husband must have taken Margery back to Connolly Avenue. After the summoning of her daughter, the poor woman had probably needed a long lie down. Was that where a ravenous spirit had found her? Curled up in bed, dreaming dreams of Alice?

'They all stomped into Dad's study and closed the door,' Henry continued. 'There was a bit of shouting and then we heard one of them—Mr Carter, I think—screaming.'

'Farter Carter screaming!' Sas boggled. 'It was just—'

'Horrible.' Henry jumped in. 'By this time, we were standing on the stairs and could see through the arch window into the back garden. The patio doors from Dad's office open that way.' He glanced at Nick, who was still pointing the vintage revolver at his head. Emma knew the house well; the explanation was for the gunman's benefit. 'I nearly screamed myself. There were half a dozen people standing like statues out in the snow, all dressed up in different costumes.'

'There was a kid with one eye all messed up,' Sas said. 'Like someone had stuck a hot poker through it. Then this posh-looking woman in a big dress and white wig. Her throat was cut from ear to ear.'

'They're ghosts, aren't they?'

Nick lowered the gun a few centimetres. 'What happened next?'

'We watched as they . . . ' Henry trembled. 'Melted through the doors.'

'Now everyone in the study was screaming,' Sas said. 'Then it all went quiet. We were still on the stairs when the study door opened and Mr Torve came wandering out.'

'Not wandering,' Henry corrected. '*Staggering*. Dad turned his head and looked at me, and I knew it wasn't him. There was someone else behind his eyes.'

'What did you do?'

'Ran! We got over the gate before they had a chance to stop us.'

'I don't think they had any interest in stopping us, those ghosts already had their bodies.' Henry looked from Nick to Emma. 'We saw it happen over and over again, even in St Jerome's churchyard. The church had been opened for midnight mass and there were hundreds of people shouting and trying to squeeze inside. I guess they thought being on holy ground would protect them. It didn't. A whole army of ghosts stormed right through the open gate and started attacking people.'

'They pushed their hands into their faces. It happened to everyone, even . . . ' Sas was close to tears now, 'the babies and the little kids.'

'We went to Sas's to find his mum.'

'She wasn't there.' And now the overgrown boy looked as if he was about to throw up. 'She can't move by herself, Emma. One of those *things* must have got her. We've seen them attack people in wheelchairs. After they've done their melting trick the people get up and walk away.'

Nick nodded. 'The transformation back to the spirit's original form. The process can mend damaged tissue, even cure diseases. So how did you two make it through?'

Up until this point Sas had kept his hands behind his back. Now he brought forth a pair of rusty metal bars.

'When the dead 'uns were squeezing through the church gate, one of 'em got shoved up against the railings. Thing shrieked like it was on fire. We reckoned the metal must have hurt it somehow. There were a couple of loose railings around the back of the graveyard.'

'We've been using them as weapons.'

'Smart,' Nick approved. 'What d'you say, Emma, think we can trust them?'

She had been watching the boys very carefully. Even with Henry and Sas's memories at their icy fingertips, it seemed unlikely that two spirits would fall into the easy patterns of speech shared by these lifelong friends. She rushed forward, embraced her cousin and pulled a blushing Sas into the hug.

'So what led you here?' she asked. 'You've seen the green light, anyone sensible would run a mile in the opposite direction.'

Henry shuffled uncomfortably. 'Dad always liked to know where Mum was, so a while back he set up the GPS on her phone. Soon as we left home, I tried calling her. She didn't answer but her GPS was still transmitting. It's coming from somewhere close by.'

'Julia's *here*?'

Emma squinted at the ecto-blaze shining through the trees. Was it possible that her aunt had been playing the role of double agent? That meek, mousy woman pretending to spy for the Circle while all the time working for Rowan Rhodes? If so, what had they done with Bob? Maybe Rowan had insisted her ever-logical husband be brought along so that he could witness the power of the ghost machine.

'Now it's your turn,' Sas grunted. 'What the hell's going on?'

'The dead have returned,' Nick said.

'D'uh!' Henry rolled his eyes. 'What can we do about it?'

'I have an idea, but I'm going to need your help.'

'Course. We'll do whatever it ta—'

The words died on Henry's lips.

Silhouetted in the throbbing green spaces between the trees stood a host of unmade spectres. Twenty, thirty, perhaps as many as fifty ghosts, all of them new arrivals from behind the gates. All of them hungry.

Nick passed Emma the revolver. 'You remember what to do?'

'Safety off, aim and shoot.'

'That's the idea. Got those railings handy, boys?' He took his own iron bar from the pocket in his coat. 'Good luck, everyone.'

Gaping mouths.

Ravenous eyes.

Soul-crushing fingers.

The dead swarmed into the forest.

28

BAM. The head of a Civil War soldier vanished in a mist of ectoplasmic gore.

BAM. A leering gentleman in Edwardian frockcoat took a blast in the shoulder.

BAM. BAM. BAM. A one-legged butcher in a bloody smock; a snaggletooth crone with wild white hair; a girl not much older than Emma, barefoot and dressed in a torn Iron Maiden T-shirt. The revolver kicked hard, twisting her wrist with every shot. Taking more bullets from Nick, she told herself this was simply a matter of survival. And yet . . . *He* had once been just like these hungry shades. Would she have put a bullet in his brain without feeling at least a twinge of pity?

To her left, Sas and Henry were busy hacking with their iron bars. They were not skilled fighters like Nick, but what they lacked in experience they made up in fear-fired frenzy. The broken railings swept high and low, jabbed at soft stomachs and plunged into yielding throats.

Nick's hollowed-out bar was slick with ectoplasm, his hands gloved up to the wrists with green. At his feet lay a pile of unmade, their limbs intertwined and their mouths shrieking. Emma wondered if they knew who he was. A soul that had escaped the gates ought to understand their longing to be whole, and yet he cut them down and sent them back. She imagined the hatred they might feel towards him, and shuddered.

He was turning towards her, words forming on his lips, when his body stiffened. With hands held out in a gesture of surrender, he spoke.

'Dead of the gates, hear me. Through these two brothers, I address you all. Those with new bodies and those still hungering for flesh, *listen*.'

The silence behind her could mean only one thing. Even so, when Emma turned and saw her suspicions confirmed, the shock was no less brutal. Pinned against a tree, Henry stared at them with large, wondering eyes while a ghostly hand pressed into his face. The possessing spectre's jaw was missing and his head was so battered and dented it looked like a roughly plumped pillow.

On the ground next to Henry, Sas writhed as a ghost went in search of his soul. It was odd, seeing the strong boy so completely overwhelmed by a kid half his size. Dressed in coal-black rags, the chimney sweep pushed his soot-stained fingers into Sas's flesh.

There were three bullets left in the Colt. She tried to press the weapon into Nick's hand but he pushed it away.

'I can't keep doing this,' he said. 'Can't you see, Emma? It's killing me.'

She *could* see it: the desolation in his eyes, the well of sadness so deep a heart could drown in it. He did not clearly remember his time behind the gates, but he knew the pain of the unmade. He wanted to help them, but how and at what cost?

'They share a kind of consciousness,' he said. 'Right up until full possession, they can sense things experienced by their brothers and sisters.'

'Like a hive mind,' Emma whispered. 'So what's the plan?'

'I'm going to speak to them, but you have to promise me something—whatever happens now, you won't try to stop it. This . . . ' He took a deep breath. 'I think it always had to happen. Maybe that was why Wolfe told my father about the dagger, so that *I* would remember. Maybe it's why he put the knife in among Pop's possessions, so I'd find it and know what to do . . . if the worst came to the worst.'

Fear winged through Emma's mind like the black bird from her visions.

'Nick, what stupid idea have you got in that head of yours?'

'Do you want me to save your cousin? Do you want me to save every soul in this town?'

'Of course, but—'

'Then no more questions.'

His gaze moved through the spaces around her, and Emma felt the wind sigh between her fingers. Nick turned and addressed the unmade:

'I am your brother Nathan Medway, and for sixty long years I dwelled among you in the prison of smoke and glass. Hear me, for I have the power to set you free.'

The little sweep and the badly injured man looked up at him. They were listening, and through them, the entire host of the dead.

'There is something you yearn for more than the return of a physical body. I know because I yearned for it too. In the coldest reaches beyond the gates, I'd dream of it. But there seemed only one way out: a necromancer's summoning.' He took a step towards the ghosts. 'I know the secret of your tired hearts. You want peace, and I . . . '

He dropped down onto his haunches beside the sweep.

'I can give it to you.'

Nick whispered something in the child's ear. Whatever the secret, its effect was instantaneous. Both ghosts released their spectral grip. Henry sank to the ground with a weak sigh while Sas shuddered and closed his eyes. They both appeared to be sleeping.

'They're all right,' Nick reassured her. 'It's just shock.'

'*Nathan Medway . . .* '

'*Our brother . . .* '

'*Unmade soul made again . . .* '

'*Is it true?*'

'*The secret?*'

'*The dagger?*'

'*The peace?*'

Thousands of voices echoed through the open mouths of the man and the sweep.

'There's a simple way to test my words,' Nick said. 'You each have the power of prophecy, tell me if what I say is possible.'

The dusty head of the sweep and the misshapen head of the man sank to their chests. It was as if they had fallen into a trance. Emma went to check on Sas and her cousin. Like Nick had said, the boys seemed to be in a state of shock.

'You're offering them peace,' she said, 'but what does that mean? Nick, I'm scared.'

'No more questions.'

'But I have to know. You have to tell me—'

'*The prophecy is confirmed. The boy speaks true.*'

This time the voices had joined in a single chilling chorus. Emma took Nick's hand and held on tight, as if she were afraid that an invisible tide might rise up and sweep him away.

'*It is agreed. The lost souls of the Lake will wait until the promise is fulfilled.*'

'I must find the ghost machine,' Nick said. 'Redirect the signal.'

'*And then make the sacrifice.*'

The dagger. The sacrifice. A path to peace . . .

'No!'

Emma's cry echoed among the trees. The truth was there, shimmering before her, bleak and hateful. It couldn't happen, not this, not now, not when she had only just found him. She could feel the old darkness rear its head and start to nibble at the edges of her life. Could hear the Richie voice calling out to her: *Did you really think I'd left you for good? When he's gone you can tell me all your hopes and dreams and we'll laugh about them together. Say goodbye, Emma. It's time you returned to pain and pavements . . .*

'No,' she repeated, 'you can't.'

'There's no other way. This is how it must be.'

He reached down to his belt and slipped the dagger from its scabbard. The jewelled hilt glittered like spilled blood in the ghost light.

'The Blade of Osiris. It was one of Randall Wolfe's most prized possessions. Once we find the ghost machine, I can redial using a different set of mystic numbers, this time placing a call through to a different kind of afterlife. Then I'll use the blade to—'

'NO!'

The darkness crept over her and the Richie voice chuckled.

'They need someone to guide them, Emma. They can't find the light on their own.'

'Then let me do it. Give me the knife and I'll—'

He pressed his lips to hers. A kiss as soft as a tear.

'Even if I was monstrous enough to let you take my place, you couldn't do it. Only those that have experienced death can guide a host of lost souls.'

'And the knife?'

'My soul is bound to this body in the same way a latched spirit is bound to their loved one's aura. There are only a few ways in which my soul can be separated from its vessel. The Blade of Osiris is one. One life to save thousands, isn't that a fair price?'

'Not to me. Never to me.'

'So you say, but I know you better than that.' Nick smiled. 'Come on, the ghost machine's waiting.'

She looked on in a daze as Nick covered Sas with his jacket and Henry with her coat. The sweep and the man stood sentinel over the boys, their mouths gaping. It was an eerie sight, like a picture plucked from the pages of a dark fairytale.

Nick took her hand. Like the guiding spirit he was about to become, he led her through the last of the trees and into the snow-slabbed car park. It took a moment for Emma's eyes to adjust to the glare of the ecto-light. How strange she hadn't guessed their destination. Of course there was only one place in that part of the town that Rowan could possibly have taken the ghost machine.

The Kinema by the Lake.

Piercing the clouds, the green spear plummeted down and stabbed through the roof of the old cinema. Under its glare, the car park was filled with the famished souls of the dead. Hundreds, perhaps thousands, had heard the promise of peace and drifted back to the site of their summoning. On seeing Nick and Emma, the horde parted and made a pathway to the Kinema's pillared entrance. It was like walking through a nightmare: all those strange and hungry people pulled together from every corner of history. And then the hand of the boy she loved, drawing her on to the moment of his sacrifice . . .

The tentacles of ectoplasm that they had seen reaching through the Lake sprang from the Kinema's open door. Beyond stood the darkened lobby with its rich red wallpaper, framed film posters, and the wide, sweeping staircase that led to the balcony. Despite being the cheapest seats, the balcony tier was where Richie had always preferred to sit. He said it made him feel big, which for a little person was important.

The thick ribbons of ghostly energy ran out from the auditorium's swing doors and across the lobby's faded purple carpet. Emma and Nick stepped carefully over each twisting tentacle. Behind them, the dead had crowded around the entrance, silent and watchful. Their hopes for peace rested on Nick, but if he failed them there was at least the consolation of warm bodies waiting out in the snow.

They reached the swing doors. From inside the auditorium came the murmur of voices and the distant ring of an old-fashioned telephone.

'What are you going to do to her?' Emma swallowed. 'I . . . I know why she did it. She loved him so much she couldn't let him go. Rowan's hurt a lot of people and—'

'I won't harm her, but this has to stop. No matter the cost, the machine's link to the gates must be severed and the dead guided into the light.' He took the Blade of Osiris from his belt. 'You understand, Emma? *No one* can interfere.'

She nodded and together they stepped inside the auditorium.

The veined skin of the marble walls, the rows of wine-red seats, the plush velvet curtains covering the screen, every surface was bathed in ectoplasmic light. Emma's eyes dazzled. She saw the scene in snatches: a small table set up on the stage in front of the curtains. The green spear reaching through the ceiling and touching down at a point just above the tabletop. The silhouette of a woman, Aunt Julia, hunched over the table, something in her hand—the receiver of a candlestick phone.

As Julia's features became clear, Emma saw the terrible strain etched onto her face. She had thought it possible that her aunt was Rowan's willing accomplice, but if that haunted expression was anything to go by then this was far from the truth. And where was Rowan? There was no sign of her on stage. Why wasn't she operating the machine herself? Emma hadn't seen her mother for over a year. What if something had happened to her? Some injury that meant she couldn't work the machine alone . . . ?

Even before she heard the voice in the stalls, Emma realized the truth.

Someone who needed help working the ghost machine.

Someone whose fingers could no longer operate the dial.

Someone who had recently been injured.

'Again! Again! Again!'

Julia looked down from the stage, exhausted and hollow-eyed.

'I can't. The voices are so . . . *Please* . . . '

'He's not coming through! You must concentrate harder.'

'I am, but I just can't—'

'You were always weak!' The voice sneered. 'That's why you married that bully of a husband. You need someone to boss you around and tell you what to do. Even when we were kids, you needed me to take charge and give you orders. Well, here are your orders—do it again! AGAIN! AGAIN! AGAIN!'

Emma could hear the madness tearing at the corners of each word. How well he had hidden his insanity from her. But perhaps the deception had been quite straightforward.

After all, they had been virtual strangers for over a year. If she'd taken the time to look into his eyes, really *look*, would she have seen madness dancing there?

When she called his name, he rose from his seat and turned bright eyes upon her.

'Emma!' Bob smiled. 'You've come! It was all for you, sweetheart. All for you!'

29

Oranges . . . Her thoughts flew back to the night they had questioned Henry about his experience in the ghost train. All he had been able to tell them was that the mysterious necromancer had smelt of oranges.

Another memory: Bob sitting at the kitchen table, telling Emma that Henry had got an A in his lab practical. The experiment had been to separate limonene, a hydrocarbon that, when broken down, produces a strong citrus smell. Bob had been overseeing these experiments all week—his lab coat would have been saturated with the aroma of oranges.

'The name in the ledger.' She turned to Nick. 'I assumed it was Rowan because she was involved with the supernatural. But "Dr R. Rhodes": *Robert* Rhodes . . . '

His strictly scientific mind had blinded her to the truth, but now she came to think about it, the whole thing made a twisted kind of sense. Rowan might have been the expert in folklore and myth, but it was Bob who revered the man most closely associated with the ghost machine. Even a foot-note like the fabled spirit telephone would not have gone unnoticed.

She moved slowly down the aisle.

'All those departmental meetings. All those late nights.'

'I was busy tracking down the device,' he nodded. 'And then, when I found it, I had to learn how to use it. Though it was a supernatural machine, I applied the scientific method of observation and experiment.'

'How did you find it?' Nick asked. 'You have no contacts in the occult world.'

'I had my wife.'

Emma stopped dead. 'Then Rowan was involved.'

'I've not heard from your mother since she abandoned us.' His smile became a sneer. 'But I knew a little about the Lysanna group she'd studied. I sent a letter, asking if they had any knowledge of Edison's machine. A few months later, I received a reply. Just a piece of paper with the address of a Mr Edgar Dritch.

'At that time I still had no real hope that the thing existed. A device for communicating with the dead? Edison had clearly been playing a prank on a couple of naive journalists. But if there was even a possibility . . . I turned up at this grubby little backstreet shop and rang the bell. An elderly gentleman answered and introduced himself as Mr Kitsune, Dritch's personal assistant. He said I was expected. I hadn't made an appointment, how could Dritch know I was coming? Kitsune said nothing, just led me into the Phantasmagorium . . . '

Emma had now reached the end of Bob's row. Insanity as bright and alien as a distant star sparkled in his eyes. She recalled something Nick had said early in their investigation: *It's like the machine's being operated by some desperate lunatic.*

'As I walked through the avenues of that horrifying place, I really thought I was losing my mind. All the things I'd based my life on were torn from under me and I was cast adrift . . . Dritch himself wasn't there, but my guide showed me to the machine. The telephone had pride of place, and yet when I asked how much his master wanted for it, Kitsune said the machine was mine, free of charge. There was only one condition.'

'You had to use it,' Nick said.

'And keep using it, until I found him.'

'Why did you start your experiments at Funland?'

'I had no idea if the machine was dangerous, so wanted to test it somewhere out of harm's way. The amusement park was perfect. Kitsune had given me instructions for dialling the numbers and directing my thoughts towards the gates. Imagine my surprise when, at that first attempt, a spirit came through. I watched from the adjoining chamber as Hiram Sparrow manifested out of thin air. I found myself frozen with fear and wonder, unable to help Henry as he tried to escape . . .

'After that, I had trouble with the machine.' Bob frowned. 'The calls were placed but the ghosts didn't manifest. I thought that perhaps it was my fault—I wasn't concentrating clearly enough on the spirit I wished to summon. This conclusion was proved correct when I used the machine on the last day of term. I thought that the summoning had failed again when I happened to glance out of the window and see the spirit of Adam Carmichael staring up at me. I rushed out to meet him . . . ' He shifted his broken arm and winced. 'You know the rest.'

'After the accident you couldn't use your hands. That's why there was a lull in spirit activity.' Emma looked to the stage. 'But then Julia came to stay. You bullied her into operating the machine for you. That conversation in the kitchen . . . '

She thought he had been asleep in the sitting room, but what had she really seen? Just a bundle of blankets piled up on the sofa. What if Julia hadn't been speaking on the phone but talking directly to Bob? Seen that way, the conversation was turned on its head: *I told you I would think about it and I have. I'm sorry, but the answer's no. You say you're acting from the best of intentions, but you don't know what you're dealing with* . . . After her refusal, it must have taken Bob a few days to wear his sister down.

Emma made her way along the row and stood before the wreck she had once called 'father'. He wasn't to blame. He didn't understand about the unmade and their dark longings. He just wanted his son back. The son *she* had taken from him.

'I'm sorry. This is all my fault.'

'No, Emma, don't you see? This is why I brought the machine to the Lake, to prove that none of it was your fault.'

'Listen to him.' Nick placed gentle hands on her shoulders. 'Let him speak.'

Robert Rhodes smiled through his grief. 'Do you think my beliefs are the most important thing in my life? Emma, I would abandon every certainty if it meant I could grasp that fragile and impossible hope.'

'What hope?'

'That one day you'd come back to me. My lost child.'

'But Richie . . . '

'Richie was gone. I made peace with losing him, but you couldn't let him go. As the months passed, and you drifted further away, I saw that there was only one way I could save you. I had to find Richie. Had to bring him back so that he could tell you.'

'Tell me what?'

'What no one else could.' Bob looked to the stage and the blinding spear of ecto-light. 'But I've failed. Richie won't answer the summoning.'

'There's a simple reason for that, Mr Rhodes.' Nick sighed. 'Your son isn't behind the gates. He never was.'

Emma spun round. 'What do you mean? Richie died a violent death, he must be one of the unmade. Unless . . . Are you saying he took the light?'

Nick strode back to the aisle. The dagger was in his hand again as he made his way up the short flight of stairs to the stage. He spoke a few words to Julia, who glanced fearfully from the boy to her brother and back again.

'He says I have to stop. Robert, what should I do?'

For a moment, Bob looked confused. Then that insane glimmer returned and he bellowed his command—

'Take no notice! We have to find Richie. For Emma's sake, we must!'

'But he has a knife!'

'He won't use it. My son is waiting to be summoned, I know he is. Dial the numbers. Make the call. Again. Again. Ag—'

Before she realized what she was doing, Emma felt the weight of the weapon in her hand. On the corpse-strewn battlefields of the First World War, it had served Oliver Medway well. In the streets and forests of Milton Lake it had sent the unmade screaming back to the gates. Now Emma prayed that the blood-soaked Colt would be merciful. She lifted it over her head and brought the butt crashing down against her father's temple.

Bob's eyes rolled white in their sockets. Dropping the gun, Emma managed to catch him before he fell and manoeuvre him into one of the stall seats. A rill of blood trickled from the gash on his forehead, but he appeared to be breathing normally. She leant in and kissed his grizzled cheek.

'I forgive you . . . Dad.'

Dad. He was not the same father she had known; madness had stripped away much of his identity, but he was no longer just Bob, the man who'd pulled the plug.

Emma met Julia on the stairs leading to the stage. The twitching lips and shaking hands said it all. Caught between loyalty to Bob and her duty to Arthur, the poor woman had been under a terrible mental strain.

'You'll find Henry and Sas in the forest,' Emma said. 'They're unconscious but they're going to be fine.'

'Emma, I'm so sorry, I should have told—'

'There's no time for apologies. There are spirits in the car park outside, hundreds of them, but I don't think they'll hurt you. Go to Henry. Don't look back.'

She watched her aunt retreat down the aisle and through the swing doors. Whatever horrors she saw in the car park, the timid Julia Torve did not run screaming back into the Kinema. It struck Emma as yet another example of the extraordinary lengths to which a parent would go in order to protect their child.

When she reached the little table under the bright spear of the ecto-light, Nick was already at work. His index finger turned the rotary dial, inputting a combination that would break the signal to the gates. Overhead, the column began to flicker and fade.

'Nick, please just stop a moment.'

He didn't look up from the phone.

'I told you, Emma, there's no other way. Not now.'

'What does that mean? "Not now"?'

'It's too late to see . . . ' He shook his head. 'Doesn't matter any more.'

He twisted the dial for the final time and the spear of ecto-plasm vanished. With the green glow of the inter-dimensional bridge gone, only the emergency exit lights stood out as beacons of illumination.

'See what?' Emma asked. 'Just tell me.'

'I can't. If I did, if I forced you to see, then you'd be forced to choose. I couldn't ask that of you.'

He took the Blade of Osiris from the table and held the hilt with both hands, the tip pressed over his heart. Emma grabbed at his fingers and tried to prise them away, but his grip was too strong.

'Wait,' she pleaded. 'Give me time, let me think.'

'There is no more time. I made a bargain with the unmade. If I don't guide them then they'll crush every soul they can find.' He stared into the empty cavern of the cinema. 'It's all right. I'm going to take them into the light, we'll find peace there.'

'You don't know that! You said yourself, no one's ever come back.'

'It can't be worse than the gates. You should go now.'

'No. I . . . I won't leave you to die on your own.'

The first tear trickled from the corner of his eye.

'Thank you.'

He flexed his fingers around the knife.

The dagger that would separate his soul from the vessel he had taken. The blade that would cut through the strings of his careworn heart and stop its precious beat. Emma felt herself reel on the lip of that old familiar darkness. As soon as the boy from the Sparrow House fell, it would rush forward and consume her again.

The Richie voice spoke up—*Look, Emma. See.*

'I love you,' Nick whispered.

Look. Just see! The voice laughed, this time its tone light and playful. So much like him. *You can do it, I know you can.*

'I love you, too.'

Nick's chest heaved against the knife.

You can do anything. You're my sister. The daredevil, Emma Rhodes . . .

His shoulders braced, ready for the push, the shove, the plunge.

Look. See. Be brave.

Richie . . . Not beyond the gates. Not beyond the light.

Under the gaze of the Sparrow House, where his lifeblood had left its indelible stain upon the pavement, Richie's spirit had lifted out of his broken body and . . . had sought shelter. Shelter in the aura of someone he loved. But that was impossible. Bob and Rowan hadn't seen their son until he had reached the hospital, where the doctors had pronounced him brain dead. Only one person had been with him when he died, and she . . .

How could Richie shelter in *her* aura? A *terrenus phasmatis* could only go to a person they loved. Richie could never love her because . . .

'It was my fault.'

The little hand moved smoothly into hers. The hand that she had felt several times, guiding and protecting her, but which she had always explained away.

'You're so silly,' he laughed. 'Course it wasn't your fault!'

She looked down . . . and saw the face of her brother smiling up at her.

30

Nick placed the Blade of Osiris back on the table.

'This is what you meant,' Emma said. 'Who you wanted me to see.'

Nick smiled. 'He's been with you a long time.'

'I've *always* been with her.' Richie rolled his eyes. 'She's my sister. She looks after me and I look after her.'

'But I didn't. Richie, I'm sorry. It was my fault and—'

'Blimey, Ems! *I'm* telling you, it wasn't your fault. You know something?' He looked up at Nick with a conspiratorial smile. 'Girls really are thick! How could it be *her* fault?'

She met her brother's gaze. He was just as she remembered him: his light, freckle-dashed skin, the soft mop of brown hair falling over his eyes, the gap between his front teeth that complemented his cheeky smile. He was dressed in the denim dungarees and Bart Simpson T-shirt he'd been wearing on the day he died. The only feature to mar this perfect picture was the ugly gash that ran down the side of his head.

'But why didn't I see him? If he's been with me all this time.'

'Margery Glock doesn't see her daughter every minute of every day because she chooses not to. Those Milton Lake necromancers,' Nick laughed. 'They think they have to perform all those ridiculous rituals, but the power to see a latched ghost is always there. You just have to want to see it.'

'You shouldn't call people "it",' Richie frowned. 'That's rude.'

'But why didn't you tell me?' Emma asked. 'If I'd known he was here it might have, I don't know, been some sort of comfort.'

'It wasn't my place,' Nick said. 'If a person with a latched spirit is shocked into realizing its—sorry, Richie, *his* presence—then the connection could be severed. It was up to you to see.'

'And it's like he said,' Richie grinned, 'he didn't want you to have to choose.'

'Choose what?'

'C'mon, Ems, you're not really this thick, are you?'

'He's a *terrenus*, so he has the power of prophecy,' Nick explained. 'Although in most ways Richie is still a little boy, many complex ideas are now clear to him, especially those related to the supernatural.'

''S not that difficult.' Richie shrugged. 'Me being here means that you have a choice. Only one of us needs to guide the unmade into the light. 'S up to you.'

Emma felt a sickening jolt. How many times in one night could her world be turned on its head?

'Hey, don't get upset,' Richie said. 'I was just teasing. It's not really up to you, anyway. I'm doing it, and that's that.'

Nick shook his head. 'No, you're not. I couldn't ask Emma to make that sacrifice.'

'Yeah? Well, it's not up to you either, so butt out.'

The little boy turned to his sister. He appeared as he always did in her dreams, a child small for his age, full of life and laughter. But there was something different about him, too. A wisdom that had hardened the soft edges of his voice.

'I've been with you every day since the accident. I watched you cry until there were no more tears left. Then I saw you change into something I called the "Not-Emma". It was like you'd breathed in all the sadness in the world, and me, I just sat with you, holding your hand. I shouted at you lots of times, did you know that? I thought, why can't my big, brave sister hear me?'

'What were you saying?'

'Let it go. Stop being the Not-Emma and be proper Emma again. And I shouted something else, too.'

'Yeah?'

'Yeah.'

'What did you shout?'

The boy shrugged. 'I love you. I love you very, very much.'

Kneeling, Emma felt the warm arms of her brother loop around her neck.

'I love you too, Richie.'

'Very much?'

'*Very* much.'

'That's sad.'

'Why?'

'Because now we have to say goodbye.'

Nick stood over them, fingers raking his hair, exposing the jagged white scar.

'No. You'll stay with your sister, I can guide the unmade.'

Richie let out a very grown-up sigh. 'Ems, will you tell Nick or Nathan or whatever his name is, he's not my dad and he can't tell me what to do.' He turned his exasperated gaze on her. ''S like I said, I walked by your side for over a year and whatever I said or did you just kept on sinking. I couldn't help you, Ems. No one could. Not until *he* came to the Lake.' Richie held out his hand. 'You saved my sister.'

Nick took the small hand and shook it. 'She didn't need me to save her, she was strong enough on her own.'

'Maybe.' Richie bit his lower lip, as if he wasn't so sure. 'But thanks, anyway.'

He padded over to the table and spent a moment examining the ghost machine before picking it up and handing it to Nick.

'You'll have to redial,' he said. 'Tune the light into my soul rather than yours.'

'No,' Nick said bluntly.

Richie stamped his foot. 'Will you two just listen? He saved you, Emma, but you haven't been rescued yet. Not completely. You still hear it sometimes, don't you? That spiteful voice that sounds like me. It *isn't* me, never was. It's that part of you that still won't believe it wasn't your fault. I can see the future, Ems. One day the darkness will be a memory and the voice won't bother you ever again, but only if *he* stays.'

Richie took her hand and led the way down the stairs and into the half-lit aisle.

'You don't need me any more.'

'How can you say that?' her voice cracked. 'I'll always need you.'

'You need me to do *this*. Trust Richie, he can see the future now!' He sported one of his trademark grins. 'Ain't that cool?'

They reached the row of seats where Bob lay slumped and unconscious. Richie moved into the stalls and laid a gentle hand against his father's cheek.

'He just wanted to help you . . . Love can make people do frightening things.'

'When did you get so smart?'

'I was always smart, you were just too dumb to notice.'

They pushed through the auditorium doors and stepped into the lobby. On seeing Emma and Richie, the crowd of unmade ghosts formed a narrow corridor for brother and sister to pass down. Emma wondered if these fortune-telling spirits had always known that *this* would be the outcome of their Christmas summoning. Had they been aware of the little boy and the role he would play in their search for peace?

They moved through the mock Egyptian pillars and into the car park. Thousands stood in the snow, many in possession of living bodies, most still clinging to their ecto-forms. The sight of people she knew chilled Emma to the core. Although Margery Glock, Farter Carter, Mr

Merriglass, and Uncle Arthur all looked the same, it was as if Emma could see beyond their familiar features and perceive the outlandish soul beneath. It was the same with Madeleine and Lola, Chan and Miles, Mr Meadow and Miss Lucas, and all the friends and neighbours, shopkeepers and bus drivers, teachers and school kids, police officers and pensioners.

The dead rolled back like a parting sea, allowing Emma and her brother to move deep into their ranks.

'Aren't you scared?' she whispered.

Richie shrugged. 'They're just people.'

A clearing had been made at the centre of the car park. As her brother guided her into the space, Emma looked up at the sky. Like a pack of grey-skinned wolves, the storm clouds raced away over the three hills, scratching their furry bellies against the fingers of the forest. In their wake, a galaxy of stars shone down on the living and the dead.

'It's Christmas!' He swung her arm back and forth. 'Our favourite time ever.'

From some distant place came the faint ringing of an old-fashioned telephone. In the few moments that were left to them, Emma bent down and lifted Richie into her arms. He felt so light, as if he wasn't there at all. Not a real boy, Geppetto. A memory from a bygone Christmas: Emma and Richie curled up in front of the TV, watching his favourite Disney cartoon. Pinocchio, the little wooden boy who was granted the gift of life because he had proved himself brave and true. Pinocchio had been allowed to grow up, why not Richie?

The sea of spectres parted again as Nick came striding towards them.

'I've redialled using numerals to tune into the light rather than the gates . . . ' He caught sight of them huddled together. 'Emma, I can't do this. I won't.'

Richie looked up, his freckled face wet with tears. 'You're alive, aren't you?'

'Yes, but—'

'How long will you live?'

'Who can answer that?'

'I can. You've both got long, long lives ahead of you, and you're going to have lots of adventures. Me and Emma, we're both stuck in the past while the future waits just round the corner. It's time we both looked up from the pavement.'

Brrrring Brrrring Brrrring Brrrring

From the auditorium, the ghost machine called out across dimensions. Nick took the Blade of Osiris from his belt and squatted down in front of Richie.

'You're sure?'

The boy gave an emphatic nod.

'Emma?'

'I think . . . ' She found the strength to smile. 'Richie's the boss.'

Nick asked them to stand side by side, only a hair's breadth separating them.

'Richie is sheltering in your aura and the bond has to be severed. It won't hurt, but you'll feel . . . ' Nick sighed. 'Loss, like something physically taken. Are you ready?'

They nodded.

'Then stay very still.'

Starting at a point level with the top of Emma's head, he moved the knife slowly through the space between them. The keen edge glinted in the starlight as it cleaved a passage from head to shoulder, shoulder to waist, waist to feet. It met no resistance, for the only thing to cut was the cold night air. Still, Emma felt the separation. As Nick had warned, it wasn't a physical pain so much as a spiritual anguish close to grieving, but in many ways different. Emma didn't think she would ever be able to describe it: that paring of her spirit, as if the knife had slipped under the skin of her soul and had removed a weeping layer. In time it would heal, she had no doubt, for Nick would not have allowed the separation to leave a permanent wound. However, she was equally confident that she would always carry the mark of this parting; a scar no one could see, but as real as the white brand on Nathan Medway's brow.

'Step away from each other,' he instructed. 'It's important now that Richie doesn't become enveloped in your aura again.'

'I can't touch him?'

'I'm sorry.'

The ringing of the ghost machine came to a sudden stop. Emma held her breath.

Aaaaaaahhhhhhhhhhhhhhhh

A sound like the contented sigh of a dying man looking back on a life well lived. It came from the tiny golden star that had appeared above the clearing. A drop of honeyed light that hovered a few metres off the ground and which slowly, slowly began to open a tear in the fabric of the world. The star moved downwards and, much like the Blade of

Osiris, separated the inseparable. It was as if the car park, the forest, even the figures of the dead were projected onto a cinema screen, and the screen had been split right down the middle. On either side of the tear, the world seemed as solid as ever, while in the widening gap a brilliant light burned brighter than the dawn.

The light.

Although the glare did not hurt her eyes, Emma could see nothing beyond its fiery glow. Seeing wasn't important. She could feel a sense of overwhelming peace radiate out and wash across her soul. Fragments of the light moved within her, banishing darkness and healing her wounded spirit. It even soothed the fresh injury made by the knife and, although it could not remove the scar itself, it at least made the pain more bearable.

Nick stretched a trembling hand to the radiance while Richie took a few bold steps forward. All around the edges of the clearing and in the dark spaces beyond, the dead closed their eyes and allowed the warmth and fullness to flood into their empty souls.

At the tear between worlds, Richie called over his shoulder—

'Goodbye, Emma . . . Goodbye . . . '

The wavering silhouette turned to the dead.

'Are you ready?' He grinned. 'Then follow me!'

The gap swelled into a huge golden oval.

'Richie!' Emma shouted. 'Wait! I wanted to tell you—'

'I know.' Her brother's grin spread until it lit up his whole face. 'I'm brave!'

Emma nodded. 'Bravest boy in the whole wide world.'

Together they watched as the small figure skipped into the light.

His silhouette became a shadow.

His shadow, a blur.

The blur, a smudge.

The smudge, a flicker.

And then . . .

He was gone.

The dead of Milton Lake threw back their heads. Those without borrowed bodies came first. Their ectoplasmic forms lifted into air, dissolved into balls of pure white energy, and flew into the golden breach. Perhaps a hundred thousand souls followed in the footsteps of their little guide, but there was more to come. Most of the unmade in possession of bodies could not squeeze into the car park, and so had crowded into the surrounding forest. Now, with their faces turned to the Christmas sky, they opened their mouths and the invading soul was released.

They came like shooting stars, sweeping and plunging into the breach. Beneath the spectacle, Nick and Emma watched in amazement, their eyes filled with starlight . . .

The tear in the fabric of the world began to narrow. Stitch by stitch, reality was pulling itself back together. The edges grew dimmer until only a few golden beads remained. Then even they were gone.

A gust of wind played through the snow, chasing and tumbling like an excited child. The moon looked down. The stars glittered. The people of Milton Lake began to stir and blink and whisper. *What's happened? What are we doing here? What in the world?* One small boy said to his mother—

'Is it an adventure? Are we going somewhere? What happens next?'

Emma met Nick's gaze, and they smiled.

What wonderful, beautiful questions.

UNLAND

A pale imitation of the light, the sun crested the forest and threw its first rays against the iron letters. Under their wavering shadow, Emma took Nick's hand. Try as she might, she still could not think of him as Nathan, and Nick himself seemed to have adopted the alias. A new name for a new life.

She yawned and tucked her head against his shoulder. It was a little after eight o'clock on Christmas morning and neither of them had slept a wink. After the townspeople began to stir, Nick had suggested they reclaim the ghost machine from the auditorium. They found the telephone waiting on the table, its miraculous work complete. Nick placed the supernatural treasure in a plastic bag he'd found behind the concessions stand, and together they hurried to one of the emergency exits.

On their way to the door, Emma looked back at her father still slumped in the stalls. Her heart trembled and she caught hold of Nick's hand.

'I-I'm sorry . . . I can't go with you.'

'What?' He glanced back, his face suddenly stricken. 'Why?'

'It's my dad. I can't leave him like this. He needs me.'

'Emma, listen: the police are looking for you. They have evidence of your involvement in the library fire, evidence reinforced by the fact that last night you stole a police vehicle. They may even think you assaulted that cop after he tried to arrest you. How will you be able to help your father from inside the walls of a young offenders institution?'

She was about to reply when the swing doors opened and Julia came bustling in.

'Is it over? The spirits, are they—?'

'Gone.' Emma nodded. 'What about Henry and Sas?'

'Chilled to the bone, but they'll be fine. Thank you for looking after them.' She drew her cardigan around her shoulders and shivered. 'The people outside don't seem to know what's happened.'

'They won't,' Nick said. 'The brain's very good at shoving impossible things deep into the unconscious. They might have a few troubling dreams now and then, but the mystery will never be solved.'

'What mystery?'

'Why, on one snowy Christmas night, the entire town gathered together in the forest by the lake. Only a few will ever know the truth—you, Emma, Henry, Sas, Mr Rhodes, and the Circle.'

'You know all about my husband.'

'I do, and I want you to tell him something from me: this is where it ends. Necromancy is not a subject for amateurs.'

Julia took a few paces down the aisle before stopping again. 'What about Richie? Did you find him?'

'We didn't have to look.' Emma managed to smile. 'He was here all the time.'

'And now?'

'Resting,' Nick said. 'At peace.'

Julia closed her eyes. 'I'm glad. Now, Emma, there's something you should know. Last night your uncle received a call from his contacts in the police . . . '

She told the story of the CCTV footage from the Smedley fire. Emma glanced at Nick, then at the unconscious figure in the stalls. She made her decision.

'You'll look after him, won't you, Julia?' she said, her voice breaking. 'It'll be easier for me to leave if I know he's being taken care of.'

'Of course. But, Emma?'

'Yes?'

'Promise that one day you'll come home. I don't think he could live if he thought he'd never see you again.'

Emma went to her father and whispered gently in his ear. 'I promise . . . '

Beyond the gates of the once-haunted amusement park, the dawn had gilded the peaceful spires of the rollercoaster and banished shadows from the dark doorway of the ghost train. They had a few minutes until the appointed hour. Enough time for Emma to run through the argument that had dominated their long trudge up the hill.

'I just don't understand how we can hand over something so dangerous to someone so evil.'

'We've no choice,' Nick sighed. 'With Wolfe dead, Edgar Dritch is the most powerful necromancer in the world. Let's say we took the machine and ran away—'

'Sounds like a plan.'

'He'd find us.'

'But all those things Wolfe taught your father, *you* remember them,' Emma protested. 'There must be some trick or spell that could keep us off his radar.'

'Dozens.'

'Great!'

'And a hundred ways Dritch could see through them. Here's the choice—we hand over the machine or we die.'

'But think of the damage he could do.'

'I prefer not to,' Nick said grimly. 'Look, the only positive thing I can say is that Dritch, although undoubtedly evil, is at least skilled. Whatever he wants the machine for, he won't accidentally blow a hole in the gates like your father did.'

'No, he'll do it on purpose!'

'I don't think so. What possible interest could he have in releasing hordes of hungry dead?' He checked her furrowed brow. 'OK, that isn't much comfort, but we either give him what he wants or he takes it from our cold, dead hands.'

They were going round in circles. Emma decided to change the subject.

'So this hole in the gates, won't more unmade spirits try to use it?'

Nick clucked his tongue. 'It's difficult to explain in non-metaphysical terms.'

'Try me.'

'Well, it isn't really a hole and the gates aren't really gates. It's more like a breach in a non-linear containment dimension, the schism in the surface of which is linked in a temporal and spiritual way to the souls able to pass through it.'

'Huh?'

'That's why I say "hole in the gates".' He grinned. 'It basically means that the breach could only be used by spirits who had a direct connection with Milton Lake. The hole will remain, but other unmade souls won't be free to use it.'

'That's good, I guess.'

'But?'

'What about those others? The souls taken by the Night Watchmen and imprisoned. Isn't there a way to help them?'

'You're talking about billions of spirits from every period of history.'

'I guess I am.'

Nick surprised her with a kiss. 'And that's why I love you, Emma Rhodes. Someone tells you terrible things happen because that's the way of the world, and you say, "I don't accept that. Change it."'

'So what are we going to do?'

'What we can.'

The crack of tyres on snow echoed down the forest road. Kitsune was on his way.

'One more thing,' Emma said quickly. 'Why couldn't you ever hypnotize me?'

'Because of Richie.' Nick wound the handle of the plastic

bag around his big fist. 'A latched spirit in an aura interferes with the hypnotist's power of suggestion.'

'That's it?' Emma felt disappointed. 'So I wasn't very special after all.'

'Are you kidding? You're the most special person I've ever met.'

Before she could draw breath, a huge four-by-four swept through the mouth of trees and pulled up beside them. The monstrous black truck had a flatbed section at the rear, headlights the size of bowling balls, and the kind of tyres that could mow down an entire herd of cattle. Emma had to tilt back her head to get a look at the windows. Whoever piloted the beast was hidden from view behind tinted glass.

The back door opened and Kitsune slithered out like an old snake emerging from its hole. In the harsh light of dawn, Dritch's assistant looked more ancient than ever.

'You have the device?'

Nick handed over the plastic bag and Kitsune glanced inside.

'The machine was fully operational?'

'Dr Rhodes used it to full capacity,' Nick said. 'I don't think your master will have any trouble with it now.'

'Mr Dritch will be . . . glad. And now I have something for you, Mr Medway. We found it in the road and I had the driver place it in the back.'

Frowning, Nick pulled himself up onto the flatbed.

'What will you do now, Miss Rhodes?' Kitsune croaked. 'I hear tell the police are looking for you. If my master or I could be of any service—?'

'Nick's arranged for some fake documents—passport, birth certificate, that sort of thing.' As Dritch seemed to know everything anyway there was little point hiding their plans. The same contact Nick had used to provide himself with a false birth certificate to gain entry to Tennyson Academy was now working on Emma's counterfeit documents. 'We hope to get out of the country before the police start a proper search.'

There came a clatter and thump from the truck. Nick dropped the back section and hefted the Thunderbird down from the flatbed.

'Thank you,' he said grudgingly. 'I wasn't sure I'd see her again.'

'A pleasure. Well, I suppose this is goodbye.'

Kitsune held out a withered hand to Emma. Surely it was just a trick of the light—there seemed to be a tear in the old man's eye.

'Your father, was he successful? Did he find the boy? And you . . . how are you, Emma?'

She stared at him. No. That was impossible. That was just . . .

The world turned on its head for the final time.

'When I was a little girl my mum used to tell me this story,' Emma said. 'In Japanese folklore, the kitsune was a magical fox, a shapeshifter that had the ability to change its form. It could become a man or a woman, anything it liked. My mum was a doctor of folklore, so she knew all about it.'

Kitsune blinked tears from his pale blue eyes.

'The head of the Lysanna faith sent you Dad's letter, didn't she? The one enquiring about the ghost machine.'

The old man seemed to shrink. He whispered, 'Do you remember what I said on the night . . . the night I left?'

'That you wouldn't come home.'

'Not until I'd done what I could to save you . . . from yourself. I looked for over a year, searching, searching, searching through the occult world for some way to contact Richie. And then the letter arrived from your father.' Kitsune gave a dry chuckle. 'Bob had found the answer the only way he knew how—in the realm of science. Once I had the keywords "Thomas Edison" and "ghost machine", I could start a proper search. One clue led to another, and finally I found myself at the door of the Phantasmagorium.

'Dritch listened to my story and agreed that I should write to Bob. I was to give him the address of the shop, but mention nothing about my own involvement. I explained that Bob was a school science teacher and couldn't afford to pay the kind of price such a treasure would demand. Dritch laughed. He wasn't interested in money—there was something else he would take in lieu of payment. My service.'

'You agreed to work for him?'

'Until the debt is paid, I am his assistant, he is my master.'

'How long?'

'A year.' The old man hauled himself into the truck. 'For a year, I am Kitsune and nothing else. You are not my daughter and I forbid you to come looking for me.'

The withered hand reached for the door. Before he closed it completely, Emma called out—

'I'm going to be OK! And Richie's at peace and—thank you! Mum, thank—'

The door slammed shut. With a splutter of exhaust fumes and a spray of snow, the huge truck sped down the forest road and out of sight. In the stillness left behind, Emma felt the ground reeling under her feet. She needed something to hold on to. An anchor to steady the spinning world. Nick held out the motorcycle helmet.

'Are you ready?'

The boy from the Sparrow House sat astride the blue and silver Thunderbird. He released the kickstand and revved the engine—a warm and comforting growl.

'This isn't the end,' she said. 'Somehow we're going to find a way to stop Edgar Dritch. We'll be clever about it, subtle. We'll work hard, and it might take years, but we'll find a way. That's our life now.'

Nick nodded. 'A new life.'

She looped her arms around his waist and he looked back, smiling.

'Where will we begin?'

The dawn dazzled. The road waited.

'Everywhere.'

And the Thunderbird flew from the forest.

About the author

William Hussey has a Masters Degree in Writing from Sheffield Hallam University. His novels are inspired by long walks in the Fenlands of Lincolnshire and by a lifetime devoted to horror stories, folklore, and legends. William lives in Skegness and writes stories about things that go bump in the night . . .